M000113152

The
Greek
Villa

BOOKS BY SUE ROBERTS

SUE ROBERTS

The Greek Villa

bookouture

Published by Bookouture in 2024

An imprint of Storyfire Ltd.
Carmelite House
50 Victoria Embankment
London EC4Y 0DZ

www.bookouture.com

Copyright © Sue Roberts, 2024

Sue Roberts has asserted her right to be identified as the author of this work.

ISBN: 978-1-83525-354-0
eBook ISBN: 978-1-83525-353-3

All rights reserved. No part of this publication may be reproduced, stored in any retrieval system, or transmitted, in any form or by any means, electronic, mechanical, photocopying, recording or otherwise, without the prior written permission of the publishers.

This book is a work of fiction. Names, characters, businesses, organizations, places and events other than those clearly in the public domain, are either the product of the author's imagination or are used fictitiously. Any resemblance to actual persons, living or dead, events or locales is entirely coincidental.

This book is dedicated to all of my loyal readers. I appreciate every one of you.

PROLOGUE

'Bye, Thea. I will be back soon, hopefully.'

I hug my friend, who is also the owner of the bakery at the end of the cobbled street in the pretty Greek village I've been staying in.

It's been so much fun enjoying long, lazy days swimming and taking boat trips with my best friend, Evie, who accompanied me. Not to mention eating far too much cake, but hey, holidays are for indulging, aren't they? I have also enjoyed chatting to people in the local bar, practising my limited Greek vocabulary because I would love to be able to have more conversations next time.

'I hope so,' says Thea. 'You are good for my business.' She winks.

The waistband of my cotton shorts – feeling a little tighter now compared to when I first arrived – are testament to Thea's wonderful baking. Freshly baked bread and croissants in the morning, and more than a healthy interest in freshly baked baklava, have been far too much of a temptation while I have been here. Not to mention custard pie and honeyed orange cake, the list goes on. If only it didn't taste so good.

'And bye, Evie. It was lovely to meet you.' Thea shakes my friend warmly by the hand.

'You too. I can see why Claudia loves it here so much.' She smiles, glancing around the pretty street.

Thea is not only a great baker, but a fantastic chef too. When I came here alone last year, she invited me to her home for dinner and I sat beneath the stars with her family, eating and drinking at a long wooden table in the flower-filled garden. I inhaled the tantalising aroma of food sizzling on a BBQ, before tucking into lamb steaks, griddled halloumi, and soft pitta, alongside a mountain of crunchy Greek salad. Taking in the sight of distant mountains and an orange sun making its descent, I felt my spirits soar and wished that I could stay forever. As I listened to the sound of everyone's laughter, and gentle teasing, I also wished I were part of a large family. I have a brother, who I was close to growing up, but he moved down south with a girl he met at university and is now raising a family over two hundred miles away. I would have loved more siblings, especially a sister, and longed for the noise of a busy household.

Even now, I'd love my home in the UK to feel livelier. I have been single for a while now, which is fine as I've always enjoyed my own company and would never be in a relationship just to avoid being on my own, but it would be nice to have company. However, people are not always who they seem, something I have had to learn the hard way.

I glance around the village road one last time as our taxi driver loads our cases into the trunk of his car for the journey to the airport.

Thea stands at the top of the road, waving us goodbye as the sun begins to rise, ready to open the door of her bakery shop to her customers. She has already been there for the last three hours baking bread rolls and cakes for the villagers, and will have a siesta later in the day.

I wave until the car has descended the narrow street and

turns right towards the road that passes the seafront. Settling into my seat, I sigh with contentment. It's been yet another wonderful stay, renting the apartment opposite the bakery, its balcony above giving a view of the beach in Roda.

'I feel really relaxed, even though I have only been away for a few days,' says Evie.

'It kind of has that effect here, doesn't it?' I smile at my friend.

I can't help looking longingly out of the window at the view of the sea in the distance. A couple holding hands walk along a boardwalk towards the beach, maybe ready for an early morning swim, and I wish that was my morning too.

I'm not exactly looking forward to heading home to my hybrid working, splitting days in the office with working days at home.

But in the words of Arnold Schwarzenegger, 'I'll be back'.

ONE

'Oh no, poor Uncle Jack.'

'He had been unwell for a little while. But you know how private Jack is. Was... He never even told anyone he was ill,' Mum says with a sigh.

She dabs at her eyes with a tissue as she tells me how her older brother, my uncle Jack, passed away at the age of seventy-four in the early hours of the morning.

I can barely take in the news. I feel terrible, knowing I had been enjoying myself in Greece, when all the time Jack had been struggling with his health, which had led to his untimely death.

A wave of sadness engulfs me as I recall spending time with my uncle when I was younger. These days, it was more the occasional family get-together, to celebrate a birthday or anniversary, but back then he would always slip me some money 'for sweets'. It became 'for a night out' as an adult, even though I would protest, especially when I began earning a good wage, but his generosity prevailed.

'Oh, Claudia, I can't believe we won't see him again. I was

only dancing with him at his birthday party a few months ago. I feel bad that I hadn't spoken to him for a couple of weeks,' says Mum.

That's what we do when someone dies, isn't it? Start with the regrets and 'if onlys'. We always think we will have more time with our loved ones, as the alternative doesn't bear thinking about.

'Oh, Mum, don't be so hard on yourself. I'm pretty sure a lot of families see less of each other as they get older. You were a good sister to him, especially after Auntie Kathleen died.' I sit down next to Mum on the couch.

I remember Mum inviting Uncle Jack around for Sunday lunch, and her and Dad including him in their shopping trips, or drives out to the countryside. Whatever they did they included him if he fancied joining them.

'Thanks, love, that makes me feel a bit better.' She pats my hand.

'And don't forget, Jack didn't like a fuss, just as you say. He would never have told anyone he was ill, you know that.'

'You're right, I know. It was just such a shock when the hospital called though, identifying me as his next of kin from the contacts on his phone. Thank goodness he had it on him. He collapsed in the supermarket apparently. We got there last night and sat with him all night. He was conscious for a while, you know, slipping in and out so at least he knew we were there. I am glad he wasn't alone when he...' She blows her nose loudly.

'Exactly. That's something to be grateful for,' I say gently. 'You should have called me though, Mum.'

'No, it was the middle of the night. You have work to think about, me and your dad don't,' she says, dismissing the idea. 'I'm fine, we had a bit of a lie-in this morning. Poor Jack.' She shakes her head and stifles another sob.

I remind her that Jack had a good life and that at least he

didn't suffer. 'He packed a lot into his life and always did the things he enjoyed.'

'That's very true, I suppose. You always manage to say the right thing.' Mum smiles.

'I must take after you then,' I tell Mum, a lady of tact and infinite wisdom.

'One thing I do know is that he left a will,' Mum tells me. 'It's with his solicitors, who say they will be in touch when the reading is scheduled. You will come, won't you?'

'Yes, if you want me to,' I reply.

'You must do. I'm certain Jack has left you something,' Mum informs me. 'Your brother will be coming up too.'

'Of course. And, in the meantime, I will help you organise the funeral.'

It will be nice to see my brother Josh and my gorgeous nephew George, who I absolutely adore but don't see nearly enough of. No doubt it will be a whistle-stop visit though, as Josh has a busy life and a pretty high-pressure job in sales.

'Oh, thanks, love. I must confess I don't really have a clue where to start with all that. It's been a long time since we planned a funeral for your grandparents. Everything is different now.'

'Not really, although a lot of stuff can be done online these days. Don't worry about a thing. First call is to the undertaker. Pop the kettle on, Mum, I'll do that right away.'

'Use Hamiltons on the high street. The number should be in a book near the phone,' she informs me, so I look up the number. 'Brian Hamilton is a lovely man. Make sure you have him when me and your dad pass,' she shouts through from the kitchen as the kettle starts to boil.

'Mum! You're both as fit as fiddles, you will probably outlive him,' I tell her as she returns with the tea, not wanting to think about the day that happens to either of them.

'You know what I mean, it's a family business, his son already works there,' she tells me.

Just as we sit with our mugs of tea, Dad reappears from his greenhouse, clutching a bag of tomatoes. Always one to avoid any emotional talk, he slipped out to his greenhouse when I arrived, after an awkward hug and a pat on the back. Dad is a fixer though. 'Every problem has a solution,' is what he always says firmly if any problem in the family seems insurmountable.

'That was good timing,' says Dad, eyeing the tea tray. 'Any of that lemon drizzle cake left to go with it?'

'I was just going to bring that in,' says Mum. 'Do you think of anything other than food?' She rolls her eyes and my tall, slender dad, who could probably eat a whole cow on a sandwich and not put on an ounce of weight, grins.

My family are Uncle Jack's only next of kin, as he met my auntie Kathleen later in life and they never had any children. I'm pleased to be included in his will and hope he may have left me the silver owl I often admired that sat on a bookshelf in his lounge. There was a globe too, that I used to spin, and ask my uncle to test me on capital cities, which resulted in me being the top of the class at geography in primary school. Maybe playing with that globe nurtured my lust for travel, along with the world picture atlas on the bookshelf, as so far I have been to Thailand, Greece, the East Coast of America, and countless European cities, usually on long weekend breaks. Oh, and Cuba. How could I forget visiting Havana and marvelling at everything about the city, including the cool American cars. But there is just something about Greece that always pulls me back to its islands.

Later that morning, having dealt with the funeral and all the other legalities, I squeeze my mum in a goodbye hug and Dad hands me a bag of tomatoes and a yellow pepper.

'Make sure you eat properly,' Mum reminds me as she does every single time I visit.

'Course, Mum, promise,' I reassure her.

'I'll be in touch when the solicitor arranges the meeting,' she says, before closing the red front door with the pristine hanging baskets outside.

TWO

'As far as I can see, it's being processed,' I say to the almost hysterical woman on the phone, who tells me she is going on holiday in four days' time and her daughter's passport has not arrived yet and what exactly am I going to do about it? I resist the urge to tell her that maybe she ought to have applied for it a little earlier in the year and not during full-on holiday season.

I finish the call and sigh. I do love my job, despite people thinking we are magicians who can have a passport processed and hand delivered by a fairy who leaves a dusting of fairy dust on their doorstep within twenty-four hours. I understand people's desire to go on holiday, I love to go myself after all, but I just feel a little flat as it's so soon after Jack's death, and maybe I'm not possessing my usual patience with callers.

I'm a supervisor at the Passport Office, and while the days can be a bit samey, I glance out of the window and remind myself that there are far worse places to work. Plus, the pay is decent. The office is housed in a listed building, with views over the Mersey and several other magnificent buildings known as the Three Graces. It is breathtaking. And, of course, I have the joy of working from home a couple of days a week and sitting around in my loungewear.

'Fancy going for a walk at lunchtime?' my colleague Suzi asks as she finishes a call.

'Sure, sounds good,' I reply as I glance at my watch. We stagger our lunch hours, so today Suzi and I will take a break at one o'clock. The sun is shining brightly, so we will probably grab a sandwich and look for a bench somewhere to eat it. Unless we are lucky enough to find a table at an outdoor café that is.

As expected, we stroll past a few nearby eateries, where empty tables are non-existent, as shoppers and tourists enjoy an al fresco lunch in the unexpected sunshine. Instead, we grab drinks and sandwiches and manage to find an empty bench near the Albert Dock overlooking the water.

'I can't wait for next week, this holiday can't come quick enough,' says Suzi, before diving into her sandwich of Brie, toasted peppers, and salami on sourdough. Mine is chargrilled Cajun chicken. Sandwiches are so much more interesting than they used to be, and I wonder what became of the humble egg and cress sandwich.

'I hope you have a great time. I could do with another holiday.' I sigh, my mind roaming back to Corfu and those long, lazy days basking in the sunshine.

'You've only just come back,' she replies with a laugh.

'That was two whole weeks ago,' I remind her, and she rolls her eyes. 'Seriously though, Jack's passing has made me realise we should grab life with both hands. Tomorrow is promised to no one, and I know Jack would approve of my travels.'

I think back once more, with affection, of sitting in his house and leafing through an atlas, Jack telling me that if I worked hard in life, the world could be my oyster.

I do feel a little guilty about jetting off so often though, knowing some people can't afford to take a single holiday. I know I am fortunate enough to be able to make several trips to Greece a year, but the apartment I rent out there is such a bargain. It's simple, but clean with that all-important balcony. I prefer the authenticity of Greek apartments to the larger hotels and their modern interior that makes you feel you could be anywhere in the world. Thinking about it, I could probably cut back even further by spending less money at the bakery, which is a little too handy. I close my eyes and feel the warmth of the sun on my face as I look up and imagine for a split second that I am back in Greece, listening to the sound of the sea in the background.

We enjoy our lunchtime outdoors, and just under an hour later, we take the short walk back to the office, feeling refreshed. I nip to the loo and scrape my long chestnut-coloured hair into a ponytail and squirt on some more body spray. Glancing in the mirror, I can see that my holiday tan is fading a little, and I might need a couple of infills on my lashes that frame my quite large green eyes. Maybe I will work outside on the balcony of my apartment tomorrow if this weather keeps up and top up the tan a little. And count down the days until I can return to my favourite place!

THREE

It seems Uncle Jack had far more money than anyone could ever have imagined. Turns out, he and Auntie Kathleen had been big savers, as well as investing in stocks and shares, seemingly with great success. The house they bought in the late nineties has almost tripled in price too.

All his assets are to be divided equally between myself, my brother Josh, and my parents, including the contents of the house. This includes Kathleen's impressive gold jewellery collection that she had built up through her life. Jack was a lover of art too, and had purchased several valuable pieces over the years. All I can think of though is that I will become the owner of the silver owl after all. I am unable to process the amount of money I'm about to inherit.

'I knew the house was worth a bit, and about the jewellery. Kathleen mentioned that before she died,' says Mum as we sip drinks in a café not far from the solicitor's office. 'But all those stocks and shares? I had no idea Jack was into all that.'

Mum can hardly take it in. Kathleen was an only child, whose parents had long departed, and she insisted Jack's family inherit everything. She had one cousin who she couldn't bear to leave a single thing to apparently.

'He always was a private man,' says Dad, eyeing up some tasty-looking cakes in domes behind the counter. He orders a slice of coffee and walnut cake from a passing waitress, Mum and I declining having not long eaten breakfast.

'We were never really savers,' Mum laments as she sips her tea.

'Not everyone is. At least you enjoy what money you do have, and long may that continue,' I remind her.

With my windfall, I am determined to pay my parents back a little for their generosity towards me. They probably won't take it, but at least I can offer. If not, I will make sure I spoil them.

'Well, that's true. We have enjoyed our life,' says Mum.

'*Still* enjoying it and hopefully for many more years to come.' I smile. 'And so you should, you have both worked hard all your life.'

My parents are forever updating their house, which is the smartest house on the street, and they are partial to a good cruise. They were also very generous when I got my first apartment, stumping up the deposit so that I could buy in a nice area. I tried to protest, being the fiercely independent soul that I am and determined to save the deposit myself, but Dad wouldn't hear of it. He told me they would have paid to put me through university, but as I never went paying a deposit on a home was the least they could do for me. I know he didn't mean it, but his comments unintentionally made me feel like a bit of a failure, even though I have a really good job in the Civil Service.

I drop my parents off, before returning to work at home, where seated at my desk in my second bedroom that doubles as an office, the walls covered in a beach scene, I gather my thoughts.

What am I going to do with all that money? Maybe I could

decorate the walls with a new mural, perhaps a forest scene next time, and buy that ridiculously expensive, huge new sofa from that Italian interior place on the retail park. It occurs to me then that I could buy a new house. A whole freaking house! And no matter how much I try, I can't get the thought of the little white house that I came across in Corfu with the *Pros polisi* sign outside off my mind.

I must stop this daydreaming, as my thoughts drift off to the possibility of owning a place in Greece *and* a slightly bigger one here. I could sell this place and add it to the small fortune that will soon be landing in my bank account. I could buy a new car, and not have to say a silent prayer that my eight-year-old Golf will get me to my destination without conking out. It cost me three hundred quid to fix after it failed the last MOT. I could buy a brand new one if I wanted to.

'Oh, Jack, who knew you had all those investments,' I say quietly. 'Maybe you could have cashed some in, and we could have gone travelling together.' I find myself looking upwards as my eyes fill with tears. 'I'll let you know what I've been up to, when we meet again,' I tell him.

Whatever happens in the future, one thing is certain: I will be eternally grateful to my dear uncle Jack.

FOUR

In the office the next day, my mind keeps flitting back to the house on the street not far from the beach in Greece. Down a backstreet just outside Roda on the island of Corfu, it is only a few minutes' walk from the sea and a long sandy beach. A dozen houses stand in a row, the one for sale slightly grubby on its exterior with a wild garden full of thistles, and a broken gate hanging forlornly at the entrance. It stands in stark contrast to the white painted houses either side of it, that are well looked after with flowers in pots outside their colourful front doors painted in red, blue and green.

The inside is probably a bit of a project too, but then it is being auctioned at a low starting price so there would be more than enough money left over for renovating if I got it at a good price. On my last visit, before Evie arrived, I walked past the villa several times en route to the beach and would stand just staring at it. The lady next door appeared one day as I was lost in a daydream.

'You buy the house?' she asked, looking suspiciously at me with her dark-brown eyes.

'I'd love to,' I told her. 'I could come here whenever I liked.'
I sighed longingly, imagining what I could do with the place. I'd
have the exterior rendered in a smooth white, maybe some
flowers climbing the walls or trailing around a wooden arch
beyond the gate. I can still barely grasp the fact that I am in a
position to actually buy it.

'You not want to live here?' She frowned slightly. 'It is a
good street to live,' she explained in her strong Greek accent.

'A holiday home, maybe. I'm not sure I could find a job here
to actually live,' I told her. 'Or that I would be ready to leave my
family and friends back home either.'

'Hmm,' she said, before going inside and closing her front
door.

I thought I'd upset her then. Maybe she would have
preferred a permanent neighbour, rather than someone who
just came over for holidays, but to my surprise she returned
with a map of the island.

'You visit here. It is a nice place,' she said, having circled a
monastery and a Byzantine castle in the hills. 'There are nice
things in the mountains, not just the beach.' She spoke of the
place proudly.

'Thank you. Oh, and my name is Claudia. What's yours?'

'Phoebe,' she answered.

I imagined her to be around seventy years old, small, and
sprightly looking, and wearing a long dress, her dark hair
plaited. She had pretty dark-brown eyes, and small features,
and I pictured her as a vibrant, young woman, reminding me
that life slips by so quickly.

I thanked her once more for the map and stood for a while
thinking about the little white villa, although the walls were
more of a dull grey right now. I closed my eyes and imagined
gleaming walls and a traditional blue painted front door. Inside,
there would be a modern bathroom, maybe a glass sink, set

against open exposed brickwork. I would display art on white walls and have a tasteful mix of modern and traditional Greek furnishings. Windows with wooden shutters would be flung open in the evening so I could listen to the sound of the crashing waves at the nearby beach that would lull me to sleep.

'Do you live here alone?' I asked her, before wondering if that sounded a little nosey.

'*Nai*. My husband. One year ago, he passes over.' She crossed herself and I offered my condolences.

'I have a daughter who lives in Athens and a granddaughter.' Her face broke into a smile when she spoke of them. 'She lives in a village,' she told me, pointing somewhere towards the mountains.

The narrow road that the house stood on curved slightly upwards, and had maybe a dozen villas in total with a nearby taverna, a small bakery and a bus stop at the end of the road that headed into the centre of Sidari, a busy tourist resort. There was a path behind the houses on some grassland that snaked down to the beach, passing some shops and restaurants, before arriving at the main high street of Roda, lined with colourful shops and tavernas. Imagine, no more apartment rentals, I thought to myself, lost in an improbable daydream of owning this house and turning it into my dream holiday home.

'Did you want anything, or not?'

A colleague pulls me out of my daydream and back into the office to the sound of people tapping away on their computers.

'Sorry, what?'

'From the machine. I'm in need of some chocolate,' she says cheerfully.

'No, I'd better not, thanks though.' I smile at the new office apprentice, who has already made a good impression with her hard-working attitude and cheerful manner.

I answer an email, then an incoming call from a bloke who

wonders why he can't call in and collect his passport this afternoon, as the last one went missing in the post. I try to explain
that it is in the system somewhere, having only recently been
applied for, with assurances that it will arrive in due course.

A busy afternoon soon passes, and I am finally at home
nursing a latte, made in my recently purchased coffee machine,
and call my friend Evie.

'Claudia, hi, how was your day?' she asks cheerfully.

'Oh, you know, the usual. I did speak to a guy with a very
sexy voice, although all he did was complain about his passport
taking too long to arrive.'

'I'm surprised you still want to work there now that you've
come into that inheritance,' she teases. 'I think I'd be off like a
shot.'

'Of course I still want to work. I haven't come into millions,'
I tell her, even though it is a substantial amount. 'Besides, I
enjoy my job. I'd just love to buy a place abroad too. But maybe
I ought to concentrate on getting a bigger place here.' I pop a
couple of blueberries into my mouth, attempting to ward off a
sugar craving with my coffee. 'Plus, the novelty of sitting around
with a pile of money and no routine would soon wear off, even
if I did come into millions. I've read about those lottery winners
who miss their daily routine.'

'If you say so. Although I'm not sure why you would want a
bigger place over here. Are you planning on starting a family or
something?'

'Yeah, right. I haven't even got a partner. And I'm in no
hurry to find another. In fact, you're right. Thanks, Evie.'

'Pleasure. Although I'm not sure what for.'

'For making me realise that I can do whatever I choose to.
Why on earth do I need a bigger place here? I have no children,
or even a boyfriend, so all that domestic stuff is definitely a long
way off. And it's not like I can only work from the UK.'

I seriously consider the fact that I could keep my flat here, the place I have worked hard to make a comfortable home, and buy somewhere in Greece. It could work, couldn't it? I'd be more than content with that, and I would have some money left in the bank to secure my future.

I feel excitement stir in the pit of my stomach the more I mull it over. A holiday home in the sun.

Having seen the wildflowers bloom in spring, my mind goes into overdrive. I could rent it out when I'm not there for part of the summer, and still be able to eat outside into early autumn. Okay, it might be difficult getting flights after late October, but I don't mind that, as by then I go into full-on excitement mode for Christmas. My brother, his wife, and my gorgeous nephew, George, will join us this year at my parents' place for Christmas Day, as they do every year. Wherever we are in the world, we always all spend Christmas together.

'I have an idea,' I tell Evie. 'Do you fancy a long weekend in Corfu?'

'When? I feel as though we have only just come back.' She sounds surprised.

'At the end of the month?' I suggest, just two weeks away.

Evie joined me for a few days last time, towards the end of my week, as she was feeling a bit burned out.

'You do remember I'm married. And a mum,' she reminds me, chuckling.

'I know, but the girls aren't babies, are they? And didn't Nick say you should have a break occasionally? And he does have his golf weekends. Just saying.'

'You're right, of course, and, actually, the timing couldn't be better. Nick is in fact off golfing that particular weekend and the girls are going to stay with my parents in Cheshire. They're going horse riding.'

'Yay. So, you have no reason not to come then?' I ask her, fingers crossed she says yes.

'Well, let me see, I was all set to paint the bedroom ceiling and... Too right I'll come.' She laughs. 'Will the flights be pricey, though?'

'Don't worry about that, I'm paying. And don't argue. I've invited you, remember.'

'Oh yeah, and you're loaded now, I forgot,' she says, still chuckling.

'We can still be friends though, right?'

'Hmm, maybe. Unless you start frequenting high-end restaurants and walking around in haute couture outfits. Then you're on your own,' says Evie.

'Don't be daft. The bistro on the high street will always be more than enough for me. And the usual mix of high street stores for clothes.'

'Okay. I guess we can still be friends then.'

'Does that mean you will come to Corfu with me?'

'Freebie weekend away. Hmm, let me think. Oh, go on then.'

'Ah, so you are only with me for my money,' I tease.

'Don't say that,' she says, adopting a serious tone.

'Oh, Evie, I'm joking for goodness' sake. You're hardly skint.' Evie and her husband run a successful haulage business, although she told me recently that the cost of everything has shot up. 'Besides I have something to show you when we get there,' I tell her.

'Sounds interesting. Any clues?'

'Let it be a surprise,' I say, which I know will drive Evie mad as she hates surprises.

'At least give me a hint,' she pleads.

'It may involve water,' I say, throwing her completely off the scent. I was thinking of booking us a scuba diving lesson anyway, something we have both always wanted to try. And the rental apartment is near the sea, so it's not a complete lie.

'Okay, in that case, great! A weekend in Corfu sounds

preferable to painting our bedroom. Maybe I'll get a man in instead.'

'I hope Nick doesn't find out.'

'Funny.' I imagine her rolling her eyes.

'And I know it seems like a long way for a weekend, so I'll book a seven a.m. flight out, and an early morning flight back for Monday, to make the most of it,' I tell her.

'Sounds like you have thought of everything. You will at least let me pay towards the accommodation?' she asks.

'Absolutely not. You know how cheap the apartments are. Luckily, there is one available. We can stuff our face with cake and sit on the balcony watching the sun go down with a kumquat liqueur after a day on the beach.'

'Kumquat?'

'The fruits of Corfu. There were bottles everywhere in the gift shops. They were hard to miss, with that vivid orange. Don't you remember?'

'Surprisingly enough, I don't pay too much attention to bright orange liqueur these days. Maybe once upon a time, but I think I'll stick to the white wine now. But an unexpected return to Greece though, how could I possibly refuse?'

I think of the map of the island Phoebe had given to me. Maybe we can hire a quad bike and take off into the mountains to visit the castle and the monastery. Or just visit the local beaches. I guess there will be all the time in the world to explore properly, once I have my house there.

'That's my girl.' I'm thrilled Evie is coming along.

If Nick hadn't been going away golfing and the girls to their gran's, I would have probably suggested they come out too, and happily paid for the apartment. I would also value my brother's opinion on the house too, but know it would be difficult for him to get away at such short notice.

After the call, I fire up my laptop and book everything and look to see if there are any photos of the villa in Roda. To my disappointment, I can't seem to find it on the larger property sites though.

I wish I had taken the phone number of the local estate agent from the board outside the property, but never mind. Just as I'm about to give up, and accept that I can do that when I get over there in less than two weeks, I see it.

My potential dream home in Roda is there! Up for auction online on Friday afternoon at one o'clock, with a suggested opening bid of forty thousand pounds. It's hard to ascertain the exact state of the interior of the building, as the online photos are pretty dark. No doubt to disguise the reality, but even so, I find my heart beating that bit faster thinking of the possibility of that house being within my grasp. I have even met the next-door neighbour, so perhaps it's meant to be. If only the auction was after my next visit, then I would at least be able to arrange to have a look at the inside of the villa. I've seen it from the outside though, and it looks solid enough, apart from needing a good coat of paint, and maybe there is a crack or two in the walls, but it is probably just the plaster. How bad can it really be?

For a moment, I wonder whether I'm being a little selfish buying a place abroad even though it's only a holiday home, at least for the foreseeable future. With Josh moving down south, will my parents miss having their kids nearby, or is that a ridiculous notion? We're both fully grown adults after all and they both have friends, along with their respective bowling and crafting clubs. Yet I know Mum likes inviting me around for tea, and how much she enjoys having a coffee and catch-up at our favourite café on the high street once a week. Or perhaps it's me that would miss that. I've always felt close to my family and enjoy the thought of my parents being a stone's throw away, and probably overreacted way more than I should have done when Josh decamped to Essex.

Still, children fly the nest, don't they? And we never forget our childhood memories, which are wonderful even though I selfishly would have liked to have lived in a house full of siblings crashing up and down the stairs, and enjoying dinner around a huge table. I guess Josh and I were lucky to be raised in a happy home though, which I know isn't the case for everyone. I have a lot to be grateful for.

FIVE

Brian Hamilton did a great job with Uncle Jack's funeral. He dressed in a black top hat and tails and walked solemnly in front of the hearse, as Mum and the rest of us looked on with heavy hearts.

There was a good turnout of mourners, despite Jack having no children. Neighbours stood alongside blokes from the pub he frequented, and staff from the high street café he visited for breakfast. It comforted Mum knowing how well he had been thought of.

Josh and his wife, Zoe, had travelled from their home down south, and I thought my brother looked tired. My three-year-old nephew, George, behaved impeccably at the service, and tucked into pasta at the pub afterwards.

'So, how's work going?' I ask my brother as we sit nursing drinks in the pub, whilst Zoe has taken George outside to the children's play area.

'Stressful.' He takes a long glug of his pint.

'I guess a job in sales was always going to be stressful,' I remark.

'That's true, but I was always very good at it. Even though it wouldn't have been my first choice of career.'

It's a shame that we often fall into careers that aren't necessarily our dream. Josh had been a promising painter, but never really pursued it.

'It's never too late to switch careers,' I suggest, Josh only being in his thirties.

'Maybe.' He shrugs. 'But the job pays well, at least it did.'

'What's changed?'

'The economy, I guess. People aren't buying new cars as much these days, opting for hiring them, or buying older ones which means my commission has reduced,' he reveals. 'The electric car thing had a boom for a while and people were waiting months for them on order. Not so much now. I'll be honest, Jack's inheritance has come at the right time.' He sighs.

'So, what will you do with the money?' I ask.

'Pay off a load of debt,' he admits as he takes a sip of his beer. 'How about you?' he asks, a strain showing in his eyes, I can't help noticing.

'Oh, Josh, I've got this crazy idea that won't go away. I've seen a house in Corfu that I'm thinking of buying. It's a bit of a do-up, but you know how much I love it there.'

'Sounds great. You should go for it.' He smiles.

'Do you think so?'

'For sure, as long as it's a sound property. At least you had the sense not to saddle yourself with a load of debt.'

I think of Josh's large house in Essex, the two cars on the driveway, and the immaculate image they work hard to maintain. The nice clothes, the stylish home interior. They have bought into a lifestyle that involves a lot of entertaining and spending vast amounts of money I imagine. Josh glances at his expensive wristwatch which, if I'm honest, I would never have imagined him wearing. Typical of him to do the right thing though and try and settle some debts.

'Anyway, we should probably make a move soon to try and avoid the rush hour traffic,' he says as he finishes his drink.

'You're not staying over?' I ask, shocked. 'It's a long journey home, and I'm not sure you're in a fit state to drive, it's been an emotional day.'

'I can't afford to take time off,' he says honestly. 'And Zoe must be back tomorrow as she has an important meeting with a potential client. I won't lie, I am a little tired though.'

My sister-in-law works as an advertising executive in a huge office in London.

'Then you must stay over. Plus, I'd give anything to spend an extra few hours with this one,' I say as George runs back into the pub with Zoe close behind keeping an eye on him.

I place my nephew on my knee and tickle him, and he giggles.

Dad appears then, with a half-bottle of whisky and some glasses on a tray and sits down preparing for a toast to Jack.

'I'd better not. We were thinking of getting off soon,' Josh tells Dad, although a bit half-heartedly this time.

'You're heading back? Does your mother know?' Dad says, glancing towards Mum, who is chatting to the lady from the library. 'She's got your old room ready.'

These days, Josh's old room is a pleasant guest room with double bed and a sofa bed for George. I know Mum would love them to have a sleepover more frequently than they do, but accepts the fact that they have busy lives. It is Uncle Jack's funeral though. Surely Mum had a right to think that they would be staying over?

'No, it's just... well, we'll miss the traffic about now. It will be hell later.' He eyes the drinks on the tray for a second. 'But you know what? Sod it. How often do I get to see my family, and I'm burying my uncle, after all.'

He takes a shot of whisky and knocks it back in one. As he

heads to the bar a few minutes later, Zoe joins him, and I can see she has a face like thunder.

'Everything alright?' asks Mum, when Josh returns, having taken in the scene at the bar.

'Fine.' He shrugs. 'But Zoe is heading back shortly as planned. Me and George can go home on the train tomorrow, just the two of us, can't we, buddy?'

'Will you be able to get the time off work?' asks Mum, looking a bit uncertain.

'I'm pretty sure it won't be a problem, we're not that busy, and I'm at my uncle's funeral, after all. I'll give my boss a call in a minute. You like the train, don't you, George?' He turns to my nephew.

'Yeah,' says George as Josh ruffles his hair.

That night at Mum's, with a tired-out George fast asleep, Josh and I sit chatting in the lounge.

'So, go on then, I know you are going to ask,' he says as he swirls a nightcap around in his glass.

'About you and Zoe?'

My brother lets out a deep sigh.

'So, is there anything to tell?'

'Not really.' He shrugs. 'We barely see each other, both working all hours. Zoe still works when she's at home in the evening, answering emails, and goodness knows what. We seem to be bickering a lot lately,' he reveals. 'To be perfectly honest, things aren't that great right now.'

'I'm sorry to hear that. Maybe you're both just under a lot of pressure in your jobs?'

'Maybe, but we've put ourselves under pressure outside of it. Don't get me wrong, I like our home, and our friends. Well, I say friends, they are the people in the cul-de-sac really.

Somehow we lost touch with our old mates when we moved down to Essex.'

'Or moved up? They do say that happens when you start moving in different circles,' I suggest.

'I'm not sure it's moving up exactly, although Zoe insists on keeping up with the neighbours, wanting the best of everything. She spent four grand on a bloody marble-topped kitchen table.' He runs his fingers through his hair. 'Who really cares about that sort of thing, especially as we hardly ever use it.' He shakes his head.

'Well, you should do.' I can hardly believe they spent that much on a table.

'Try telling her that. Everything is for show.' He shrugs.

Listening to my brother, none of this sounds like the Josh I remember. He used to be an easy-going surfer type, who enjoyed painting and hoped to maybe sell some of his work one day. Then along came the beautiful Zoe, who turned his head, and somehow he got into sales, which he discovered he was good at. I look at my handsome brother, his slightly curly hair and that wide smile, and brown eyes that crinkle at the corners when he laughs. I also can't help wondering if the delectable Zoe has taken advantage of his easy-going nature.

'You should come and visit. Stay over,' he suggests.

'I'd really like that. You should come and stay too. You can have my bedroom; I'll take the double sofa,' I offer.

'I'd take the sofa bed,' he says, finishing his drink. 'As I would probably come up on my own.'

'Oh, Josh, I had no idea things were so strained at home. I mean, how would I? Me up here, you down there.'

'There's not much you could do, I suppose. Anyway, it's good to talk to you, sis. Why is it that sad events like funerals are the things that bring families together?'

'That's true, isn't it? I guess everyone is so busy, but we should make the time.'

'Shall we finish this off?' asks Josh, reaching for the bottle.

'Just a drop. I can't be doing with a hangover even working from home tomorrow,' I tell him.

We chat for a while longer, sharing memories of Uncle Jack until I can barely keep my eyes open.

'Right, time for bed I think,' I tell my brother. 'Or I will go past it, and lie awake for hours.'

'I know that feeling,' he admits as he swirls his wine around in his glass, and I wonder what is keeping my brother awake at night.

Outside of our respective bedroom doors, I squeeze Josh in a hug, sensing he maybe needs it right now.

'Night, sis.'

'Night, Josh, see you in the morning. Bring your appetite to the breakfast table. Dad's cooking.'

SIX

We're sitting in the lounge sipping coffee, George watching a cartoon on TV, while Mum and Dad are in the kitchen, as Dad rustles up his famous breakfast.

'Do you remember I told you that I'm considering buying a villa in Greece?' I ask Josh as I sip my drink, and visualise the white building in the blazing sunshine.

'I do.'

'Well, I've got my eye on one that needs a little work, although not a major renovation.' He's about to say something, but I chatter on excitedly. 'It's only a stone's throw from the sea, in the village of Roda. Remember all our family holidays there? Can you imagine spending time there again, whenever you felt like? I can almost feel the sun on my skin as I speak.'

My brother frowns for a moment.

'Yeah, you mentioned buying a place, and of course I loved our holidays there, but what do you know about doing up houses?' He raises an eyebrow.

'You've changed your tune, you told me I ought to go for it,' I remind him.

'I know I was enthusiastic about it initially,' he admits. 'But old houses can be a money pit,' he advises cautiously.

'Well, I can afford to get the work done professionally, and I'm okay with painting and decorating,' I say indignantly, feeling sad that he doesn't seem to be even a teeny bit excited. 'Anyway, ssh, I haven't actually mentioned it to Mum and Dad yet,' I tell Josh as Mum pops her head around the lounge door and tells us breakfast will be ready in five minutes.

'Well, it's a big thing to take on, but I guess if anyone can do it, you can,' he says, but without much enthusiasm.

'I reckon I can. I do have an eye for interior design and finding bargains.' My end of line chrome shower from a shop on the high street was an absolute steal. 'You have to admit, the flat looks good.'

'There's no denying that, but do you know any builders in Greece?' he asks. 'Or anything about Greek law. And have you seen the inside of the property?' He bombards me with questions, bursting my bubble with every single one.

'No, no and not really,' I tell him, wondering if I really am crazy to even contemplate such a project. He's right, what do I really know about building work? But then, the rest of the houses on the row look sound enough, and maybe the neighbour next door would have told me if she had any problems with rising damp or anything. Wouldn't she?

'Is there someone you can trust to help you?' he asks.

'I'm hoping Thea can point me in the direction of someone. And my potential new next-door neighbour, Phoebe. It's a shame I'm not going until the end of month though as I'd like a chance to look inside, but hey ho.'

'Wait. You're telling me you are prepared to buy a house, even though you haven't seen inside?' He looks aghast.

'Yes, but only if the price is right. Look, I've come into money and the villa could be a real bargain. The location is so perfect, it might just be my little piece of paradise.' I resist adding, *It's my inheritance, I will spend it how I like.*

'Well, it sounds like you have already made up your mind,' says Josh eventually. 'So I can only wish you the best of luck.'

'Could you be a little bit excited for me? It could be perfect,' I say, feeling disappointed by his reaction. 'It's down a side street, a short walk from the beach, and as I said you can actually hear the sound of the waves from the balcony. There's a local bar and taverna and I just know it will make the perfect holiday home. The auction is tomorrow and there is no way I am missing out.'

'Tomorrow?'

'Yes. Exciting, isn't it?' I really want him to feel at least a little bit of my enthusiasm.

'You should go for it.' He smiles. 'Really, you should, although you can't blame me for being a little cautious, I'm just watching out for my little sister.'

'And I appreciate that.' I smile warmly.

We enjoy a delicious full English breakfast and Mum even went to the trouble of making George pancakes with fruit, which go down a treat.

Glancing at a painting on the kitchen wall, I ask Josh if he still paints. It saddens me that he is going to use most of his inheritance to settle debts.

'I can't remember the last time I did,' he admits. 'When I'm not working, Zoe has usually arranged something or other with friends, or I'm just plain knackered. Especially since George has come along.'

'You should make time. A hobby like painting should be relaxing. Something to help you switch off. I remember how much you used to enjoy it,' I remind him.

'You definitely should, you always were good at painting. I remember your pictures being displayed on the wall at school,' adds Mum.

Josh would sometimes sit in the garden and sketch the trees and outline of hills in the background before filling them in with watercolours. I always thought he displayed real talent.

'Does Zoe not have any hobbies?' I ask, knowing full well she goes to Zumba classes and has regular get-togethers with her friends at a local bistro.

'Sometimes. Look, I know what you're getting at, but the job is so full-on it wipes me out. But, yes, maybe I should paint as a way of relaxation, or at least go for a run now and then,' he concedes.

'Self-care is so important. You'll be no good to George if you end up ill,' I whisper, as George finishes his pancakes.

'I know.' He nods. 'Well, that was definitely worth staying over for, thanks, Dad.' He pushes his plate away, having polished off every scrap of the delicious full English breakfast. 'And, Mum, for George's pancakes.'

'It's a pleasure, we love having people to cook for,' says Mum as I pile the plates up ready to go into the dishwasher.

It's been so good spending time with my brother and my gorgeous nephew, George, I think to myself after they have headed off to catch their train home. Maybe Josh could bring George over on holiday, when I get my place in Corfu. We could build sandcastles at the beach and swim in the clear blue sea.

I realise that I am getting a little ahead of myself. And that I can't seem to visualise Zoe coming over with him. I dearly hope that they can work things out together. It would be nice to see a glimpse of the brother I grew up with again.

SEVEN

'It's been so lovely having your brother here. It's a pity he only manages to turn up for special occasions,' Mum says with a deep sigh as she pours me and Dad a cup of tea from the pot. I've logged into work and have agreed to work at Mum's for a few hours. I know she finds it a wrench when we all leave, even though I only live a few miles up the road.

I've decided not to tell anyone other than Josh about my plan to buy the house, as they will only try and talk me out of it, but there is no way I am missing out. Properties in that area so close to the sea hardly ever come up for sale, and when they do they are completely out of my price range. As for the tradesmen, I'm sure my friend Thea at the bakery will be able to recommend someone reliable; she pretty much knows everyone in the village, and I do seem to vaguely recall her saying her nephew was in the building trade. Even so, my stomach churns over a little every time I think about joining the auction later. I hope I don't lose my nerve.

'It's a long trek, I guess. And you do know you are welcome to visit them down there,' I remind Mum. Josh often suggests this to my parents.

'Hmm,' says Mum as she switches on the dishwasher.

'What does "hmm" mean?'

'Well, I know he says that, and I'm not saying we aren't made welcome, but I always feel Zoe is putting on a show and would rather we were not there. That's why we stayed in a hotel last time.'

'You stayed in a hotel?' I look up in surprise. She hadn't mentioned that before. 'Why on earth would you do that?'

'It was fine, really. And little George would only have trotted into our room at six a.m. otherwise, so at least we had a lie-in.' She smiles. 'I'm a right grump if I don't get enough sleep.'

'I guess so. Anyway, I'm sure Josh will be back soon. Especially after one of your breakfasts, eh, Dad.'

'I hope so. That was a bit of a funny business though, Zoe going off home without him, don't you think?' says Dad as he sips his tea. 'She hardly said two bloody words at the funeral.'

'I'm sensing trouble in paradise,' says Mum. 'Did he say anything to you?' She turns to me.

'Two seconds, Mum.'

I quickly respond to an email, before taking an incoming call.

When I've finished, I continue the conversation. 'Not really,' I say, not knowing if it's my place to say too much, besides I don't want Mum worrying. 'I think maybe they are just both working too hard.'

'That's the modern world for you,' says Dad. 'All you ever hear about is stress, everyone thinking they can do it all, and I don't just mean women before you say I'm sexist. People chase the wrong things, that's the trouble, and they want everything now. When me and your mother first started out, we had a second-hand sofa and—'

'Yes, okay, love,' Mum says, heading Dad off before he begins one of his monologues about everything that is wrong in today's society. 'That's how things are these days, rightly or wrongly.'

'I still can't see Josh in sales though, although his charming manner probably yields more results than from those pushy types,' I tell Mum.

'Oh, I agree. There's nothing worse than a pushy salesperson. I still regret buying that purple dress from Next that does nothing for my colouring, even though the assistant told me I looked beautiful,' Mum says, and I laugh.

'It's funny, I still imagine Josh with his surfboard and tousled hair, hanging out on the beaches in North Wales. On holiday, charming the local females.'

'I know.' Mum smiles at the memory. 'He was always in the sea, wasn't he? Whilst you were always stretched out basking in the sun as I recall, chatting up the boys.'

I used to take my best friend at the time along to the caravan we frequented every summer, and we got to know some other families that included teenage boys. Mum was right about us chatting with them, or flirting more like: my friend and I would toss our long hair over our shoulders, mine chestnut brown, hers blonde, and hang out with them at the local funfair in the evening. We enjoyed long, heady summer days that are embedded in my memory forever.

I guess I have always loved the seaside, so it's no surprise that I have such a love of the Greek islands. The rushing of the sea as it caresses the sand, and the hot sun has always been able to soothe away any stresses in my life. The most recent being the end of a disastrous relationship, when I had finally dipped my toe into the dating scene again. It had been the first relationship since I'd split with my ex after six years together, on and off; we had long breaks sometimes, but somehow always ended up back together.

I met my long-term partner at work, when he took the desk opposite me. There was no big drama when we finally split; we had simply outgrown each other. It still hurt like hell at the time though, knowing it was over and I likely wouldn't see him again, especially as he changed jobs. We had been such a big part of each other's families that both our mums sobbed when we broke up.

I'm glad the split was civilised though, and when I looked at his wedding photos on Facebook recently and felt nothing but an affectionate memory of our time together, I knew it was the right decision.

When I did dip my toe into the dating scene again, maybe I was naïve, or maybe I was just unlucky. Either way, that last one was enough for me to consider taking a vow of celibacy.

Before I know it it's lunchtime, so I grab my laptop and head off to my flat. It's a nice morning, so I decline the offer of a lift from Dad and walk the two miles across town to my place. Imagining the steps clocking up on my daily steps app.

Passing houses with neatly mown lawns and perfect flowering borders, I close my eyes and imagine the front garden of my house in Corfu. I think of an early evening walk down to the beach, enjoying a cocktail or two at a beachside café. I'm so lucky to have the chance to work remotely, and with good Wi-Fi I might even be able to spend the odd few days working over in Greece. I try not to get ahead of myself as I imagine glancing out of the window at the distant mountains and sipping frappés.

'I'm just popping over to my villa in Greece to work from home for a few days,' I will tell my colleagues. *My* villa in Greece! I realise I am jumping the gun once more and feel panicked at the thought of anyone else outbidding me at the auction, even though I am a firm believer that if something is meant to happen, then it will. That house simply must be mine.

Back home, I open my large bag to retrieve my laptop, and laugh as I find a piece of my Mum's home-made lemon cake wrapped in foil and think of what she could do with all those Greek lemons!

I hope my parents will come and have some lovely holidays while they are both still fit, then shake my head and tell myself to keep a grip on reality. But then, it's okay to dream, isn't it?

EIGHT

I log in and take a few deep breaths as I wait for the online auction to begin. I have stuck to my guns and told no one about my plans, apart from my brother, so that nobody could talk me out of it, but I feel utterly compelled to do my utmost to become the owner of this house. I have been gifted this money and I could potentially buy a house in the place I adore, which is beyond my wildest dreams.

Uncle Jack knew about my lust for travel, and how I particularly loved Corfu, so I think he would approve somehow. Actually, he did tell me what a wonderful adventure he had in Mexico, visiting Chichén Itzá and sipping margaritas on a palm-fringed beach watching the sunset. I briefly wonder if I'm tying myself down buying a place, rather than travelling the world, although I guess my money would soon run out if I did that.

'Bricks and mortar. That's the thing to invest in.' Hearing my dad's voice in my head reassures me a little that I am doing the right thing as excitement rushes through me in anticipation.

The auction is just about to start when my mobile rings. It's Evie, but I don't have time to chat so she leaves me a voicemail saying it was nothing too important. I quickly tap out a text and tell her I will call her back shortly. Hopefully with some news.

The bidding starts at thirty-five thousand rather than the forty I expected it to, so I swallow down a little feeling of excitement as I realise it might actually be within my grasp!

An offer is immediately put in at thirty-six, so I bid thirty-seven. It's followed by another bid and soon enough we are at the forty thousand mark. Things slow down a little then, the bids only going up in five hundred amounts. I can feel the palms of my hands begin to sweat as I try and steady my breathing. I don't really want to go as high as fifty thousand, as it might cost that much to do the renovation.

I picture a courtyard with a blue gate and a huge lemon tree in a pot. A glimpse through the backyard on my last visit revealed it to be a bit of a jungle, although there is already an olive tree surviving amongst the wildness.

The bids climb higher, and my heart begins to thud even more. This is a million times more stressful than buying something on eBay; I remember the same feeling when I bid for a second-hand designer bag, and the disappointment I felt when I was outbid.

Please don't let that happen today.

The bids climb, and suddenly there is another call on my mobile. I take a quick glance at my phone and recognise the number as an electricity company. I ignore it, but then there is a call on the intercom; a delivery guy is wanting to deliver something. I wonder whether they are signs that I should not proceed? I buzz the guy in and tell him to leave the parcel in the communal hallway, thankful that it doesn't need a signature.

In a flash, the bidding is at forty-four thousand pounds, but things seem to have slowed down.

I say a silent prayer as I put in my final bid of forty-four thousand five hundred. The seconds feel like minutes, and I breathe deeply as my heart hammers inside my chest.

Then finally just as quickly as it started, the auction is over.

It takes me a moment to process what has just happened. I've only gone and done it. The villa in Greece is mine!

I let out a loud whoop before I race downstairs to collect my parcel.

Upstairs, I unwrap the box and admire the print on canvas. It's a beautiful beach scene in vivid colours that I stumbled across on a website. I thought it would look good against my freshly painted white walls that contrast nicely with my dark-wooden dining table, but the timing feels like a sign that I have done the right thing.

Thinking about it, Josh has the talent to do something like this. I do hope he begins to dabble again as he has suggested he might. I would be proud to display one of his paintings on my wall.

It occurs to me then that the painting would also look good on the walls of my house in Greece. *My* house!

I flop down onto the sofa and resist the urge to scream out loud, as the old guy across the landing would probably only knock and check I was okay if I did that. I'm bursting to tell my parents. Albeit slightly apprehensively, hoping they will approve.

I've decided to keep it a surprise from Evie until the weekend when I take her there. I will have to collect the keys from the estate agent first, and there is all the admin and costs, but I've done it.

I have bought my own little piece of paradise!

NINE

I call Josh immediately and tell him my news.

'So, you did it then? Congratulations, I can't wait to see it,' he says enthusiastically.

'Do you mean that? I'm heading over there for a long weekend with Evie next week. I mean, it's going to take a lot of hard work, but when it's done you must book a flight and come over. It might take a while to sort out a guest room though.' I realise I am babbling away ten to the dozen and imagine him smiling at the other end of the phone.

'It all sounds very exciting. I know how much you love Greece. Really, I'm happy for you. In Roda too, all those happy holiday memories from our childhood, as you said. I can't wait to come over and see it.'

'Thanks, Josh. You sound upbeat,' I tell him, and he reveals he has just sold a top of the range BMW, so is in for a nice bit of commission.

'Brilliant! Funny how money comes to you when you already have some,' I say, thinking of our inheritance. 'Ninety grand though? Who the hell has that kind of money to spend on a car?' I'm aghast.

'Erm, you,' he reminds me. 'It's just that you chose to buy a house instead.'

'Oh, yeah.' I laugh. 'And you.'

'True enough, although I will probably spend mine sorting my life out,' he says. 'Oh, and I took your advice. I bought an easel and a top of the range painting set earlier. I'm going to the South Downs to paint on Sunday. George is having a day with Zoe's parents.'

'That sounds lovely.'

I don't ask him why he and Zoe aren't spending the day together.

We wrap up the call, then I remember Evie calling me earlier and return her call. She asks me if I fancy a trip into town tomorrow as she needs a few bits and pieces for our weekend away.

'I wore my sandals out with all that walking we did last time, so need some new ones. Oh, and a new bikini. There won't be much walking this time, I hope. I'm looking forward to a rest.'

'I did tell you to pack your trainers last time,' I remind her.

'I know, but they are so unflattering.'

'So are pig's feet from walking around in fancy sandals.'

'Oi, I don't have pig's feet.' She laughs. 'Although I take your point. I'll buy some trainers. I think I saw some sparkly ones in a sale at Kurt Geiger.'

'Anyway, there won't be much walking this time, just a bit of sunbathing and shopping,' I reassure her. 'We'll have an evening drink on the terrace of the apartment. Oh, there's a great little taverna not far away that we must try too.'

Last time Evie came out we headed to the main street in Roda, shopping and eating at pretty restaurants overlooking the sea. It will be nice to explore the area around my new home again and I almost blurt that out before I stop myself.

'Can't wait.'

'Me neither. See you tomorrow. Eleven o'clock sharp outside Flannels.'

It's going to be a struggle keeping things from Evie, as we share everything, and I know I will be bursting to say something as soon as I see her.

A feeling of apprehension washes over me for a split second as I wonder whether I really have done the right thing. As Josh had reminded me, what do I know about builders, not to mention Greek law? I am going to be relying on my friend Thea to set me on the right path, which I am sure she will, so maybe there is no need to worry about that side of things. Other people buy houses abroad, don't they? It's all about having a positive attitude.

Besides, I've done it now, the house is mine and if I can't do this type of thing while I'm young and with an unexpected inheritance, when can I do it, right?

I place the phone down and think about the people I really hope will agree that I have made a great decision as I try and get a little more work done.

After dinner, I close my laptop and make the short drive to my parents' house to break the news.

Not before I take one more look at the house on the computer with more than a little bit of pride.

TEN

'Twice in one day! To what do we owe the honour?' Dad asks as he opens the front door, a banana in his hand.

'I have something to tell you,' I say, feeling inexplicably terrified. Didn't my dad always say to invest in property? So, I'm not sure why I feel so nervous. Maybe it's because I don't actually know whether or not I have invested in a money pit. I tell myself it doesn't look too bad on the photos though.

My mum switches the volume down on the television, her expression a mixture of concern and surprise.

'Well, come on then, don't keep us in suspense. What do you have to tell us? Although I'm not sure why you didn't tell us earlier.'

'Because I have only just done it.' I swallow hard.

'Done what? For goodness' sake, spit it out,' says Dad, reaching over for a two finger Kit Kat.

'I've bought a house,' I say brightly.

'Have you really? Well, that's wonderful news. I've always said, haven't I, put your money in bricks and mortar,' says Dad with approval. 'Oh yes, a very sensible thing to do with your inheritance. I'm sure Uncle Jack would approve.'

'Oh, I agree, love, that's wonderful. I did wonder whether you might buy a bigger place. Your flat's lovely, but there's something about having a whole house,' says Mum. 'So where exactly is it?'

I decide to tell them quickly. Rip the plaster off.

'It's in Greece.'

'Greece!' Mum exchanges a look with Dad, open-mouthed. 'You've bought a house in Greece?'

'I have. You know how much I love it there. And before you ask, I'm not emigrating, it's going to be a holiday home. I only paid just under forty-five thousand pounds. It's a bit of a renovation project, although nothing too drastic. At least I hope not.' I can hear myself babbling.

My dad gives a low whistle as he runs his hands through his thick head of greying hair.

'Well, you've always been a bit impulsive, but I think this takes the biscuit,' he says finally. Mum is silently absorbing the information. 'But actually, why not? I hope it has a spare bedroom for me and your mum to come and stay.' He nods, warming to the idea.

'Of course it has! And you would be made more than welcome. It will be just like going on holiday all those years ago,' I tell them enthusiastically.

'I'm a bit shocked, I won't lie, but yes, we know you love Greece, we all do,' agrees Mum. 'A holiday home, hey? I've often thought about having one of those. Well done, love,' she says, and I breathe a sigh of relief that they don't think I have gone stark raving mad.

'I'm going over next weekend for a few days with Evie, so I'll send you some pictures. I'll be getting builders in, but you know, Dad, I will always appreciate your input.'

'Maybe leave it to the professionals.' Mum raises an eyebrow and glances at Dad.

'How was I to know those boards were completely rotten?'

he says, referring to the time he decided to replace the bathroom floor after a flood and Mum screamed at the sight of Dad's legs dangling through the ceiling during an episode of *Coronation Street*.

'Oh, I'm so excited, and I'm glad you don't think I'm crazy.' I breathe a sigh of relief.

'Not at all. Me and your mum have been talking about a cruise in late summer. Maybe we could choose one that docks in Greece and come and have a look at your house.'

'Sounds wonderful. Although you don't usually get enough time on land on a cruise. Maybe fly over when it's finished. I won't have loads of time to be there myself, I have a job here remember.'

Which is why I am relying on Thea to help me find suitable builders. People I can rely on. I can use most of my annual leave to oversee the project, but I need people on board who I can trust to carry on with the work in my absence.

'It is exciting,' says Mum. 'And whether it's home or abroad, I'm pretty sure property is always a sound investment.'

Hopefully she's right.

I fire up my laptop up and show my parents pictures of the villa. There is an outdoor stone staircase leading to a bedroom with a wooden balcony that looks completely rotten, but I can already imagine it with hanging pink flowers trailing down towards the garden from a brand new wrought-iron balustrade.

'Oh, I can see that being really pretty when it's finished.' Mum clasps her hands together. 'And Roda is such a lovely village, isn't it? There was once quite an expat community there, I believe, although I don't know if that's still the case.'

'Probably, but I don't mind if there isn't. I could probably do with brushing up on my very limited Greek anyway, although I guess a Google search would tell me if there are any groups. It might be a good way to make friends.'

I went on several holidays to Roda with my parents when I

was younger, that led to a lifelong love affair with Corfu. Some days we would take the bus down to busy Sidari and Mum would browse the souvenir shops, whilst Dad would 'get us a seat' at a restaurant with an outside table overlooking the sea for lunch – no doubt furtively sampling the baklava with his coffee before we returned. Mum would always buy a gift set of olive oil and herbs for our neighbour who kept an eye on the house, along with a touristy tea towel showing a map of the island. Even now I can't resist a browse around the souvenir shops as it always evokes such pleasant memories. It's just a brilliant place to go and relax and switch off from everything in the world.

'Right, that's me off then.' I leave my parents' house for the second time that day and head off home.

I never realised just how much their reaction would mean to me, but I'm so relieved they don't think it's a bad idea. A text pops through on my phone as I arrive home. It's from Josh.

Have you told Mum and Dad about your plans yet?

Literally just this second. They like the idea. <heart emoji>

Cool. I thought they might. Who wouldn't like the chance of a free holiday to Greece? <smiling emoji>

I feel the need to flick through some photos of Uncle Jack and myself, and silently thank him for the gift of my inheritance, which came totally out of the blue.

There are photos of us on bikes, riding through Delamere Forest. It's where he met my auntie Kathleen, when she served us at a tiny coffee hut at the end of a footpath in the pouring rain. They chatted about the native birds in the forest, when he remarked upon seeing a woodpecker, and discovered a shared love of wildlife. Six months later she had upped sticks and moved to Merseyside to be with him, perhaps partly due to the fact that he lived in a village that had wetlands close by and every type of wading bird you could possibly wish to spot. It was joyful to see how in love Jack and Kathleen were, especially later in life.

Putting the photo album away, I silently thank Jack for inspiring my desire to travel as memories of playing with the globe in his front room come rushing back again. I know how lucky I am and feel grateful to Jack for ensuring I have money for my future. If only there was something that could guarantee you won't get your heart broken again.

ELEVEN

'Passport, tickets, money, bank cards,' I repeat over to myself as I zip up my bag for the flight.

Evie's husband is dropping us at the airport early, en route to taking the girls to their grandparents' place in Cheshire.

'I bet this is a lot more exciting than painting and doing the gardening,' says Nick as he drops us off. 'Although it was your idea to do that, not mine.' He laughs, probably making the point that he isn't an uncaring husband who has his wife painting whilst he's playing golf. As if he needed to tell me that.

'I expected you to organise something fun for yourself,' he reinforces the point. 'I was surprised you wanted to paint the ceiling.'

'I know and I appreciate that, but with not long returning from Greece, I felt a bit guilty going again so soon,' Evie says. 'But as you are going golfing, I did think about going out with the girls from work, but then my best friend stepped up and insisted I go along with her on an all-expenses-paid weekend.' She laughs.

'Well, have a great time. I'll miss you,' he says warmly.

'Yeah, right, after you've had a few on the nineteenth hole, you'll forget I exist,' she tells Nick, who places his hand on his heart and protests.

'And I don't keep tabs on how many times you go away you know, as long as it's not every weekend.' He winks.

'As if I would.' She reaches up and kisses him on the lips.

'You never said you had been invited out with your work friends,' I say as we head off into the airport.

'Oh, I know, but it was a *Magic Mike* tribute thing for a hen do. I'm past the age of watching gyrating men thrust their pelvis in your face.' She laughs.

'Did you ever enjoy that sort of thing?'

'Not really,' she admits. 'I always thought it looked rather unhygienic, rubbing cream on their bodies and asking women to lick it off.' She gives a little shudder.

I'm not surprised by her comment as this is a woman who used to take her own bottled water into restaurants, such was her fear of germs. 'You never know, they might fill bottles with tap water and charge for it. I can't take the chance, not with my delicate stomach,' she would say in her defence.

Many a time we had to make stops so she could use a loo somewhere, the rest of our taxi passengers sighing inwardly – and not always inwardly – due to her anxious tummy, each time vowing she would never drink again.

She seems a lot better these days, but that was after several years of having every test known to man performed by her GP, who concluded she was a picture of health. One or two friends at the time even dared to suggest she was a bit of a hypochondriac.

'It's anxiety,' I told her one evening when she had been to the loo twice before the starter had arrived in a restaurant. 'It must be if there is not actually anything medically wrong with you.'

'Do you think so?' she asked, wiping down the table and the arms of her chair with an antibacterial wipe.

'I do.' I raised an eyebrow as she put her wipes away, the air suddenly filled with the vague scent of pine, which I hoped the waiter didn't think was my perfume.

'You think I'm a nutcase,' she'd said, and I told her no, she just needed to do some more relaxation and stop thinking about it so much. Mind over matter. But, of course, it is never as simple as that. Thankfully she discovered swimming and enjoyed it so much that she magically was able to build up her stamina and was overjoyed when she could manage over sixty lengths without shitting herself in the pool. It was an epiphany. From that day on, she was – almost – cured.

'I'm shattered. These early mornings are a thing of the past for me at the weekend,' says Evie as we board the plane and settle into our seats. 'I'm usually only climbing out of bed at ten thirty, about the same time as the girls.' She laughs.

'Better than getting up in the middle of the night with babies, hey?'

'No kidding,' she says, yawning. 'And I don't think the girls were too happy being dragged out of bed so early either, but they're young, they'll survive.'

I can't ever imagine waking during the night for an infant, surviving on only a few hours' sleep, but then can anybody? I guess when the time comes, you just get on with it and I like to think a good audiobook would get me through the night feeds. If that time ever comes for me.

An hour into the flight, Evie is dozing and a while later, it seems so have I, as the captain is soon making an announcement about making the descent into Corfu Airport.

'Wow, that went quick, have I been asleep?' asks Evie, before tying her long blonde-highlighted hair into a ponytail.

'Asleep? The rest of the passengers had to put their headphones on to drown out the sound of your snoring.' I shake my head.

'You're joking!' She looks mortified.

'Nope.'

She fishes her sunglasses from her bag and places them on, maybe in the hope no one will recognise her in the airport terminal, whispering and laughing at the snoring woman.

The handsome guy at the passport kiosk spends several seconds looking at me, and I resist the urge to give him a sultry look, or even a wink. Then I remember that my embarrassing passport photo bears no resemblance to my current look. These days I wear a long, layered cut and not a slightly out of control perm.

Stepping outside the airport building, the hot sun seems to work its way upwards, massaging my legs before landing on my face that I turn towards the sun, relishing the heat.

'Oh, it's good to be out of the UK, isn't it?' I sigh, putting all thoughts of the dreary weather back home out of my mind.

'It is. I'm so sorry I never got the chance to paint that ceiling though. Not!' Evie giggles as we go and collect the car, a nippy little Fiat Uno. We skirt through part of Corfu Town, taking in the hustle and bustle of traffic, and resolving to return to the Old Town and amble though its maze of streets, until we are out on the highway, that soon gives way to a coast road.

'I can't believe I'm here again.' Evie fiddles with the radio and the sound of Greek music fills the air. She makes me giggle as she sings words she has no idea of the meaning of, with real feeling.

'I'm thinking you should watch Greek TV if you want to learn the language,' she advises me. 'I once saw a travel programme where this guy in Syria said he learned American purely from watching movies.'

'I'll be sure to remember that.' I raise an eyebrow, and wonder whether he spoke in an American accent.

'I'm dying to see what this surprise is,' she says, reminding me that I have managed to keep the house purchase a secret. 'You did say it was something to do with water, so I've been imagining all sorts. I thought maybe a boat trip to another island, but as we are only here for the weekend, I can't imagine you would do that,' continues Evie, trying to prise information from me.

'Just wait and see.' I smile, and she huffs.

I hope she doesn't think I have taken leave of my senses. I'm even less sure she will set foot inside the place, as she likes things clean and shiny, and I know it will be anything but. She also hates spiders, but then, so do I. Maybe I will have to take some photos of the inside and show them to her.

She sings the chorus at the top of her voice and has me laughing.

'What do you suppose that means?' she asks, before typing into Google Translate to discover it means 'You are my one and only'. 'Imagine some gorgeous Greek bloke whispering that to you.' She sighs and I remind her she is a happily married woman. 'I am, and I know I'm lucky, but after sixteen years together it isn't all moonlight and roses, you know.'

That's the thing with relationships, isn't it? It's not like in the movies, where people seem to be in a state of constant lust. The chemical that first attracts us to each other wears off over the years. At least for most people. So, what you are essentially left with is friendship, so you need to make sure you actually like the person you are with, and share some common interests. And work hard to keep the romance alive too, I guess.

We drive along roads flanked by fields, some with olive groves in the distance. With the window down and the Greek music playing, it's suddenly as if I am on an entirely different planet, away from work and all thoughts of the comings and goings of daily life back home neatly filed away. The roads are bordered with yellow and red wildflowers growing beneath a hot sun and a brilliant blue sky.

In no time at all, we turn into a side road and at once glimpse the beach at Roda, with its orange and white umbrellas flapping gently on the sand and I feel my stomach turn over with a mixture of nerves and excitement.

As we pull up to the apartments, Thea is getting out of her car carrying bakery supplies, and smiles broadly when she sees us.

'It is good to see you back so soon.' She places some boxes on top of the car and gives us both a hug.

The owner of the apartment is away right now, so had left the key with Thea for us to collect.

'It seems we can't stay away. We are just over for a long weekend this time though. Oh, and we must have a snack as we have just arrived,' I tell her, following her into the shop.

Trays of cakes and bread rolls are displayed beneath glass counters and have me drooling. Sticky squares of baklava sit alongside honey and nut cake, lemon and orange cake and Thea's speciality, fig bread. We take one of the loaves, along with a slice each of a honeyed pistachio sponge, and some bottled water from the fridge.

We head across the road and, after nipping to the small nearby supermarket for ham and salad, assemble lunch on the apartment balcony that has a glimpse of the beach.

'Can you imagine owning a holiday home in a place like this,' I comment as I slide a cube of salty feta into my mouth and admire the view.

'I can. That is all I can do though, imagine. Besides, I don't think it's very accessible in the winter, is it? And the weather can change a bit in Corfu.' Evie takes a glug of cold water.

She has a point, but I don't suppose I was thinking of being here over the winter. Unless, of course, I can't bear to tear myself away from the beautiful home I envisage creating, then I could take an internal flight from Athens.

'Anyway, eat up, we need to go and collect something.'

I feel the nerves in my stomach, hoping Evie will approve of my, some might say, impulsive purchase.

'Collect something? Is this part of the surprise you've been talking about?' Evie eyes me suspiciously.

'It might be. Actually, yes, it is.'

'Ooh great. Let's go,' Evie says, finishing the last of her water and picking up her bag.

'After that we can hit the beach if you like,' I suggest.

'Shall we unpack first and grab our beach stuff then?' she asks.

'No, we'll come back and do that. We're not going far,' I say, with a little touch of mystery.

Outside, Evie expects us to climb into the car, so is surprised when I tell her we are walking. Five minutes later, we turn into the street next to a bike hire shop and I glance at my watch, my heart beating wildly. We enter the cool estate agent's office with a marble floor and a young estate agent dressed in a blue short-sleeved shirt and dark trousers greets us with a smile.

'*Kalispera.* You are Claudia?' He recognises me from a video call and greets me with a welcoming smile.

'I am, and this is my friend Evie.'

'Congratulations on your purchase.' He smiles, handing me the key. 'I hope you will be very happy here.'

'Happy with what?' Evie looks confused.

'The villa, of course.' Now it's the estate agent's turn to look puzzled as he glances from me to my friend.

'It's a surprise,' I explain and he nods a little uncertainly, probably as he takes in Evie's mouth that is gaping open.

Outside in the blazing sunshine once more, Evie appears to have been rendered speechless.

'You've bought a villa here in Greece?' she says eventually, an excitement in her voice almost reaching fever pitch. 'Is this the surprise?'

'No, I'm marrying a Greek bloke tomorrow who I've been messaging, I wondered if you could be my bridesmaid... Of course the villa is the surprise!'

'Oh my goodness! Wow, well this really is a surprise. Have you used your inheritance money?' She looks a little doubtful.

'I have. I just thought, when would I get an opportunity like this ever again?' I tell her brightly.

'That's true. Oh, I can't wait to see it. But why are we staying in an apartment if you have a home here?' she asks, looking bemused.

'Well, it isn't exactly finished yet. In fact.' I pause for a minute, anticipating the shock. 'It isn't what you might call exactly habitable right now.'

'Oh, please don't tell me you have bought an old ruin,' says Evie, her cautious enthusiasm having completely evaporated.

'Not an old ruin, no, but it does need some work. I bought it from an online auction, it was an absolute bargain, so I couldn't resist,' I say, full of positivity.

'There's usually a reason for that,' she says, unconvinced.

'Oh, where is your sense of adventure.' I laugh, trying to convince myself as well as her, I realise. Not for the first time I wonder whether I might have made a huge mistake. 'Anyway, come on, it's literally a five-minute walk from here. The sea is almost within touching distance. There is no way I could afford a fully restored house in such a location without having to renovate it.'

'I guess not. Lead the way,' says Evie, painting a smile on her face that doesn't quite reach her eyes.

TWELVE

We walk in the bright sun, the sound of the sea in the background, passing people enjoying their day. A couple on a quad bike zip past and crowds of what appear to be locals at this time of year make their way across zebra crossings to the beach opposite. The sight of the spring sunshine glistening on the water immediately lifts my spirits.

A few minutes later, we take a turn across a small patch of wasteland opposite a church, where the road curves upwards. I feel inexplicably nervous as I pass the neat houses, almost holding my breath, wondering what I will find inside as I clutch the front door key tightly in my hand.

'Ta dah,' I say, when I stop outside the house, its front garden sprouting some sort of green weed with white flowers and, despite the sunshine, the walls look decidedly dull. There's a crack snaking down from the bedroom window to the floor. Was it there the last time?

'Is this it then?' Evie looks decidedly underwhelmed.

'It is,' I say proudly. 'I can hardly wait to get inside.'

I open the creaky gate and she follows me into the garden, along the neat path. I could have sworn the path to the front door was overgrown with weeds last time. I imagine the locals clapping their hands with joy knowing the dilapidated old villa has been bought; I'm sure they are fed up with looking at such an eyesore. An old lady across the road appears with a broom in her hand, sweeping the non-existent debris in the road and watching us. I lift my hand and wave and she waves back, smiling, before continuing her sweeping.

'I like that,' says Evie, eyeing the stone staircase to the balcony off the bedroom. 'It's quite romantic. Remember Richard Gere in *Pretty Woman* scaling steps to his love?'

'That was a fire escape in Downtown LA. I'm not expecting someone to come along on a white charger and do the same thing here.' I laugh. 'I think my new neighbour across the road would have her binoculars out if that happened.'

I tentatively push the key into the door and find myself in a front room with a stone floor. There's an old blue-and-white larder style cupboard that looks quite retro, which I am surprised isn't in the kitchen. I open it, and the drawer is jammed with something that, at first glance, I think is some paper, but when I look closer I see that it is an old recipe book, its pages yellowed with age. Maybe I can ask Phoebe to translate some recipes.

'Hey, look at this.' I show Evie the book, and she wrinkles her nose at the dusty paper. 'Maybe I could make us something out of this book, when the kitchen is up and running.'

The walls are in dire need of painting, but first impressions aren't as bad as I expected, apart from a few broken floor tiles that can be replaced. I push the window open and the wooden window frame crumbles like dust in my fingers, and a feeling of concern creeps over me. Will I uncover more problems as I explore further? Maybe I have behaved impulsively and Josh was right to exercise caution after all.

If first impressions in the lounge were okay, the kitchen is a different story. At least I think it's a kitchen, as it's a tiny space and there isn't a single cupboard in sight. It's now clear why the blue larder cupboard was standing at the end of the lounge, beyond the kitchen door. A sorry sink stands in a corner of the room, overlooking the wild rear garden.

Up the creaking stairs, we discover a bathroom suite in an interesting shade of blue with some contrasting brown wall tiles. The pine beamed ceilings feel oppressive, but once painted white they should be just fine. But it's the damp spot on a bedroom floor that has me worried. I glance up at the ceiling where there is also a damp pattern spreading outwards. That needs sorting before the autumn sets in for sure.

'So, what do you think then?' We're standing outside, just as Phoebe appears from next door.

'*Kalispera*. So, you buy the house?' She smiles as I introduce her to my friend.

'I did,' I tell her, praying I have done the right thing. I console myself with the fact that I have enough money to pay for a roof and maybe a ceiling. That must be the biggest spend I will face, surely?

She nips inside her home and returns suddenly with a crucifix. 'To keep the house safe,' she says, placing it on a window ledge. 'But, of course, I will also check everything is okay, after you leave.' She smiles.

'Thank you, that is very kind.'

'Do you have the builder?' She nods towards the house, and I tell her about asking Thea's nephew.

'*Nai*, he is a good boy.' She smiles approvingly. 'I also know people if you need.' She speaks her words carefully, trying hard to master the English language, which is generally good with just one or two grammatical errors.

Two old gents wearing flat caps stroll slowly by then and wish us a *kalispera*. Phoebe says something to them in Greek, and they smile and wish me good luck as they move on.

'Is it just old people on this street?' asks Evie, glancing around.

'Maybe not,' I say, looking over her shoulder at a bloke who has just walked out of a house opposite with a gorgeous chocolate-brown Labrador. She turns to see the good-looking bloke dressed in a tight black T-shirt and denim shorts, who appears to be striding towards us.

'*Kalispera*,' he says, placing the sunglasses he is wearing on the top of his head.

'*Kalispera*,' I reply, painting on my brightest smile while unconsciously standing straighter.

'You are the new owner?' he asks, glancing up at the currently not so attractive villa.

'I am.'

The delightful dog jumps up at me then, and I give it a friendly stroke.

He nods slowly. 'And the work, you will do some of it yourself?' he asks doubtfully.

'Well, some of it, obviously. But this is just a viewing trip. I'm hoping Thea at the bakery will help me recommend some builders. She mentioned her nephew being a builder.'

'He is indeed.'

'Oh, do you know him?'

'I do. I am the nephew.' He smiles a gorgeous smile. 'My name is Dimitri, I am pleased to meet you. Both.'

'Pleased to meet you too. This is my friend Evie.'

'Oh, and this is Prudence.' He introduces the delightful brown dog.

'Ah, she's adorable,' I comment as she wags her tail wildly. 'I love her name.'

'She is actually my aunt's dog, named after a deceased relative we were all fond of.'

He takes in the state of the house then.

'Surely you are not staying here?' he asks in surprise.

'No, of course not, we are in some apartments around the corner. So, what do you think? Can you help? Do you have a lot of work on at the moment?' I bombard him with questions, keen to get things started as soon as possible.

'If I say I am not busy, you will say I am bad builder. If I am too busy, you will worry it may take some time. I am not sure what to tell you.' He smiles, a most delicious smile.

'Maybe just tell me the truth. Can you do the work or not?'

'Of course. I usually work with my friend Yiannis, he is a little older but very experienced. Sometimes I call in some local labourers if it is a big job, or one that needs doing quickly.'

He eyes the exterior wall and I ask him about the crack.

'Just plaster, I am sure. The outside you will want painting anyway, I assume?'

He reaches out and touches the line in the wall, and as his T-shirt rises I see a smooth, tanned stomach and have to avert my eyes.

'Oh yes, I want a white, smooth stomach.'

'Stomach?' He raises an eyebrow.

'What? I mean finish. Stomach? Maybe it's because my stomach has just given a little rumble, haha,' I babble, praying I am not blushing. 'You know, a smooth finish on the walls, white and smooth.' Oh my goodness I'm blushing, I know it.

Dimitri grins and gives me a knowing look.

'Of course,' he says, glancing at his watch. 'I must go to work now, but maybe later I can have a proper look around?'

We arrange to meet him back here at six o'clock this evening.

He climbs into a van, and I hear some Greek music from his radio as he has the windows down. He raises a hand and waves as he sets off around the corner.

'Oh my goodness, that's Thea's nephew?' says Evie. 'He's gorgeous and he's your new neighbour too. That's handy, having a builder over the road.'

'As long as his work is good, that's all I am interested in,' I tell her, and I mean it, despite admiring his obvious good looks. I've worked hard in my job to become a supervisor and have made a lovely apartment back home and I would like to do the same here. I like my life, I enjoy my hobbies, that include walking and cooking, I have a couple of good friends at home and work and my folks are close by, so this place needs to add to all that, not take away. Besides, Dimitri probably has a wife or girlfriend lurking somewhere. Just like my last boyfriend did.

'Anyway, come on. Business talk later, but now as promised let's hit the beach.'

It's early May and the perfect weather for spending the afternoon on the sand, listening to gentle music pumping from the bar.

Watching the rolling waves, I think of how I have bought a house here and for a minute feel simultaneously adventurous and foolhardy. Have I been reckless? Come late October cheap flights won't come to the island, as Evie has pointed out.

One year, in late October just before the flights stopped, I spent the most beautiful week here walking in the foothills. The stunning scenery with its gently changing foliage was a sight to behold, a blanket of orange and mauve moss mingling with ever-green trees. I passed villages and outlines of castles and ancient buildings on the top of the hills and watched birds circling above. It was so wonderful and not something I would have considered in the summer months, in the sweltering heat.

I'd hooked up with a local walking group on that visit, who walked for miles during the cooler months in the spring and autumn, discovering footpaths off the beaten track, and drinking home-made ouzo in gardens offered by locals, who proudly showed off their allotments. One time, the walk leader had to return with her car to accept the abundant bags of courgettes, corn and tomatoes gifted to us from the bumper autumn harvest.

Lying on sunbeds beside each other, Evie receives a photo on her phone of the girls on horses at some local stables with their grandmother. She sends one back of the two of us, raising a beer, the sea in the background.

'I hope Nick is enjoying his golfing trip. Where is it he's going?' I ask.

'Scotland. St Andrews. He's been wanting to play that course for a while now, so when someone in work suggested a golfing weekend, he jumped at the chance.'

'Never fancied taking golf up yourself?' I ask as I sip my cold beer.

'I did try it once, literally once, but couldn't even hit the ball. When I finally did it disappeared off into a pond. No, I'll stick to the gym if I fancy a bit of exercise.'

Finishing the beer, and with the warm effects of the sun and the early start this morning, I can feel my eyes becoming heavy. Maybe a small siesta is in order before meeting Dimitri at the villa, and then out somewhere nice for dinner.

When I wake, what I imagine to be a short while later, Evie is nowhere to be seen. As I look around I see her walking towards me from the bar with a couple of bottles of water. Glancing at my watch, I am shocked to discover I have been asleep for over an hour.

'Did you have a sleep?' I ask, sitting up and stretching my arms out.

'Nope. I read for a bit, but then I did sleep for a while on the plane. I went for a swim, actually. I had forgotten how much I enjoy swimming. I thought I would get us some water instead of more beer, if you want to stay awake later. I'll save myself for a cocktail with dinner.'

'That sounds like a sensible idea,' I say, sitting up and grate-fully taking a glug of the bottled water.

'What type of restaurant do you fancy tonight? There's that

fish one we went to last time, although I did spot a new one opposite the pirate bar, if you fancy it?'

'I don't mind. Yeah, let's try somewhere new, give them a bit of support, hey?'

'Let's do that.' We tap our bottles of water together.

We hang around for another hour, making the most of every minute of the warm sunshine on the relatively empty beach as the summer season hasn't quite started up yet, before we return to our apartment. As we walk along the busy road we meet Thea carrying a straw basket presumably on her way to the shops.

'*Kalispera*. I see you have been enjoying the beach?' she says brightly.

'Yes, it's lovely. Oh, and I met Dimitri earlier. I didn't realise he lived on the same street as the house I am buying... Have bought.' I still need to get used to the idea that I own it.

'Ah, so you met him. Although he does not live in that house. He is looking after my sister's dog this week as she is away on holiday. Has he agreed to do the work?'

'Fingers crossed. I'm meeting him outside the house later.'

'He will do a good job and he has plenty of builder friends,' she reassures me. 'Anyway, enjoy the rest of your day,' she says, placing her hand warmly on my arm as she departs.

'Oh, and I have some honeyed orange cake left,' she shouts over her shoulder. 'I know how much you like it. Shall I save you some?'

'You are a bad influence,' I tell her jokingly.

The thought of Dimitri not actually living across the road gives me a twinge of disappointment and I give myself a talking-to. I have only met this man once. And know absolutely nothing about him.

THIRTEEN

I take a shower, then take the short walk to the villa with Evie. Dimitri is nowhere to be seen, but just as we arrive he pulls up in his van. This time he is covered in dust, his denim shorts and black T-shirt covered in a light film of what looks like plaster. He is with an older, leathery-skinned man with twinkling eyes and a smiling face who he introduces as Yiannis.

'His English is a bit what you might say... restricted.' Dimitri frowns, searching for the right word as Yiannis runs his hand over the walls of the house.

'Limited?'

'Yes, limited. Maybe my own is not as perfect as I think.' He smiles, but I am struggling to concentrate on his words. His dark hair that was tied back this morning is let loose now, the light curls almost touching his shoulders. But it's his smile that captivates me as it could literally light up a room.

'Thank you both for coming. I guess you would like to take a look inside then. I'm still worried about that though,' I say, pointing to the zigzagging crack down the building. 'There's nothing more off-putting than a big crack,' I say and Evie sniggers like a schoolgirl.

'I can imagine,' he says, keeping completely straight-faced. 'Although I am sure it is superficial. The building will be rendered anyway, yes?' he asks.

'Yes,' I say as I imagine my smooth, dazzling white villa and hoping it doesn't take up most of the budget.

Upstairs is where the problems are though. The damp patch stretching outwards is water coming through the roof I am told, and Dimitri tells me they will need to investigate further. They point and prod, speaking to each other in Greek, before heading to the van for a pair of ladders. Yiannis scales the ladder like a man half his age, followed by Dimitri. After waiting for what seems like forever, Dimitri gives me the news that the roof will need to be completely replaced.

Heading into the second bedroom, he bounces on a slightly soft spot and Yiannis shakes his head. 'New floor,' he announces as I feared he might.

The small bathroom looks solid enough, it just needs ripping out completely and replacing.

'You don't like this colour,' Dimitri teases, looking at the bright-blue bath suite.

'Strangely enough, no. Or, surprisingly, the brown tiles.'

They take their time assessing the premises, including the rear yard with the stone steps leading to the upper floor.

'I would like a pretty balcony there, maybe something with a nice filigree pattern. I'm thinking French doors opening out onto the balcony,' I say, my imagination running away with me, along with the budget for the build probably.

'We can do whatever you like. I have a couple of other jobs to finish, but I promise that in two weeks' time we will start, and it will have our full attention,' Dimitri reassures me.

We decide that the roof is the first and foremost job and I agree to return for two weeks in the near future as I feel I need to be there to oversee the first part of the project and draw up some plans.

Phoebe appears once more after Dimitri has left and invites me and Evie in for a drink. We were about to head off and change for dinner, but it seems rude not to accept. She is going to be my new neighbour after all.

We step inside her cheerful home, with white walls, a dark sofa draped with a colourful tapestry throw that she proudly tells me she made herself. The floor is terracotta stone, and a wood burner stands in the corner for the cooler months, which is something I want for my home.

'Maybe not tea,' she says, changing her mind as we sit down. 'As it is a little hot some fresh orange juice, maybe,' she offers, and we gratefully accept. She gestures us into the small but pristine kitchen and lifts a contraption from under a counter, the like of which I have never seen before. She loads it up with several oranges and pumps the handle of the manual orange juice maker and soon hands us each a glass of freshly squeezed juice.

'Now I definitely want one of those,' I say.

'Ooh me too. I love fresh juice in the morning,' agrees Evie.

It would be great to have fresh juice back home and I wonder if I might be able to find a machine on Amazon.

'One day, I will take you to the store to buy the machine,' she offers, her English far better than Yiannis', although not perfect. Maybe we can help each other, and I will learn more than the usual morning and afternoon greetings, as well as please and thank you.

She asks us a little about our life, taking an interest in our work and Evie's two children.

'No children for you?' she asks, pushing some biscuits towards us. I feel rude declining, as I don't want to spoil my meal later, so take one out of politeness. My goodness, why do they taste so good? Evie happily polishes two of them off, much to the delight of Phoebe. My friend is one of those people that can eat anything and never put on an ounce of weight. Even after she had the twins, she was soon back to her pre-pregnancy weight.

'No, not yet,' I tell her, wondering if I ever will become a mother. It's not something I have yearned for up to now, but who knows further down the line? Women are choosing to have their families later these days, I tell myself.

She asks if we have plans for tomorrow and tells us she will be going to church in the morning. 'It is a beautiful church. I will pray for good luck in your new house,' she tells me, and I thank her.

Half an hour later, we stand to leave, and Phoebe wishes us a good evening.

'She's a nice lady, isn't she?' says Evie as we walk back to the apartment.

'She is. I wonder whether she might be a bit lonely, but then there seem to be plenty of people in the street she chats to. I noticed the woman of a similar age across the road as well.'

'I'm sure she has friends. Didn't she say she has church in the morning? She must have some friends there, surely?'

'I'm sure you're right. Maybe it's just genuine Greek hospitality she is showing us.'

A few doors along, a young couple emerge with a tiny baby in a pram and a toddler and smile warmly at us, so it seems there are not just older people living here, which feels nice.

Back at the apartment, we change into dresses and head off along the main street as the sun begins to set behind the hills. It's a little quiet, but a few families and couples are enjoying the start of the better weather and stroll along dressed smartly in summer bright colours, skin gently glowing from a day spent on the beach.

Boards outside restaurants offer up fresh fish dishes, beef stifado, and home-made moussaka. A colourful beach kimono in a shop window catches my eye, but I bought one similar last time I was here, so I rein myself in. I could happily buy clothes every time I step into a shop, but I have so many I will save my shopping for interior soft furnishings, once the renovation is complete. I dare to imagine how it might look and feel a tinge of excitement.

Kostas from the gyros café and the lady from the clothes shop I frequented on my last trip are having a chat outside a shop and approach us as we pass.

'Welcome back, ladies,' says Kostas warmly.

'Thank you.' I can't help noticing the way Kostas looks at Evie and she looks a little coy, glancing at him but saying very little. I tell them excitedly all about my new house purchase.

'That is wonderful!' The lady from the shop claps her hands together. 'We must have lunch in the cooler months when the shop is quiet and I can close it for an hour or two,' she says, and I thank her, feeling grateful that I have made another friend already.

The new restaurant we have chosen is already half full, mainly with locals, but we are lucky enough to get a table over-looking the beach, as a family with two small children leave.

'I still cannot believe you have bought a house, here, you lucky thing,' says Evie as we sip some cold water, along with some olives a waiter has placed in front of us.

'Neither can I.' I gaze dreamily across the water and sigh. A boat is gliding along in the background, its twinkling lights on deck illuminating the rapidly darkening sea. It's a world away from back home, the calmness being a perfect antidote to the bustling city and noisy traffic. I love both of these settings though, and can hardly believe that I will have the opportunity to flit between both worlds.

We share a bottle of crisp, white wine, and our delicious meze arrives. There's hummus and tzatziki dips, *dolmades* in tomato sauce, along with chicken skewers, and halloumi bites. There is also a tasty-looking Greek salad and some olive bread.

'What was that with Kostas?' I ask, biting into a salty piece of halloumi.

'What was what?'

'I saw the look you gave each other.' I raise an eyebrow and she fiddles with her napkin.

'I'd say you're imagining things.' She laughs, taking a glug of her wine.

'Okay fine.' I dive into my food.

'Although, actually, I do find him attractive. We chatted a bit last time I was here,' she reveals casually.

'Did you?'

'Yeah. Remember the day you weren't feeling too well?'

The day in question I was suffering with a hangover, regretting a third ouzo in a karaoke bar, after drinking wine.

'I'd prefer not to.' I pull a face and she laughs.

'Well, anyway, I went out, you know, window shopping, and I had a gyros at the café. He served me and we got chatting as it was quiet. I always caught him looking at me after that whenever we walked along here,' she reveals. 'He's really nice.'

'So is your husband,' I remind her. 'Is everything alright with you and Nick?'

'Yes, it's fine.' She plays around with her food a bit. 'It's just... Oh, I don't know; we've been together for so long we're more like mates these days,' she reveals. 'I mean I was nineteen when we got married, and we had already known each other for four years. Sometimes I wonder what on earth I was thinking.' She gazes out across the water. 'The girls are older now, doing their own thing most of the time. No doubt they will be off in a few years.'

'Oh, Evie, is everything okay? I think your story is so romantic, not many people marry their childhood sweethearts.'

'Yes, everything is fine, don't worry.' She pours us more wine and paints on a smile.

My heart breaks at the thought of her having doubts about

her marriage going forward, although she did marry very young. I love Nick as much as Evie and have always envied their relationship. They've always given each other space, she's sitting here with me right now after all, and he's golfing in Scotland. But maybe they do their own thing a little too much.

'I imagine marriages go through many stages. Maybe you just need to inject a bit more romance into things,' I tentatively suggest. 'When was the last time you had a romantic weekend away together?' I ask, thinking that the girls seem to go to their gran's so that they can explore separate hobbies.

'Not sure. Oh, Claude, don't worry, just because I fancy a local café owner, it doesn't mean I'm thinking of jumping into bed with him.' She grins.

'Ah, so you do fancy him.' I point my finger at her, and she rolls her eyes and laughs.

'No harm in a bit of harmless flirtation, is there? Maybe it just feels nice to be paid a little bit of attention, that's all.'

'I'm not sure many people flirt after years of being together, but I'm sure Nick still fancies you.'

'Well, I'm not.' She places her wine glass down. 'I had my hair coloured last week and bought a new dress to go to his aunt's fiftieth birthday party and he barely noticed.'

'He never noticed your highlights?' I ask, surprised.

'Well, yeah, but he never said much, just, "Have you had your hair done?" Not even followed up with "It looks nice", or "It suits you". He never pays me compliments these days, even though I always tell him if he looks nice.'

'Have you told him how you feel?'

'I did, actually, the day after the party.' She dips bread into some hummus. 'I told him I felt like I had gone to a lot of effort for the family party, and he never appreciated it.'

'What did he say?'

'He hugged me then and told me I always look beautiful, and that he always thought actions spoke louder than words, which of course is true. But he didn't really do anything either. I guess I just feel a bit taken for granted.' She shrugs.

'Does he ever plan dates or anything?'

'He used, and so did I, but I guess we've been so busy with the business and the girls, we don't focus on us,' she admits. 'When we do have nights out, it's usually with a group of friends or business associates.'

Evie and Nick kindly invite me along to some of their get-togethers.

'Look, I'm no marriage expert, how could I be? I'm resolutely single. But I imagine you must have to work at it a bit, especially in a long marriage. I think you should find a gorgeous hotel and book that weekend away,' I tell her firmly, and she promises me that she will.

We finish our delicious food and head to a local bar with neon lights flashing across a small dance floor, with promises of no more marriage talk. We are only here for the weekend after all, so intend to make the most of things. We chat to a couple of girls from the North East, who tell us they got a bargain price holiday in early season, and join them for a dance on the dance floor, before topping the evening off with a cocktail. A couple of blokes are glancing over at us, locals I think, but I don't make eye contact.

It's just after eleven o'clock when we say our goodnights to our new friends and stroll back towards the apartment, as the restaurant owners place food boards inside, ready to close for the evening. A group of young men are chatting outside the gyros café and glance over at us as we pass. Just then, Kostas emerges from inside with some food for the boys and waves us over.

'*Kalispera*, ladies. Would you like anything?' He gestures to an empty outside table.

'Are you hungry? It's ages since we've eaten,' coaxes Evie. I am a little peckish, which often happens after a few drinks, but I know the real reason she wants to be here. And I don't want to encourage her. But what the hell, I'm not her keeper. What harm can it do?

Kostas, who is maybe forty years old and good-looking, serves us chicken gyros and as the last customers leave, he dims the lights in the café and joins us outside. The air is a lot cooler now, especially being so close to the sea. Evie, who is wearing a sleeveless dress, gives her arms a little rub.

'Are you cold?' Kostas goes inside, then returns with his zip-up hoody from a chair and drapes it over her shoulders.

'How long are you here for?' he asks, seeming to direct this question more at Evie I can't help noticing.

'We leave the day after tomorrow,' I tell him, wiping my mouth, having finished the tasty chicken snack.

'You are only here for a short time?' He seems surprised.

'Yes, it's a bit of a whistle-stop tour to show Evie the house and sort out some builders,' I explain.

'But soon enough you will be a regular visitor to the café, now you have bought a villa here, won't you, Claudia?' says Evie.

'I'm not sure about being a frequent visitor, however delicious your food is. This place isn't good for my waistline,' I tell Kostas with a smile.

'Ah, but I only use fresh ingredients. Healthy. We Greeks live long lives.' He winks.

Evie can't seem to take her eyes off Kostas as he chats to a waiter who has just emerged from the café, after clearing up. The young man says goodnight, before firing up his moped and driving off into the night. I notice the little looks exchanged between Evie and Kostas and think it is maybe a good thing we are leaving the day after tomorrow.

We finish up and stand up to leave, the only sounds in the street now coming from the occasional passing car, or people saying their goodnights from a bar at the end of the road.

'*Kalinychta*, ladies.' Kostas takes our hands and shakes them. His hand lingers a while longer in Evie's, his gaze fixed on her.

We take the short walk home and I can't resist taking a detour past the road with my house, and it's completely silent. A few stray cats cross our paths as we walk, streetlights gently illuminating the road. It's so quiet, it is just possible to hear the sound of the waves from the beach, and I dream of the day when I can sit on my newly installed balcony and relish those sounds, the voile curtains gently fluttering in a warm breeze.

'You okay?' I ask as we approach the holiday apartment, noting Evie has barely said a word.

'Yes, I'm fine, just a little tired. It's so gorgeous here, isn't it?' She sighs. 'I'm so envious of you.'

'Well, it's lucky I have two bedrooms. You know you will be welcome over anytime.'

'I know that. And don't you worry, you won't be able to get rid of me.' She smiles and despite our close friendship, I do hope Nick will be joining her. I'm buying a huge sofa bed for the lounge, so the girls can join them too.

'I'm pleased about that.' I link her arm as we walk. 'I'm sure you will all love it here,' I say as I glance up at the silvery moon in the clear night sky.

FOURTEEN

'What do you fancy doing today then, after I've met with Dimitri? I was thinking we might go into Sidari, I remember that beach bar you liked.'

'Sounds good.' Evie has been chatting to Nick on the phone this morning and seems in a brighter mood.

'How's his golf weekend going?' I ask.

We're sitting on the balcony, drinking orange juice and eating croissants and some Greek yoghurt.

'Pretty eventful apparently. One guy got disqualified from the event for cheating, and another ended up in hospital after drunkenly falling down some steps outside the clubhouse and breaking his ankle.'

'Oh no. Who knew golf could be so dangerous?'

'I know. At least he called me though, which is a first when he goes away.' She laughs and I wonder when they became so disconnected, even though I never got that impression when they said goodbye at the airport.

'Right. I won't be long.' I glance at my watch as I finish my breakfast and cross the road to Thea's. Dimitri is already standing inside in his work gear, chatting to Thea, ready to head off for the day.

'*Kalimera*,' he greets me warmly.

'*Kalimera*,' I say, returning his smile.

He takes his phone from his pocket and shows me some figures that, thankfully, are not as eye-watering as I expected.

'I can make a start on the roof soon. But I am afraid I will need a little money upfront for materials,' he tentatively asks. 'I hope you don't mind.'

I hesitate for just a split second, having read back home that it is not something that is encouraged.

'I'm sure my aunt can vouch for me.' He holds his hands up. 'It's just that the price of wood and building materials has increased in price and my supplier I am afraid likes a hefty deposit.'

'Not a problem.' I reassure myself that everything will be alright, and, of course, I have come to know Thea well. I tell him I will transfer the money if he gives me his bank details, which he does.

'I will see you in two weeks. Let me know when you arrive,' he says. 'And don't worry, everything is in good hands.' As he shakes my hand and heads to the van, I notice Yiannis sitting in the passenger seat, and he waves.

'Yiannis, I didn't see you there. How are you?' I stroll towards the van.

'I am okay. A little pain in my back, but I am getting older.' He smiles as Dimitri climbs up beside him into the driver's seat.

'You come out of a bakery empty-handed?' I can't help remarking to this Greek god, and Dimitri laughs.

'I like to look after myself, although I do indulge occasionally. No one can resist temptation the whole time.' He holds my gaze with his dark-brown eyes, and I feel the heat rise in my cheeks.

'Have a safe journey home,' he says as he starts up the

engine. 'Actually…' He hesitates for a moment, before adding, 'It does not matter, I will be in touch with you soon.' I can't help wondering what he was about to say.

Back at the apartment Evie is ready and we set off to head into Sidari. The sky is blue, and it feels like it is shaping up to be a beautiful day.

'Actually,' I say, noticing a place that hires quad bikes and mopeds. 'Do you fancy leaving the car here and hiring a moped? Maybe after Sidari we can take a little ride out somewhere.'

'I thought you said there would be no sightseeing on this trip?'

'I said no walking. It might be fun, but not if you don't fancy it. We can have a pool day if you like?'

'I'm joking. Hiring quads does sound like fun.' Evie smiles.

There is a small pool at the apartments, although thinking about it I wonder if maybe I ought to be at the villa, at least trying to have a go at tidying the garden a little and pulling up some weeds. But then again, I don't want to ruin Evie's weekend. I will get properly stuck in in a couple of weeks, along with Dimitri and Yiannis, and maybe a couple more workers, who he mentioned he employs on a casual basis. Fingers crossed my employer will let me have the time off. I'm pretty certain no one else has holidays booked, and I can work from here for a few days if I need to.

As neither of us particularly like riding pillion we decide to hire a moped each and are soon scooting along the main road towards Sidari. Driving out of the main street in Roda, we pass a tourist office offering trips into Corfu Town and boat trips across the water. Shops display football shirts of every country on rails outside on the street, alongside vibrant beach towels and floaty summer dresses. It's still a little quiet as the shop owners slowly open up their stores ready for the summer onslaught of visitors to the island.

We drive on past half-built hotels and buildings with graffi-tied walls, before the landscape changes to roadside villas painted in various pastel shades with elevated pools looking down across the valley. Gardens are filled with lush green plants, some with palm trees. In the distance, cypress trees can be spotted perched high on hills alongside tiny white churches. When a car driver rounds a bend rather quickly though and almost in the middle of the road, it reminds me to keep my eyes firmly on the road ahead.

Presently, we approach the main strip of Sidari, and slow down as a trickle of early season tourists walk along a road that has no significant path, walking inside a yellow painted line.

Recalling our favourite bar, we park in the car park at the rear of the restaurant that has views over the beach. After being shown to a seat, we order a drink just as Evie receives a message on her phone and smiles.

'Is that from Nick?' I ask, sipping a strawberry mocktail through a straw.

'No, it's from the girls actually.' She turns the phone towards me to show a photo of them in a restaurant having Sunday lunch with their grandparents, pulling funny faces for the camera. I'm not sure why I'm so fixated on Evie being content with Nick and staying married. Maybe it's because my own parents have been married for so long. Or maybe it's because I can't stand cheats, and the thought of Evie being tempted fills me with dread.

I push away the memory of the guy who I thought just might have been the one, after discovering he didn't believe in dating someone exclusively. A fact he failed to mention to me.

We enjoy lunch, a huge Greek salad, and some calamari, drizzled with lemon juice, before taking a stroll along the beach front. It's busy being the weekend, with local families as well as tourists swimming and enjoying water sports in the lovely weather, warmer than usual I was told by Thea in the bakery.

We sit and watch the world go by for a few minutes, then take a walk along the main strip, passing bars with people sitting outside drinking and chatting. I stop and linger for a moment at my favourite jewellery shop as their selection of silver rings and bracelets displayed outside on a stand catches my eye.

'Why don't you treat yourself?' says Evie as my eye falls on a stunning bracelet with an amethyst stone at its centre, which just happens to be my birthstone. 'You have just come into an inheritance after all.'

'I have, haven't I? You've convinced me,' I say, trying it on for size.

It's such a reasonable price for silver that when Evie goes to explore the inside of the shop, I purchase one with her birthstone on it too. Perusing lots of shops, selling all the usual touristy souvenirs, but with hidden gems amongst them – I buy a gorgeous olive wood bowl for my new house – we eventually stop for a cold drink at another restaurant that overlooks a section of the beach.

'Fancy driving back to Acharavi Beach? It's on the way back to Roda. We could spend a couple of hours there if you like?' I suggest.

'It's a shingle beach though, isn't it?' Evie points out. 'I prefer the beach at Roda, if I'm honest.'

I wonder if that also includes a stroll along the main street to catch a glimpse of Kostas.

'That's fine. I just thought it would make a change, that's all.'

'Okay, sure.' She smiles. 'Let's make the most of the time we have here.'

We head along the road once more, and a couple of blokes on quad bikes toot their horns at us near a junction, before turning around and heading our way. When we pull up at the beach, the two very confident guys ask if they can buy us a drink. I'm flattered, of course, as I think Evie is, but don't think we can be bothered. I glance at Evie to make sure.

'Thanks, but we're meeting someone here,' I say, and the guys shrug and head for the beach bar and immediately get chatting to a couple of young women sitting on bar stools sipping a drink.

'Look at those abs though.' Evie lowers her sunglasses and glances over at one of them, as he lifts his T-shirt over his head, and I shove her on the arm and laugh.

We find a couple of sunbeds and order some soft drinks from a passing waiter.

I'm stretched out beneath the glorious blue sky, feeling the delicious warmth of the sun on my skin, when Evie suddenly reaches over for my hand and takes it in hers. 'I'm glad you're my friend,' she says. 'You always watch out for me, don't you?'

'I'm glad you're my friend too.' I give her hand a little squeeze. 'And you look out for me too, it's what friends do, isn't it?'

'Yeah, but when I think of how anxious I used to be, you always made me feel grounded, talked common sense to me. I must have been a right pain in the backside, a bit of a hypochondriac even, according to some and maybe they were right. Not to mention a clean freak.'

I don't mention the time she brought disinfectant to a B and B that was already squeaky clean and proceeded to clean it from top to bottom. Or the fact that she brought a sleeping bag to sleep on top of the covers.

'You were not a pain,' I reassure her. 'Anxiety is a real thing. You couldn't help that. But I believe we should all try and find something that shifts the focus, relaxes us a little. In your case, it was swimming. I like to make stuff.'

I bought a craft book from a market stall a few years ago, and have made some pretty items, such as keyrings and cushions that I have given as gifts. 'And eat too much cake probably,'

I say, adjusting my black bikini top that just about holds my ample boobs.

'You've got a gorgeous figure; I love your waist. I look like a boy.' She laughs looking down at her toned midriff and slender legs that I would kill for.

'Besides, I can't take all the credit for helping you, the cognitive behavioural therapy helped. And Nick and the girls,' I remind her.

'And the tablets. I was reluctant to take them, but I know they did help in the beginning,' she recalls. 'But you're right, of course, my family and the counselling sessions help, but I just want you to know that I couldn't have a better friend and I'm grateful.'

'You don't need to thank me,' I tell her, although I am so pleased to hear how much she values our friendship.

'But I want to. You're the one who really gets me,' she says, which makes me feel a bit emotional. 'And don't think I haven't noticed you trying to steer me away from Kostas.' She raises an eyebrow.

'Have I?' I reply, not very convincingly.

'You have. But you needn't worry, as I said it's just nice to be flirted with a little. I like that you care though.'

'Of course I care. I would hate you to make a mistake that you would live to regret.'

I remind her again that every long-term relationship changes into something more comfortable over time. 'But that doesn't mean you stop trying to keep the spark alive. Don't forget those weekends away, picnics in the sun, whatever it takes to remind each other why you fell in love in the first place,' I advise. I don't add that it's preferable to taking up with a love rat, as she is well aware of the dreadful mistake I made.

'Maybe you ought to be a marriage guidance counsellor,' says Evie.

'No, thanks. It's different with close friends. I'm not sure I could be telling strangers what to do.'

'Anyway. I agree me and Nick need to spend some time alone together. You're a bit of an old romantic deep down, aren't you, despite what happened with that... that rat you met online,' she says, angry on my behalf. 'Sorry, I didn't mean to bring him up.'

'Maybe I am. I do believe in happy ever after, but I can't even think about another relationship right now. Anyway, how did we end up talking about me when we were talking about you?' I laugh.

I think of my cheating ex who was bored with his fiancée, as they had been together since they were teenagers and fancied a little bit of fun before he committed to marriage. But I am determined not to let it sour my opinion of all men, even though they are strictly off the menu for now. I've grown to like my own company these past months, and it would take someone very special to change my current happy, single status.

'I do know what you mean, and I love my family with all my heart and couldn't imagine a life without them,' she reassures me. 'I guess we are both so busy with the business, romance is sometimes put on the back-burner. We're pretty exhausted most of the time, but you're right that we really ought to make the time.'

'You should delegate more, instead of having to work weekends. No wonder you are both exhausted.'

Evie and Nick do work a lot. They built up their haulage business from nothing, and work long hours. 'And while we're at it, if you can manage breaks apart, surely you can manage them together once in a while, now that the girls are older.'

'Duly noted. You always were the voice of reason.' She smiles. 'Here's to our friendship.' She lifts her juice glass.

'I'll drink to that,' I say and we tap our plastic juice-filled tumblers together before settling down onto our beds to enjoy the sun.

Watching the swimmers and the people on pedaloes, I still can't believe I will soon be able to regularly experience this type of thing on Roda Beach, just a short distance from my own holiday home. Well, as soon as the refurbishment is finished, that is. I close my eyes and feel the warm sun wash over me, once more feeling grateful to be doing something most people can only dream about.

Back at the apartment in the late afternoon, I receive a text from Dimitri telling me he will be heading to the builders' merchant for materials on Monday, and wishing me a safe trip home. I deposit some money into his account, batting away any feelings of caution.

'What's up?' asks Evie, maybe noting my look of uncertainty.

'Oh nothing, just Dimitri wishing us a safe trip home. I've just sent some money up front for some building materials for the roof.'

'Surely you're not worried about that? He's Thea's nephew,' she reminds me.

'No, no, of course not, you're right.'

'He's pretty hot though, isn't he?' she says.

'Evie, what are you like! And is he? I never really noticed.'

'Yeah, right.'

'Okay, there is absolutely no denying that he is handsome, but I am more interested in his building skills, thank you. I'm spending good money, I need to keep my practical head on.'

She smiles then as a text pings through on her phone. 'Ooh it's Nick. And he says he will take me out for breakfast when we get home, before we head off to work. Is that romantic enough for you?'

'It's a start. He must be missing you.' I smile.

'He must be. He never usually does anything spontaneous like that. In fact, he's never usually even one for breakfast.'

'Well, it's nice that he's making an effort. Maybe his ears

were burning or something when we were chatting.'

The following day we take a drive into a mountain village and stop for lunch in a pretty restaurant in a picturesque village, the outside space bursting with flowers in pots overlooking a deep valley.

Later, we browse the narrow, cobbled streets of the virtually self-sufficient village, taking in the rows of vegetables growing in gardens, and cats lazing on stone doorsteps. We make sure to stock up on some Greek herbs and my favourite honey from a small local shop.

After enjoying a swim at the apartment pool in the late afternoon sunshine, it's soon time to pack for our flight home.

Whilst Evie is in the shower, I take a walk round to my new house already counting down the days until I return. As I stand staring at it, visualising how it might look after the renovation, I feel thankful I have managed to sort out a builder.

Phoebe appears then, wishing me a safe flight, and reassuring me once more that she will keep an eye on the house.

'Thanks, Phoebe, I appreciate that. See you soon.'

In the early hours of the morning, we trundle our suitcases out in the driveaway to load into the car.

It's always a wrench to leave this place but soon enough I will be back and overseeing the start of the renovation project.

We take the familiar route, me really wishing I could stay a little longer, and are soon back at the airport. I don't know why, but I can't quell a slight feeling of unease, praying that I haven't bought a money pit. I know that the price of building supplies has dramatically increased worldwide, but I just feel a responsibility to get everything right, as I am using Jack's money, and I want him to be proud of me. I take a deep breath and tell myself I am fussing over nothing, as we head to the departure lounge, ready to board the plane.

FIFTEEN

'Enjoy your breakfast.'

I hug Evie and Nick, who has dropped me home after the flight. It's just after seven in the morning as we have jumped back two hours. I'm not looking forward to going to work today, although, luckily, I did sleep for virtually the whole flight.

'We will. Don't go getting used to being taken out for breakfast, though, hey.' Nick winks at Evie, and I mouth the word 'hotel' when Nick isn't looking.

Back at work, I manage to get through the day fuelled by coffee, before heading to my parents' house to tell them all about the house.

'You'll have no money left at this rate, booking all these holidays,' says Dad, reading his newspaper in the lounge after his evening meal, while I tell him my plans.

'The apartments cost next to nothing, and I have my wages as well as my windfall, remember.'

'Do you want us to pop over with you?' offers Dad. 'Have a look at the place. Maybe I could even lend a hand.' Mum is shaking her head and grimacing in the background.

'What your father means is, we were thinking of going over to Corfu for a week in the summer. We never did visit the Achilleion Palace when we last went over. Perhaps we should leave the builders to it, for now though,' she suggests.

'Isn't the Achilleion Palace the place that was used as a location for a Bond film?' asks Dad, folding his paper and putting it away, hopefully putting aside any ideas of helping with the villa renovation.

'That's right. *For Your Eyes Only.* I read about that,' I tell him. 'And actually, I haven't been there either, so maybe I'll come with you for a day trip.'

'You can't go skiving off from your own building project,' Dad jokes, laughing.

'I don't need to be there all the time, I'm paying the builders,' I remind him. 'I'm sure they will know what they are doing.'

'Oh, but you don't want them taking the mick, having extra-long tea breaks and all that business.' He shakes his head.

'Can you just imagine your father being on the building site?' Mum asks me when Dad has retreated to his greenhouse. 'He'd be a complete nightmare, telling the other builders how it's done.'

'You're probably right.'

'Maybe you should just email photos to us from a safe distance.' She chuckles. 'Although we will come and have a look at it. It's probably better if I'm with him, to save the builders.' She winks.

'Of course, Mum. Yiannis doesn't have the best English, so maybe he wouldn't understand Dad anyway.'

'What about the other bloke, Damon is it?'

'Dimitri. Oh, his English is very good. A lot of the young people who work in building and tourism have a good grasp of English.'

'Just as well. You don't want anything to be lost in transla-
tion when it comes to a house refurbishment.' Mum frowns.

The mention of Dimitri's name makes me think of his broad
shoulders and dark wavy hair. Oh dear, this really must stop.

I have a very definite vision of how I want the place to look
and hope the builders will share it too. I imagine a filigree black
metal balcony and a water feature in the garden next to the
olive tree that will need cutting back. I can't believe the roof will
have to come off first though. I feel slightly nervous as I take in
the extent of the work that needs doing, and just hope that the
house doesn't reveal any nasty surprises as the work progresses.
I wonder what I will be able to do to help, other than tidy up,
and place debris into skips? At least the builders won't be
expecting endless cups of tea as there is no electricity at the
villa. Maybe Dad's right though, being there means at least I
can ensure the building work stays on track.

My new house purchase is the talk of the office at the
moment, everyone telling me how envious they are and asking if
I will be hiring it out with mates' rates. I never thought about
sub-letting the place as I want it to be a home from home filled
with my own clothes and personal items, although maybe I will
consider it for close family and friends in the future.

The following two weeks drag as I watch the clock that
surely must be running out of battery and is on a go slow. Even
the days when I am working from home seem to be endless.
Finally, it's the day before I'm due to set off and I'm packing a
bag when my phone rings. It's Josh.

'Hi, sis. When are you off then?' he asks. We'd chatted for
over an hour after my last trip, and I told him all about the
house.

'Tomorrow, for two whole weeks,' I tell him, feeling a little
flutter of excitement.

'Sounds great. Don't forget to send some photo updates.'

'I will do.'

'Actually, I was just wondering, would you mind having a house sitter for a few days?'

'Are you talking about you? Of course I wouldn't mind. I prefer the flat not to be sitting empty. Is everything okay though?' I ask anxiously, as I hear as him sigh at the other end of the phone.

'Yeah, don't worry. I just thought I might bring George up to see Mum and Dad and spend an extra day after the weekend. I have a couple of days' annual leave to use up.'

'And Zoe isn't coming with you?'

'No, it's full on at her work, she can't get the time off. I thought I'd take George to Chester Zoo,' he says, brightening. 'He'd love it there; I know I did when we were kids,' he says, instantly evoking memories.

'Well, you're very welcome to stay. Aw, I'm sorry to be missing George though, and you, of course. Unless you can get up here tonight that is?'

'Great, if you're sure? Zoe has a night out planned anyway, a leaving party in town with the work gang. I can be with you about six, if that suits?'

'Perfect. See you later.'

'Great, sis. And I'll drop you at the airport tomorrow morning if you like, George will have me awake early.'

'Thanks, Josh. I will see you later. Just one thing though, why aren't you staying at Mum's?'

'I can't deal with the questions for a whole weekend, about why Zoe isn't with me. I'll call them in the morning, invite them to the zoo before I head back.'

'Fair enough. Safe journey.'

The rest of the day passes quickly, and just before five, Josh arrives and after dinner we head to the local park for an hour to tire George out before bed. While George explores the playground, we sit on a bench and chat, and Josh opens up about the cracks in his marriage, admitting he isn't happy.

'But I'm thinking you kind of guessed that.' He sighs. He jogs over to George then, who needs a lift up onto a climbing frame.

'I did. We can talk later, if you like, when George is asleep.'

After spending an hour at the park, we head back to the flat and George is soon safely tucked up in bed.

'So, what are you going to do?' I ask Josh as I take a sip from a small glass of wine.

'That's the thing, I don't know.' He runs his hand through his hair. 'Zoe could never afford to buy me out, or vice versa, and if I contribute to the mortgage I couldn't afford somewhere to rent, especially down south.' He swirls his wine around in his glass.

'Things are that bad then?'

''Fraid so. It's sad, because I remember us being really happy in the early days of our marriage, but I feel like I've been acting a part in a film these past few years,' he admits. 'I don't quite know what's happened to us, but we are both pretty miserable. Sorry, fancy burdening you with all this the day before you head off to Greece.'

'It's fine, don't apologise, you have to talk to someone. I think you've done the right thing coming here for a break, give each other a bit of space.'

'Maybe.' He gives a forced smile.

'And if things don't work out, have you considered moving back up north?' I ask.

'I've thought of nothing else but being so far away from George would break my heart.'

'I get that. Well, you and George are welcome here anytime, you know that. And I'm sure Mum and Dad would tell you the same thing. Whatever you decide, you know we will all support you,' I reassure him.

'I know. Thanks, sis. It feels good being here.'

We head to bed then, and I can't help wondering why relationships are so complicated. Not for the first time I think that when it comes to affairs of the heart, things are far easier when you are on your own. And it would take someone very special to change my mind about that.

SIXTEEN

'Bye, Josh, and have a wonderful time at the zoo, George.'

'Nanny and Grandad are coming too,' says my brother and George replies with a loud, 'Yay.'

'They'll love that. I hope you all have a lovely day.'

I give Josh and George one last squeeze at the airport when I am dropped off. 'And remember, I am only ever at the end of a phone if you need a chat,' I tell my brother and he nods.

I plug my earphones in ready for the journey and soon enough I am walking on Greek soil once more and taking a taxi to the house. It's a driver who I vaguely recognise from one of my previous visits.

'It seems you can't stay away, huh?' He smiles through his rear-view mirror that has some rosary beads hanging from it.

'It's true. Do you live in Roda?' I ask, thinking I have seen him around.

'*Nai*. In the village.' He smiles.

'Then we will practically be neighbours. I have bought a house there,' I tell him excitedly.

'You buy a house! You must really like it here.' He smiles.

'Although, you know it is not the same in the winter. Many restaurants close,' he informs me as we drive.

'Don't worry, I know all about that. I will be spending my summer holidays here, and occasional weekends, overseeing the building work. The villa I have bought needs renovating.'

'I wish you good luck,' he says cheerfully. 'Do you have good builder?' he asks.

'Yes, a nephew of a friend I have made here. His name is Dimitri.'

'Ah, *nai, nai*. Dimitri and Yiannis, they work very hard,' he tells me, which is reassuring to know. It also makes me realise what a tight community it is as everyone seems to know each other. I can't wait to get to know everyone a little more too.

Saying goodbye to the taxi driver, I settle in once more to my holiday apartment and have a quick shower and change. I'd received a message from Dimitri yesterday saying the removal of the roof had started, but even so when I arrive at the house I gasp in shock. There is just a stone square and a huge wooden structure above, surrounded by scaffolding. I arrive just as Dimitri is descending a ladder.

'*Kalimera*.'

He smiles a dazzling smile and wipes his dusty hands on his black T-shirt before shaking mine.

'I see you have the roof off. How's it going then?' I ask, hoping all is well.

It looks alarming but it's reassuring to know that the work appears to have started in earnest.

'Pretty good. Would you like to see?'

I follow him upstairs and as I turn to enter the bedroom, he pulls me gently back by the arm.

'Please, do not step in there. At least not without a parachute.' He pulls a face.

'Wait, what?' I cross the landing and as I open the door I

find myself staring into a gaping hole where the floor once was and gazing down into the kitchen area.

'The floor. It was no good. Rotten floorboards.' Yiannis shakes his head.

'What, every single floorboard?'

'Almost all of it,' says Dimitri. 'The villa had been empty for a long time, there was lots of damp and some woodworm too.'

For a split second, I wonder whether I have employed cowboy builders, finding a problem with everything, ripping up floorboards and telling me there is woodworm, before pulling myself together. Dimitri is Thea's nephew, for goodness' sake, and didn't the taxi driver just give him a glowing endorsement? All the same, he might have mentioned the rotten floor to me before ripping it all up.

'And do not worry. The floorboards I buy very cheaply from a friend who has a timberyard. Would you prefer if I tell you everything we do when you are not here?' Dimitri asks reasonably and probably noting my serious expression. 'Also, I could not have known how bad it was, until we began working on it,' he adds, which is a fair comment I guess.

'No, really it's fine. I understand that. Maybe just tell me how much things will cost as they crop up, so I can keep a running total.'

I don't want him thinking I have unlimited funds, no matter how healthy my current bank balance is.

'Of course. I promise you I am not, what do you say, a cowboy,' he says, tapping into my thoughts. 'The floorboards are the only extra cost at two hundred euros. Everything else is already included in the total quote I have given you,' he reassures me.

'Okay, great.' I smile my brightest smile, embarrassed by the fact that he might think I find him unscrupulous. 'I want this to be my dream home after all, so if anything needs doing, just let me know the cost. Anyway, I am here now so I can tell you exactly what I want.'

'Good. Because I am here to give you exactly what you want,' he tells me in a non-suggestive way, but even so I feel my stomach do a little flutter as he looks at me with those deep-brown eyes. He looks even more gorgeous than he did last time and those broad shoulders. Has he been working out more since the last time I was here?

Walking around downstairs, I point out things I would like, including a window seat that will look out over the rear garden. I imagine myself sitting reading inside, on the days when the weather is too hot to be outside.

I can hear Yiannis and the two young apprentice builders who have just arrived, whistling along to the sound of Greek music coming from the radio they have brought with them.

I sit with Yiannis and Dimitri, sketching out some ideas, before telling them about the wrought-iron balcony rail leading to the bedroom that I dream of, and they look at each other and smile.

'What's so amusing?' I ask.

'You know a stone wall may be more practical,' suggests Dimitri. 'It can be very rainy in the winter.'

'And wind,' adds Yiannis, doing a theatrical whirlwind impression. 'From beach.'

'Salty deposits from the sea may ruin your pretty balcony. It could even end up rusty. But, of course, it is your house.' Dimitri shrugs.

'Well, maybe it is just a romantic notion,' I grudgingly admit. 'But a stone wall is just so boring.'

'It is your house, if that is what you want, you should have it,' Dimitri concedes. 'I am not a metal worker, but I know someone who is. Maybe you could visit his yard with me and look at some examples of his work and give him a sketch of your ideas?'

'Sure, okay, that sounds like a good idea.'

I'm quickly learning that my own ideas of a house here, and what is actually practical, may be two different things, yet I yearn for a pretty holiday home near the sea.

Phoebe appears then at the front, with a huge melon cut into pieces on a platter. It's almost noon and the sun is getting up fiercely in the bright-blue sky, so the melon is gratefully received by the men, who make short work of it.

'And if they get tired. The ouzo,' Phoebe advises with a wink. 'One shot, to revive, no more.'

'Thanks, Phoebe. Definitely no more. I don't fancy managing a bunch of drunken builders,' I say, and she laughs.

The lady across the road with the dark curls is outside once more, brandishing her brush and sweeping some fallen leaves from a tree. I wave over and she waves back.

'Is she your friend?' I ask Phoebe, noting there seems to be very little interaction with the women, even though they appear to be of a similar age.

'No,' she tells me flatly.

'Did you fall out?' I ask Phoebe, who says she needs the empty melon platter, before turning and heading back into the villa.

'I tell you sometime,' she says as I follow her, letting me know the subject is closed.

'So tomorrow. You will be busy here?' she asks.

'Yes. I am kind of making sure everything is going okay, although I must admit I feel a bit like a spare part.'

'A spare part of what?'

'It's just a saying. It means I feel a bit useless.'

'Tomorrow it is Sunday, my granddaughter and her son, they come here. We drive out for a picnic to a nice park. Would you like to come?' she offers.

'That sounds really lovely, Phoebe, thanks.'

I'm sure my absence from the project won't be felt for a few hours. Besides, is there anything more important than getting to know my new neighbours?

Phoebe heads inside then, glancing briefly at the lady across the road, who turns her back and walks into her house, and I wonder what has happened between them.

A few hours pass, and other than me brushing up and placing lots of wooden debris into a skip and nipping to a local shop for iced cold water, there isn't an awful lot that I can do. Soon enough it's time to pack up for the day.

'Phoebe reminded me it is Sunday tomorrow so I take it you won't be working?' I say to Dimitri as the day draws to a close.

'Normally, no, but I will be here in the morning with Yiannis,' he reassures me.

'Right. Well, Phoebe has invited me out for a picnic with her granddaughter, if that's okay?'

'Absolutely not,' he says flatly. 'You are the project manager, I believe is the title.'

'But I'm sure you can manage, I—'

He bursts out laughing then. 'I am joking. You are the boss. Have a nice time.'

'Right, well, yes, thanks I will, although I will be here to check in. I hope it doesn't rain.' I glance up at the gaping hole in the roof, although the builders have already begun placing wooden slats across it.

'It is May,' says Dimitri, smiling as he heads to his van with Yiannis. 'There should be no rain. And it is unusually warm,' he reminds me.

He takes a wallet from his pocket and pays the two young labourers in cash, and they head off.

'See you tomorrow, bright and early if you have time,' says Dimitri, putting his sunglasses on and letting his hair loose from the band it was in. I feel almost guilty agreeing to go out with Phoebe and her granddaughter tomorrow, but at least I will be here for a little while, and I am paying them to do the job after all, I remind myself.

That night, I climb into bed exhausted after a shower, and smile at some photos Josh has sent me from Chester Zoo. Mum and Dad have beaming smiles on their faces, and I hope they have enjoyed a lovely day. It must be so nice for them having their son and grandson around to have a day out with, not something they can do on a regular basis given the distance between them. I sink into the bed with its freshly laundered white cotton sheets and I am soon out like a light.

SEVENTEEN

The sun streaming through the pale curtains has me rising the next morning at six thirty. I make myself a coffee, then push the door open to the small balcony. To the left I can glimpse an allotment area being used by some of the locals, where they grow courgettes, corn, tomatoes and a variety of fragrant herbs. Next to that, a caged area has chickens that are already awake and clucking. I lean over the balcony and on the right side, I can see the white church, with its dark bell tower. It's so beautiful and quiet at this time, although the sudden sound of a cockerel crowing loudly breaks the silence. Straight ahead, I glimpse the sea as the sun begins its ascent, a gentle orange hue rising slowly above the horizon.

Sitting on the tiny balcony, I think of how this place is a world away from back home, where my balcony there gives a view of apartments, and a railway track. Tonight, I plan to sit here and read a book, and realise it's been so long since I've actually done that back home, often starting one but never having the time or being in the right frame of mind to finish it, with so many distractions around, including Netflix and the temptation to scroll through social media on my phone. I vow never to meet anyone that way again though, after my last miserable experience.

I dress and shower, then nip to the bakery for some cake for the picnic.

'Kalimera,' Thea greets me brightly. 'So how is the build going?' she asks as she finishes serving a local with some bread rolls.

'Good, I mean, it's early days really, and I probably shouldn't be sneaking off for a picnic with my new neighbour, but it's such a gorgeous day.'

'You are paying the builders to do the job for you,' she says, echoing my own sentiments and making me feel better. 'And I am sure they can be trusted. My nephew is a good man. He must be, to be working on a Sunday.'

'Of course.' I smile, selecting some slices of cheese and spinach pie called *spanakopita*. I buy a cake topped with icing and a jelly sweet for Phoebe's great-grandson too. 'And I'm very grateful.'

'Have a good day. I will check on the house later if you like?' offers Thea, but I don't want the guys to think I am checking up on them.

'Don't worry about it, but thanks anyway,' I tell her as I head off.

I knock at Phoebe's with the food at eight thirty and she receives it gratefully, before putting it in her fridge until her granddaughter and great-grandson arrive.

'Did you have a lie-in?' Dimitri teases as I arrive at the villa. It's something I am learning he seems to do rather a lot, although I realise that work starts early before the sun gets up in the afternoon.

'Well, it is Sunday.'

'For some of us,' he replies, a grin on his face. 'I am teasing, I hope you have a nice morning at the park.' He smiles. 'It is good that you trust us to get on with things.'

'Of course I do.'

'Oh, and I hope you have your mosquito spray, especially if you go near the lake in the park.' I don't think he is joking about that, but luckily I do have a spray in my bag.

I pull on some gardening gloves and get stuck in pulling up some weeds from the rear garden.

'You don't want to ruin your outfit, please leave it to us,' says Dimitri. 'By the way, you look nice,' he adds, flicking his eyes over my knee-length white cotton dress; my hair is loose and over my shoulders this morning.

'Thank you.' I almost add, 'So do you,' but as he is in his usual work gear, it doesn't seem appropriate.

An hour later, Phoebe appears outside as a young woman is walking up the slight incline of the road, holding a young boy's hand. She has almond eyes, and her blonde-highlighted hair is tied back. Phoebe introduces her granddaughter Sofia when I join them.

'Nice to meet you,' she tells me outside the gate. 'And this here is Jason.' She introduces the adorable little boy who politely says hello. 'I hear you will be my grandmother's new neighbour,' she says warmly.

'Eventually, yes.' I gesture to the house next door, with the half-constructed roof and surrounded by scaffolding. 'And it's nice to meet you too. I'm Claudia.'

'Gaia,' says the little boy as he greets his great-grandmother and runs into her arms. She speaks to him in Greek and covers him with kisses.

A short while later, we take the walk down the sloping road to Sofia's car that is parked at the bottom. Phoebe insists I sit in the front seat next to Sofia, whilst she sits in the back with Jason.

Sofia is so easy to talk to, I feel like I have made another new friend, although she tells me she lives around a forty-minute drive away in a small village.

'I invited my grandmother to live with us, but she loves Roda. I cannot say I blame her.' She smiles. 'I would like to live around here too, but we could never afford a house here,' she tells me, which makes me feel guilty for having the means to buy a holiday home here. I wonder if I will be viewed with disdain, like those people who buy second homes in Cornwall and the Lake District, forcing prices up and the locals out?

I try not to think about that as we turn out of the village. As we drive through tiny hamlets, Jason is chattering excitedly and pointing things out in the distance. He laughs at a braying donkey, its head hanging over a fence in someone's front garden.

Soon enough we are on the open road passing verdant fields and rolling hills with farmhouses dotted in the distance. Eventually we arrive at a pleasant-looking park, fronted with wrought-iron gates and a giant palm tree.

It's so beautiful inside the park, with tall trees and grasses surrounding a large lake, the sound of birdsong gently trilling in the trees. Sofia has bought a small scooter out for Jason and he whizzes along the footpath ahead of us so fast that she often has to call out to him to wait. After ambling along the lakeside in the beautiful sunshine, we arrive at a picnic area of wooden tables shaded by trees, where Phoebe produces a Tupperware box filled with cold meats and olives, along with bread, and some cheese and spinach parcels and sets out the picnic. The sound of water can be heard from a small waterfall rushing over some rocks.

'Gosh this is lovely, it's like being in the middle of a forest,' I remark.

'It is a lovely way to switch off I think after a busy week, after this we can walk through the botanical area. There are so many different plants, medicinal ones too,' Sofia informs me.

'We have some lovely parks in England, of course, but we don't often get this kind of weather to enjoy them.'

'I cannot imagine the sun not shining, especially in the

summer,' says Sofia. 'The winter can be wet though, which is of course the reason for all these glorious plants.' She glances around at palm trees, lush plants with colourful flowers, and tall, leafy shrubs.

We dine on delicious food, and I bring out the cakes from Thea's bakery, which are gratefully received. Jason's eyes light up, but Sofia tells him he can enjoy cake only after he has eaten some of the picnic food.

When we finish, Jason gleefully eats his sponge cake with the jelly sweet on top, before Phoebe takes him to the water's edge to feed the ducks with some leftover bread.

'Are you married?' I find myself asking Sofia as we sip lemonade, wondering why her husband isn't accompanying her on a Sunday visit to the park.

'Yes, but my husband works shifts,' she explains. 'He is an ambulance driver, and sometimes he is required to work on a Sunday. But I am used to it now.' She shrugs. 'I guess people get sick every day of the week, but the job pays quite well.'

'Do you go out to work?' I ask her.

'I used to. But you know, when Jason was born I decided to stay at home until he went to school. I was thinking of returning to work, he has now just started, but then...' She rolls her hand over her stomach.

'You're pregnant?'

'Almost three months. My grandmother is superstitious, so probably would not tell you yet. Next week, three months pass, so I am sure she will let you know then.'

'I'm so happy for you.'

'Thank you, Claudia. I am happy you move next to my grandmother, she gets a little lonely since my grandfather has died and doesn't have a lot of close friends, although she does chat to the neighbours. She is no longer friends with Eliza across the road.'

'Yes, I've seen her outside her house and we have waved to each other, but we haven't officially met.'

Just then, Phoebe returns from the lake with Jason, so Sofia changes the subject and once more I wonder why the two women are no longer on speaking terms.

An hour later, having taken another stroll, we make our way back to the car park.

'Thank you for inviting me today, I've had such a lovely time,' I say as we drive back towards Roda. Jason is playing with a little windmill I bought him from the café shop in the park after we had nipped in to use the loo.

'That was very kind of you,' Sofia says as we drive. 'He can plant it in his garden for when the wind blows. It will remind him of the sea near his great-grandmother's house.'

Arriving back in the village, Sofia heads inside to have tea with her grandmother and I thank her once more, before nipping next door to check on progress, but there is no one to be found.

'Hello,' I call throughout the building, my voice bouncing off the empty walls. Walking into the kitchen area, I come face to face with Dimitri and almost jump out of my skin.

'Oh, my goodness, I thought there was no one here.' I can hear my own heart thumping through my chest.

'Would that be a good thing, as you are paying us to do a job?' He smiles.

'No, I guess not, but you did say you would only be here for the morning. Where are Yiannis and the boys?' I ask.

'The boys would never work on a Sunday,' Dimitri tells me, as he wipes his hands on a rag. 'I persuaded Yiannis to come in for a few hours this morning whilst his wife visits church. He must be home for the family meal though, or his life will not be worth living.' He smiles.

'Of course, I'd almost forgotten. Maybe it's because

Sundays are not really days of rest back home, although I guess builders don't work on a Sunday there either. Honestly, thanks, I really appreciate you being here,' I tell him gratefully.

Glancing upwards, I can see more wooden beams criss-crossing the ceiling and that it is almost finished. 'I can't believe I never even questioned you being here today, it being Sunday. Thank you. I owe you a drink,' I say brightly.

'Okay. I know somewhere nice,' says Dimitri, wrapping some tools in a canvas cloth.

'What, right now?'

'Yes. I could use a cold drink. Unless you mean, like out for a drink, as in a date.' He raises an eyebrow.

'Absolutely not,' I almost shout, then feel rude for feeling so appalled by the idea. 'I mean, I appreciate you coming out today, so I think a drink is in order. Lead the way.' Did Dimitri really think that I was asking him out?

Dimitri can't seem to keep the smile from his face as we walk down the road and turn left, rather than right towards the main street of shops and restaurants. Passing several village houses and a small supermarket, we eventually arrive at a white-washed bar with several dark wooden tables and chairs on a terrace outside. An old wooden rowing boat is filled with flowers and creates a welcoming feel.

Inside, I take in the interior of rough white stone walls, some photos on the wall. It is quite busy with families out relaxing and sharing a drink together.

'This is our local bar,' he explains as we take a seat on two bar stools and Dimitri speaks to the barman in Greek and orders us a drink, which I quickly take some euros from my purse and pay for.

'This is nice,' I say. Glancing around as we both sip an ice-cold Corfiot beer, I notice black-and-white pictures of the old port are dotted around the walls, along with a ship's wheel. An old wooden rowing boat is filled with flowers and looks brilliant against the white walls.

'The people in the village gather here. Maybe it could be your new place, do you call it a local in England?'

'Yes, that's right.' The thought that I could visit regularly getting to know people here excites me. 'Do you have evenings out in the main street too?'

'Of course.' He smiles. 'But most of those shops and bars close when the tourist season ends. This is for the villagers all year round.'

As we chat, several people pass and say hello to Dimitri and nod and smile at me. When Dimitri drains the last of his drink, he stands ready to leave.

'Well, thank you, Claudia. That was exactly what I needed after a hard morning's work, but now I must go.'

Feeling mellow with the drink, I could have happily sat here for longer with another beer, chatting to him, but it's clear Dimitri needs to leave. I order myself another drink and take it outside to sit at a table that gives a side view of the beach in the distance, and the church across the road. I watch Dimitri head back towards the street of my villa, remembering he is staying at his aunt's house looking after her dog. I suddenly wish that my house was completed. Maybe then I could have strolled home with him, perhaps invited him inside for coffee. I remind myself that he is my builder, and that even if he was single, which I don't actually know if he is, it would be a total mistake to mix business with pleasure. Not to mention the fact that romance is definitely not something I am looking for. Far better to admire him from a distance, I think, a bit like my favourite movie actor.

'May I join you?' a man asks, jolting me from my daydream. I can't help glancing around at the empty tables and wondering why he has chosen to sit opposite me.

'Sorry, I am just being friendly. I never noticed you here

before.' He holds his hands up and I feel rude for thinking he might be about to hit on me. 'My name is Eric.'

Eric, an older guy, who is definitely something of a silver fox with warm-brown eyes, shakes me by the hand.

'Nice to meet you, I'm Claudia,' I tell him.

'You have French heritage? Claudia is a French name, I believe?'

'No, I think my father just liked the name. Mum seems to think he had a thing for an actress called Claudia.' I smile.

'So are you here on holiday?' he asks as he sips his beer.

'Yes,' I tell him. 'But I usually head down to the main strip near the beach.'

I don't feel it necessary to tell everyone I meet about my half-renovated villa with a cement mixer in the yard.

Eric is so easy to talk to and the time quickly passes by. He tells me about the village and how he has lived here all of his life, and that not many tourists frequent the village bar, even though the beer is better.

'Well, I can't disagree with you,' I say, finishing the last of my delicious local beer. 'It was good to meet you, Eric, maybe I will see you around.'

'Maybe you will.' He smiles. 'Enjoy the rest of your holiday.'

'Thanks, bye, Eric.'

That evening in the apartment, I sit and watch the sunset on the balcony and feel blessed to have met some lovely people today. Hopefully, tomorrow it will be full steam ahead with the roof of the house and we will begin to see some real progress. It's hard to envisage the finished product, as the villa currently resembles a building site. There are brushes, buckets and lengths of wood everywhere as well as a cement mixer. I think about the blue wooden, crumbling back door with a metal insert that I would like refurbished; thinking about it, I must rescue it from the tip. I recall Dimitri teasing me when he said would I ask him out on a date, and despite everything I close my eyes and imagine how it would feel to be wined and dined by him, at some romantic restaurant overlooking the sea, twinkling lights everywhere. I give my head a shake and flick on the movie channel to an early George Clooney film, where he is in a clinch with an impossibly beautiful lead actress. Far better to have an active imagination when it comes to romance. That way you will never get your heart broken.

EIGHTEEN

Monday morning, after a breakfast on the balcony, I head over to the house and Yiannis has already arrived and is standing on the top of the roof, but there is no sign of Dimitri or the young men.

'*Kalimera*, Yiannis,' I call up. 'Are you okay?'

'Yes, yes, I am okay.' He waves down.

'Where are the others?'

'Maybe they come soon,' he says, whistling as he hammers some nails into a wooden beam.

Maybe? I think to myself. I thought Sunday was the day of rest, not Monday, and wonder what on earth is going on. I busy myself sweeping dust from floors and pulling up weeds in the rear garden and more than an hour later Dimitri arrives.

'Having a late start today?' I try to keep the sarcasm out of my voice as he did work yesterday, but time is money on this project. Dimitri seems unfazed by my comment and just shrugs.

'I was down at the harbour, to check out the boat. You are aware the tourist season starts fully in a couple of weeks.' He pushes his sunglasses to the top of his head.

'Yes. What do you mean about looking at the boat?'

'I have a boat. I take the tourists out on trips in the summer season across the water.' He takes a swig from a bottle of water before scrunching it up and tossing it in the skip.

'I'm aware the season will soon be in full swing, but I didn't realise you had another job,' I tell him, disappointed that he will not be giving my villa refurb his undivided attention.

'Most of the islanders are involved in tourism. My work on the house will maybe slow down a little. This is why I will always work Sundays in the meantime,' he explains.

'So, you're saying work on the house will stop when the tourist season is in full swing?' I ask, horrified.

'It will not stop completely. Yiannis will still be here.'

Much as I am grateful for the hard work Yiannis puts in, he is an older man who works more slowly than the others. I might need to go and talk to Eric from the bar last night, who during our conversation mentioned that he was a retired builder.

'What about the casual labourers?' I enquire about the young workers with a feeling of rising panic. I had hoped that the renovation work would be continuing steadily when I head home, but now it would seem that the builders have summer jobs.

'They work in their family restaurants down at the beach,' he tells me, looking at the floor, unable to quite meet my eyes. 'Maybe I should have been clearer about all of this.'

'Yes, maybe you should.'

Like when you agreed to take on the work, I think, realising that this could drag on forever.

'Don't worry. Most of the work will be done soon, I promise. If not, we will continue properly at the end of September, it goes a little quieter then and by the end of October no one comes here at all, apart from a few people who fly over from Athens.'

'End of September?'

This is not good news, and I'm now considering asking my dad over, maybe even my brother.

'I hope I do not give the wrong impression. I will still work here after the day is over on the boats, but not as many hours.'

'But you will be completely exhausted.'

I don't want to have to employ new builders, but then again where would I find any, as it appears everyone takes on their summer jobs? I realise I am feeling desperate even thinking of asking Dad over here. He's a little too old for any sort of heavy labouring, although he would never admit to that. I wish Dimitri would have mentioned this when he signed up for the job, although perhaps I should have asked more questions. Maybe I really can coax the guy I met at the bar out of retirement.

'How long for the roof to be finished?' I ask, thinking at least the house will be protected from the elements.

'A few more days. It is not a large roof, it will be finished before you head home,' he tells me, and I feel a sense of relief that at least one of the major jobs on the villa will be completed.

I can't believe I have been so stupid. Why didn't I do my research? Perhaps it would have been easier to have bought a place on the Costa del Sol.

'Maybe you had better crack on then,' I say, returning to the rear garden, taking out my frustration on the weeds growing between the cracks that I attack with such force the trowel bends. It seems my anger has been productive though as two hours later, before the sun reaches its height, I have filled a wheelbarrow with grasses, and a tidy crazy paved yard is revealed, with the olive tree at its centre neatly cut back. I've brushed and hosed it all down, revealing the white between the grey concrete flags. I am sitting on a bench taking a break, when Phoebe pushes the rear gate open.

'*Kalimera*. You would like some?'

She is brandishing a huge jug of home-made lemonade with ice and glasses, for all of us to enjoy.

'Thank you, that will go down really well,' I say, wiping my perspiring face with a tissue.

'You have been busy, very nice.' She glances around the tidy yard and nods approvingly.

'Maybe I will pitch a tent and live in the garden then, because I have no idea when the house will be finished.' I tell her about the builders having summer jobs.

'Everybody work near the beaches in the tourist season, always busy.' Again, I wonder why no one really discussed this, but I can't pin this lack of communication on anyone else, despite my frustration.

I call Dimitri and the other builders down for some of Phoebe's delicious lemonade.

'I am surprised we are allowed a break,' Dimitri teases, taking the drink and glugging it down, as do the others. 'But come, take a look up, most of the roof beams are on now.'

I'd been so busy in the yard I'd barely glanced above even though the banging had continued above my head.

'We are about to put the last few beams across but first we need you to hang the *gouri* from the beams,' Dimitri tells me.

'The *gouri*?'

'Yes. It will bring you good luck in your new home. It is symbol for new beginnings. May I?'

He pulls a red ribbon with a tiny metal house at its centre from his pocket. 'I bought this for you, for good luck in your new home.'

'Thank you, Dimitri, that's so kind.' Despite the worry over the ensuing build I am touched by his thoughtfulness.

'You must be the one to tie it around the beams as you are the householder,' he instructs.

He stands behind me then and guides me up the ladder towards a flat platform. I almost stumble at one point, and feel his hand on my backside for a split second as he steadies me, which almost makes me lose my footing even more. Glancing down, I notice Phoebe below with a huge grin on her face. I carefully tie the good luck charm around a beam at the centre, before descending the steps feeling flushed in the face, which may not be entirely down to my hard work in the sunshine.

Several hours later, the final beams of the roof have been nailed in and the crew break for lunch.

The builders take some slices of *spanakopita* from tubs and glug down water, whilst Dimitri seems preoccupied with scrolling through his phone. He takes a call and with a slow smile spreading across his face, he begins a conversation in Greek with someone as he strolls a short distance away.

Phoebe appears out of her front gate carrying a basket before heading to the local shops.

'Tonight, you would like to have dinner at my house?' she offers.

Phoebe always says, 'You would like,' rather than 'Would you like,' which kind of feels like she is telling me I will enjoy something. I will possibly correct her when the time is right; in return, I hope she may teach me a few Greek phrases.

'Actually, yes, thank you, Phoebe, that would be really lovely.'

'Good. I will make the cheese pie. My mother's recipe.'

'Wonderful. I will see you later and thanks.'

'Tomorrow, we will continue working on the roof,' Dimitri tells me as he returns from his phone call. 'After that, the work inside will maybe not take so long,' he assures me.

'And the outside rendering?'

'As soon as the roof is finished, we will begin. I will have that done in no time at all. Even faster if you like it rough.'

'Pardon?'

'A rough texture on the walls.' He gives me a sidelong grin. 'It takes longer if you want a smooth finish.'

'Oh right, I see. I guess I would like it smooth, but I will have a think about that, especially now that time is of the essence.'

I'm about to apologise for my earlier frostiness, but remember how laid-back everything is here in Greece, including deadlines. I must keep reminding the crew how important it is to keep the building schedule on track before the influx of tourists.

'So you are okay?' He looks at me a little doubtfully.

'Yes. I will have to be, I guess. Truthfully, though, I didn't realise my workforce would disappear in the summer, but never mind. I trust you enough to know you will work hard while you are here.'

'That is good to hear. And you have my word that I will. We all will.'

When the building work has finished for the day, Dimitri and Yiannis head towards their van and Dimitri takes some cash from a wallet and pays his two young labourers as he does each day. There is no contract I realise, which means they can disappear whenever they need to. Before they leave, Dimitri asks me if I am busy later.

'I am having dinner with Phoebe, she invited me earlier,' I tell him, suddenly wishing I was free. And wondering if he is going to ask me out.

'I see. I was going to ask you to run a hose of water over some of the newly laid cement on the stone terrace upstairs. It can crack in the heat if it is not watered,' he says, before picking up his tool bag. 'But I can come back and do so.' He smiles.

'Oh. Right, yes.' A silly feeling of disappointment runs through me, and I feel like such an idiot. Of course Dimitri wouldn't be asking me out; he will have a girlfriend, why wouldn't he, he's gorgeous. Besides, am I really thinking about a holiday fling with my builder? A bit of fun? I really must stop watching those romantic movies. I firmly file any thoughts of romance into the corner of my brain and get a grip on reality. If only he wasn't so damn attractive.

'Have a nice night then, see you in the morning,' he says, before firing up the engine and disappearing around the corner in a cloud of dust.

I take a bottle of water outside into the garden, watching the olive tree gently waving its branches in the late afternoon, and that's where I answer a video call from Mum.

'Hi, lovely, how are things? Is the weather nice over there?' she asks.

'Hi, Mum. Oh, it's gorgeous, look...'

I turn my phone around and show her a view of the beautiful blue sky, the tip of the mountains in the far distance. I also show her the garden, which last time she saw it was a bit of a jungle.

'Ooh you have worked hard, and the weather looks lovely. We had a nice time at the zoo on Saturday, didn't we, George?' she says to my nephew. 'It was threatening to rain all day but thankfully it didn't. Are you going to tell Auntie Claudia what your favourite animal was?' she asks George.

'The monkeys,' says George, pulling a face and making monkey sounds at the camera and making me laugh.

'I'm glad you had fun, George, I'll see you soon.' I blow him a kiss and he gives me a cheeky grin before blowing me a kiss in return, and my heart swells with love.

'Hi, love, how is the building work going?' asks Dad, who appears then, munching on an apple.

'Good, but I'm not sure for how much longer.' I tell him all about the second jobs the builders have once the tourist season is in full swing. 'Probably my own fault for not asking enough questions.' I sigh.

'Maybe I should come and give you a hand after all,' he says, and I almost take him up on the offer.

'Don't worry, Dad. The guy in charge of the build has

assured me they will work hard at every opportunity, so I have to put my faith in them.'

Mum and Dad drift off then, telling me *Countdown* is about to start so I chat with my brother, who tells me what a great weekend they have had, and how he hadn't realised how much he missed his home town.

'So, you stayed an extra day?'

'I did. I hate it when we have to rush off, and George will only be missing a morning in nursery. I'm making the most of it, before he starts school in September.'

'I can understand that. Anyway, I hope all goes well when you head back. Perhaps you need to sit down and have a conversation with Zoe, see if you can work things out,' I tell him, thinking about little George, although of course I want my brother to be happy too.

'I know, I will. Thanks, sis. Talk soon, enjoy the rest of your time there, not jealous a bit.'

He pans the camera round the room and everyone waves before I hang up. I feel blessed to have such a wonderful family and can't wait to have them all over here to enjoy a nice holiday. In the meantime, it's time to head back to the apartment and get ready for dinner with my new neighbour.

NINETEEN

A drone of crickets in hedgerows fills the air as I walk past the village church and the grassy area that leads down towards the beach. Children are playing football and feral tabby cats lounge beneath trees with white painted trunks, a common sight, especially along village roads, so that motorists can see them in the dark, I'm told. In no time at all, I am turning into the road, where I see Phoebe standing outside talking to a couple of people. As I draw closer, I can hear their raised voices and unsmiling faces.

Phoebe shakes her head at one of them, and guides me inside, not before I hear one of the men saying, 'Noise, too much noise.'

'Oh my goodness, are they complaining about the building noise?' I ask, mortified by the thought of having angered my new neighbours already.

'*Nai*. But I tell them it will soon be done, do not worry, although maybe the builders could start work a little later?' she suggests.

'Oh gosh, yes, of course, I will speak to Dimitri. Maybe eight o'clock is a little early.'

I'm not sure I would like to wake up at that time in the morning to the sound of hammers, drills and cement mixers. I'm aware the builders have been starting almost as soon as the sun is up, sometimes not finishing until late in a desperate bid to get the work finished before they depart to their other jobs, but I don't want to get on the wrong side of my new neighbours before the project is even finished.

'People rise early in the morning,' she tells me honestly. 'But they drink tea, take early walks. They like peace.'

'I completely understand. I will talk to the builders.'

I try not to get too upset about their comments, but I guess they have a point. The builders were already working when I arrived well before eight yesterday.

'I hope you like pie,' she says then, placing a huge filo pastry-topped pie down in the middle of the table.

'I do, but I don't think that's like any pie I have ever made, it looks amazing,' I say, taking in the thin golden layers and the delicious smell.

She cuts into it, and I hear the crunch before chunks of cheese, leeks and red onion ooze out as she spoons it onto a plate. There is a Greek salad and some bread too.

'It's as delicious as it looks, Phoebe,' I tell her as I dive in. 'It must have taken a while to make. Is there a herb in it?' I ask, not quite able to place the flavour.

'I have the time.'

'Yes, I suppose you do.'

'It is a good herb to use.' She pours me a glass of lemonade.

'Oh, I see, you have the *thyme*.' I smile at the misunderstanding. 'Well, it tastes lovely.'

'I grow the thyme.' She points to a terracotta pot on the windowsill, alongside a pot of basil.

'Thank you for making me so welcome, Phoebe. I hope the other people in the street will be just as nice,' I say as I polish off more of the delicious food. 'I don't want to upset anyone.'

'Do not worry. The house was a mess and they want to see it fixed up, though they don't want the noise.' She rolls her eyes and laughs. 'A lot of old people live on the street, but they like the young people here. They give the place energy,' she reassures me.

We chat easily and she asks me about my family back home, and I find myself telling her all about my inheritance from my uncle Jack.

'Which is how I came to buy the villa. I would never have been able to do that otherwise,' I tell her as I sit back stuffed, having eaten every last morsel of the pie.

'Your uncle has left you a great gift. He must have loved you all very much.' She places her hand over mine.

'He did. I have nothing but lovely memories of my uncle. Family is so important.'

'Maybe we raise a glass to your uncle.'

'That's nice, we will. To Uncle Jack.'

She crosses herself and says a little something in Greek that she tells me is a prayer to keep Jack and her husband safe in heaven.

I head off later before it gets too dark, and as I turn a corner I run into Dimitri.

'*Kalispera*,' he greets me with that winning smile.

'*Kalispera*. How are you?' I ask.

'I'm okay. I am glad I have run into you actually.' He falls into step with me as I head towards my apartment. 'It would seem we have been making a little too much noise with the building work. I have spoken to the neighbours, the elderly residents mainly, to let them know we will start work at nine o'clock. Is that okay with you?'

'Oh yes, that's wonderful. I was going to text you and suggest the very same thing. And are they okay with that?'

'They are,' he reassures me. 'Well, it's been a long day, I am off home for a beer. Actually, would you like to join me?' He lifts the carrier bag he is carrying as we arrive outside my apartment.

'What? Back at your place?'

'Yours is closer, if you want to invite me in,' he suggests, with a cheeky grin.' Maybe you can tell me more of what you would like.' After a pause, he says, 'In the house.'

I hesitate for a second, but as the night is quite young, I agree. I have nothing else to do for the rest of the evening other than search for a TV channel that I can understand.

'Sure. A beer on the balcony sounds good as it's such a lovely evening.'

Outside in the balmy evening we sip our beers and take in the lights as they slowly come on in the bars and restaurants, a faint sound of music from somewhere. The sea is slowly darkening, with lights from boats gently dancing across the water. A plane is heading towards the airport, reminding me that there will soon be an influx of holidaymakers on the island.

'I'm not sure I could ever get tired of this view.' I sigh, content with food from Phoebe's and feeling more and more mellow with every sip of beer.

'It's pretty special, isn't it, but maybe we take everything for granted, even living in the most beautiful place.' He takes a sip from his bottled beer and gazes across the rooftops.

'Maybe. I know that we don't always appreciate what is right in front of us, that's for sure,' I agree. 'So, have you always been in the building trade?' I ask, attempting to find out a little more about him.

'Yes. It was a natural thing for me as my father was a builder, and I would help him when I was young. After school, at weekends, I learned everything from him. I am sure I am not as good as him though.'

'Now you tell me,' I joke.

'Don't worry, I am good. Of course, but my father is a master,' he says proudly. 'He has retired now.'

'Does he fancy coming out of retirement? When the tourist season starts?' I joke.

'When I say he has retired, I mean from the building work. He will also be taking tourists on the boats when the season starts.'

'Worth a try. So, what happens when the season ends?' I'm intrigued to know.

'We finish building projects, paint our houses, do a little sea fishing. When the real winter sets in we play cards and see more of our families. Well, most people do. I never refuse a building project in the winter though, although it can rain quite a bit.'

Dimitri explains that for a lot of people a summer income has to last throughout the winter months. 'So, if the tourists don't come, it can be a hard winter, but everyone helps each other out.'

That's the nice thing about village life, I guess.

An hour later, I stretch out my arms and yawn.

'That is, I believe, my cue to leave,' says Dimitri, standing. His silhouette looks so good in the faint light on the balcony, his hair touching his shoulders, those broad shoulders, that full mouth. It's definitely time for him to leave. I walk him downstairs from the upper floor.

'Goodnight. See you in the morning,' he says as I see him outside.

'Goodnight. And thanks for the beer.'

'The pleasure was mine.' He smiles and as he strolls off I think of how much of a pleasure it was for me too.

TWENTY

Early the next morning, I head to Thea's bakery and buy up lots of the morning's fresh offerings as I think it's time for me to go on a bit of a charm offensive.

The builders are already at the house, but no sound of drills or hammers can be heard yet. Taking a deep breath, I knock on the doors up and down the road, offering pastries and cakes. Phoebe's estranged friend smiles and embraces me, which comes as a surprise.

'Do you speak English?' I ask her and she tells me she speaks a little.

'Sorry about the noise. When the villa is finished you are invited to a party, with the other neighbours. Will you tell them that?'

'*Nai, nai.* Do not worry. That house has been a sore eye.'

'An eyesore,' I correct her.

'Ah, I see. Eyesore, *efcharisto.*'

The other neighbours have congregated outside, and the older ladies whisper to each other.

'Okay,' says the oldest lady. 'We come to your party. Maybe I teach you how to make the best cheese pie,' she says proudly, which brings verbal protest from Phoebe and two other women. Just then the couple with the young children walk past and wish us all good morning.

'You are renovating the house I see,' says the pretty dark-haired lady, who looks around my age.

'Yes, although we are starting a little later in the morning now, sorry about the noise,' I tell her and she waves her hand.

'It's fine, we cannot really hear it too much at the end of the street. Besides, I am awake early.' She nods to her toddler in the pushchair.

'Well, you are very welcome to come over for drinks when the villa is finished. At least almost finished, which is maybe all I can hope for at this time of year.'

'Thank you, I will look forward to that. Oh, and we did a renovation too,' she tells me in a low voice as I walk towards the pram to say hi to her little boy. 'And they complained also. Now? We are all good friends,' she says, which I find very reassuring.

Back at the build, work has started, including the work on the roof. Yiannis begins the plastering and skimming of the outside walls and the noise of a concrete cement mixer drones and whirls as the sun begins to creep higher in the sky. The men work so quickly, I have faith that the main work will be complete by the time I head home.

It feels particularly warm today, and after a couple of hours, I notice the young labourers wiping their brows and flagging a little and figure maybe it's time to bring out the ouzo. I nip to a shop and return with a bottle and some shot glasses, much to the delight of the workers.

'Yamas,' I say, raising a shot glass and grimacing slightly as I take a shot, encouraged by Dimitri. I also hand some slices of watermelon around and a short time later work is resumed, the builders refreshed. I remember Phoebe advising to give no more than one shot, just as a little pick-me-up.

'I think maybe you did the right thing at the right time,' Dimitri tells me. 'What do you call it, hair of the dog?'

'Hair of the dog, yes. Wait, are you telling me the boys are hungover? No wonder they were flagging after two hours, and I don't mean literally,' I say, glancing at the broken flagstones on the floor.

'It is a little warm today, although I did notice them in the bar last night watching football, when I went to buy some beers. They are young! Maybe I should not tell you that.' He pulls a face, seemingly regretting dobbing them in. But I guess he's right, they are young men after all.

'And you didn't feel like joining them?' I ask, wondering why he was heading home to drink alone, at least until he ran into me.

'They are nineteen years old. I cannot keep up.' He smiles.

It's hard to gauge his age as he looks young, but he has a maturity that belongs to an older man. As I am pondering this, he inadvertently tells me he is twenty-nine years old when he mentions doing the same thing himself ten years ago when he was their age. So, Dimitri is five years younger than me, although I'm not exactly sure why that has even crossed my mind.

'I remember one occasion when I stayed awake for almost two days,' he says as he checks on the cement. 'There were two parties I didn't want to miss. I was working three jobs at the time in the summer, until all hours of the day and night. It would kill me now approaching thirty.'

'Nonsense. You're still a young, fit man and thirty is no age. I bet you could still go all night,' I say, before wondering why on earth I said that.

'Do you think so?' he asks, a smile playing around his mouth.

'Dancing, partying, you know what I mean. I'm sure you could keep up.'

I lower my gaze and concentrate on scrubbing a low wall at the front of the property in preparation to paint it, wondering why I manage to always say the wrong thing and get myself into a spin, when I hear an almighty crash followed by shouts inside the house.

At first, I think they are making the usual building noise, throwing old things into the skip, before Dimitri downs tools and races inside with me in hot pursuit. Please don't say I am about to face some sort of building disaster; I'm not sure I could cope with it.

My worst fears are confirmed, as the sight in front of us has me covering my mouth in shock. Yiannis is suspended through the ceiling covered in dust, his leg seemingly trapped. I have a flashback to my dad and his mishap in the lounge. I scream then loudly, as the whole ceiling suddenly gives away and the room is covered in a cloud of dust.

Thankfully, Yiannis lands square on a mattress that had been brought downstairs from a bedroom ready to go in the skip.

'Oh my goodness! Yiannis, are you okay?' I rush to him in a panic, my heart racing.

'I think so. Maybe God is watching. He saved me,' he says, glancing upwards with his hands joined together.

Dimitri helps him slowly to his feet, and he visibly winces in pain.

'It is my back,' he says, rubbing at it with a look of pain on his face. 'I think maybe I work no more today.'

'I will take him to the hospital.' Dimitri springs into action.

'You don't think he needs an ambulance?' I ask, worried about any damage to his spine.

'No ambulance.' Yiannis dismisses the idea as he allows Dimitri to gently guide him to his van. 'I have a soft landing.' He raises his hands heavenward once more.

I selfishly think of the ceiling and try my best not to burst into tears.

Dimitri gives instructions to the labourers to carry on in his absence, shaking his head when they reply in Greek.

'I think they were hoping for an early finish. I told them not a chance. Especially as we are now one man down.'

'Thank you. Oh, I hope Yiannis is going to be alright, thank goodness that mattress was there to break his fall.'

Maybe someone was watching over him as I was going to place the mattress into the skip this morning, but never got around to it.

Phoebe appears outside then, fussing and asking if there is anything she can do.

'Not unless you know another builder. Or maybe say a prayer for me when you go to church. Because if this house is going to be finished anytime soon, I think we are going to need a miracle.'

That evening I pour myself a glass of wine and the tears I have been holding in all day fall freely. When Evie calls, I tell her all about the build.

'Oh my goodness! I hope Yiannis recovers quickly. What a nightmare though.'

'I know. The season will be fully up and running soon, and I'll have a half-renovated house.' I take a slurp of wine. 'And, actually, he will be okay. Dimitri called earlier telling me he has a slipped disc, so it's strong painkillers and plenty of rest.'

'How bloody inconsiderate of him,' she says, making me laugh.

'Oh, I know I sound selfish, Evie. I think I'm just panicking. He was a little slower than the other builders, but definitely the driving force with his years of experience. Saying that, I did meet a bit of a silver fox at the bar the other night who once worked as a builder. Maybe I could try and coax him out of retirement.'

'Ooh interesting, I'm sure things will work out, try not to worry. Anyway, I just called to tell you about a night away with Nick. We booked a lovely hotel, and I even invested in some new underwear. It was wonderful, just what we needed. Thanks again for reminding me that marriage needs working at from time to time.'

'I'm so glad things are working out, although I knew they would. You and Nick are made for each other.'

'I know, and I can't believe how stupid I was, drinking in all the attention from Kostas. Just as well I never did anything stupid. We're going to try and get away once a month, or at least go out for dinner. The girls have been rolling their eyes at us, saying we are like a couple of teenagers, but I think they are pleased really.'

'I'm certain they are. There's nothing kids want more than their parents to be happy. Anyway, I'm off to watch a YouTube tutorial on how to render the outside of a house,' I say only half-joking. The days are ticking away and it's a pretty big job.

Dimitri calls me an hour later and tells me that Yiannis will be out of action for at least the next couple of weeks. Even then, he won't be able to climb any ladders or get involved in any heavy lifting or working.

'That's awful, I hope he isn't in too much pain. But I won't lie, this has got me really worried about the build,' I tell him.

Dimitri gives a deep sigh. 'I know, but I promise we will work quickly. I have to tell you though that the labourers have only one more week before their family restaurants opens.'

'And you don't know of anyone else who needs a job?'

'Not really, as I say all hands are on deck for the tourists soon. I know that my father has no desire to work these days as he is enjoying his retirement, apart from helping his friend on the tourist boats sometimes. It is less hard work, I suppose.'

I think of my own father then, and my brother. I realise I'm getting desperate when I even imagine Phoebe brandishing a saw and a spirit level.

This can't be happening! Once more I wonder what I was thinking buying a villa online without viewing the interior. I've watched enough of those house-buying programmes to have known this. I could end up ploughing all of my inheritance into this project, I think to myself as I feel my stress levels rise. Why couldn't I just be content with coming over here and renting the holiday apartment?

I calm myself down by breathing deeply and telling myself that at least the roof is almost in place, so the house will be protected from any sudden downpours of rain. The kitchen has already been demolished and disposed of, awaiting delivery of some new units tomorrow. Dimitri assures me they will take him no more than a day or two to install, but the main problem now is the ceiling above the room that will be the lounge. It will be alright, I tell myself. Everything will be just fine.

'Really, that is not a big job,' Dimitri tells me, when I mention it, but I think he really is just trying to stop me from becoming hysterical. The outside rendering is still unfinished – the other huge job which was being overseen by Yiannis. Suddenly it all feels like an impossible task and despite my best efforts at being positive, I pour myself another glass of wine and sob my heart out.

It probably wasn't my best idea to walk around to the villa after two glasses of wine, to fully take stock of the situation. At least the rear garden is looking nice though, I think to myself as I push the gate open, thinking the flaking paint could do with another coat. The wooden bench set against a wall could probably do with a coat of paint too, maybe in the same colour.

I sit down and glance up at the house, glancing at the scaffolding in place ready for a job that will be completed goodness knows when. Not for the first time, I wonder why on earth I even thought about buying a renovation project. But then, sitting here in the balmy evening close to the ancient olive tree, I can already feel my senses being soothed. I have already made friends here and can't think of a nicer place to have a holiday home. I tell myself that everything will be alright in the end and conjure up some positivity that I normally have tons of.

I stand to leave, when a spider the size of a saucer scurries towards me and my scream echoes around the neighbourhood as I jump onto the bench. A few seconds later, the back gate bursts open and in strides Dimitri.

'Claudia, are you alright? I was just walking past, and I heard a scream.'

'Yes, yes. It was just the size of that thing.' I look through my hands and point to the walled area of the garden, but of course the spider has long gone.

'Was it a snake?' asks Dimitri unperturbed.

'A snake? You're telling me there are snakes?' I ask, horrified.

'Yes, but they are all pretty harmless. Nothing to worry about. So, it wasn't a snake?' Dimitri asks.

'No, it was a spider. The biggest I have ever seen in my life.' I give a little shudder as I think about it.

I take in Dimitri's appearance then, his hair tied back, the white patterned short-sleeved shirt, and smart jeans. He smells good too.

'What are you doing here alone anyway?' he asks, a puzzled look on his face.

'I don't know.' I shrug, feeling a bit silly. 'I just wanted to see how far things had come and assess the damage. And see what I could do to help.'

I don't know exactly what I was thinking, but I didn't feel like sitting home alone this evening.

'At this hour?' He glances at his watch. It is almost eight o'clock.

'Maybe.' I can feel the tears threatening behind my eyes again, but manage to pull myself together.

'Anyway, thanks for calling in. Please don't let me keep you, as you are obviously on your way out for the evening.' I muster up a smile.

'If you are sure you are okay. Maybe I will walk you home first.'

'No, really, it's around the corner, and it's still light,' I say breezily. 'But thank you anyway.'

'Please, try not to worry.' He turns to me. 'Tomorrow the floorboards will be laid in the bedroom and the kitchen units will arrive. I will work until midnight if I have to,' he says and I feel filled with gratitude.

'Thank you, Dimitri,' I say in a small voice. 'Maybe I will walk with you a little way before I go home. You can watch out for any more spiders.'

TWENTY-ONE

We turn right at the bottom of the road as the orange sun slowly begins its descent. As we reach the white church overlooking the grassy area close to the apartment, we say our goodbyes. Dimitri tells me he is meeting a friend at a restaurant on the main street, even though I never asked.

'That sounds nice.'

'It's better than spending the evening alone.'

His eyes lock with mine and I feel that familiar fuzzy feeling.

'Well, have a nice evening. And thanks for responding to my scream.'

I suddenly feel a bit daft; I'm an independent woman who has bought a house in Greece for goodness' sake. Why on earth should I be bothered by a spider? They don't bother me back home.

'Anytime.' He smiles, still making no attempt to move. 'Enjoy the rest of your evening too.' He lingers for a split second, before he walks off.

'Thanks, and don't drink too much,' I call after him, before biting my lip and wondering why I said that, coming across like his mother, but he just laughs. 'I mean, hangovers can be costly, as less work gets done,' I tell him in an effort to explain myself.

I study him for a minute as he walks away, watching his confident, yet easy-going stride and I'm mortified when he turns around and clocks me watching him. He raises a hand as he continues on, and I dash inside my apartment.

Once inside, I grab a drink of water and curse myself for letting Dimitri have this effect on me. Maybe if I google local paint shops it will cool me down.

I discover one in Sidari and decide I will head there on the bus tomorrow and buy some paint to refresh the gate and the garden bench. Maybe I can distract myself from thinking about the bigger jobs if I tackle the small ones. I might also look for some interior shops to get some ideas for the finished project too.

I flick through the TV channels back at the apartment, and find a channel showing nineties films in English, and settle down to watch an action film with Nicolas Cage. Deciding to wake early in the morning, I resist any more wine and sip a bottle of water, until my eyes feel heavy. An hour later, the television is nothing more than a drone in the background, and I drift into a sleep.

The sun is up early, and I shower and take my usual morning coffee on the balcony and stare across at the view that never fails to lift my spirits. The church bell is gently ringing out on the hour and I realise it is eight o'clock, and the building work will not begin for another hour. Before I do anything this morning, I will head out to the local supermarket and grab a few provisions. Walking along, taking in the sights of the early morning risers taking a walk, and vans dropping food off in shops, I feel the breeze through my hair as I near the sea.

'*Kalimera*.' Kostas is outside his gyros shop, rolling out the sunshade for the outside eating area.

'*Kalimera*, Kostas. How are you?' I ask as I walk past.

'I am very good.' He smiles. 'You?'

'Yes, I will be, thanks. I won't lie, I am slightly concerned about the progress of the house build.'

'You mean with Yiannis having the accident? Yes, I hear about that from Dimitri. I get the feeling he will work hard to put things right,' he says and I wonder what Dimitri has told him. 'So how is Evie?' he asks, setting out some plastic tables and chairs.

'She's very well, just back from a romantic weekend with her husband,' I can't resist telling him and he smiles.

'I am glad she is happy. She always looked, maybe a little sad,' he says, and I can't help thinking that he wouldn't have minded being the one to put a smile on her face.

'I think she had a lot on her mind. You know how it is, a busy family life and a business to run.'

He nods before wishing me a good day.

Coming out of the small supermarket with my bags a short while later, I bump into the young woman from the house at the end of the road.

'Good morning.' She smiles brightly. 'I am glad I ran into you. Are you free for that coffee? You can take that look around the house,' she offers. 'Oh, and my name is Ria.'

'I'm Claudia. And, yes, thanks, that would be wonderful. I'm heading to a paint shop later and I may be able to get some inspiration from your house, if you don't mind.'

'I would be flattered.' She smiles again. 'I just have to go in here for a few things.' She gestures to the general store. 'Then I will walk back with you.'

She reappears quickly from the shop and we take the short walk back together to her house.

'Why did you choose to buy a villa in Roda? Are you familiar with the area?' Ria asks as we walk.

'Yes, we had many family holidays here. I have wonderful memories playing on the beach with my brother and with friends I made at the hotel.'

Glancing at the seafront hotel that has a different name these days, a flood of happy memories come rushing back. I was eight years old the first time we came to Roda, and I remember my mum pulling a face when the waiter served us octopus, although maybe the story stays in my mind as it has been retold so many times at family gatherings. Mum thought the calamari was a type of onion ring and almost passed out when she realised what it was. 'My palate was never that exotic,' she would laugh. 'The most adventurous thing I'd eaten was a beef bourguignon on one of our cruises.'

'Are you from this area?' I ask as we pass the church.

'A few miles from here, in a very quiet village. I wanted somewhere closer to the beach for our children and a little livelier for them to make friends, although it does go very quiet when the tourist season ends,' she informs me as we approach the beginning of the road. 'The house was at a bargain price, so we couldn't let it go. It was maybe in the same state as the one you have bought.'

'That is interesting. But I agree, it is all about location, which is exactly why I was drawn to the house.'

The thought that her house was in a similar state encourages me and I can hardly wait to get inside and have a look.

Ria puts the key in the door, and the first thing I notice is the bright, white painted hallway and the beautiful green and white mosaic floor tiles.

'Is that an original floor?' I ask, admiring it.

'Not at all. It's a very clever floor covering.' She smiles at my reaction as I bend down and stroke the patterned floor covering.

'It looks amazing, just like the real thing.'

I follow her into a lounge and gasp. It's simply stunning with white walls once more and teal-coloured curtains. A sofa in a soft mustard-matching colour dominates the room, and a dark-wood bookcase holds a few stylish ornaments and a couple of well-placed reading books.

I follow her into the kitchen to discover gorgeous cream units and oak worktops that have a slightly curved edge.

'Olive wood,' she tells me before I can ask. 'My father-in-law saves wood from old trees in his olive grove. I guess I am very lucky that my husband is a carpenter.'

'He is? Would he like to work on my house?' I'm half-joking, although I guess I am trying to gauge a reaction.

'He is very busy with his work at the moment. He works for a large furniture company,' she tells me. 'Although, maybe when your villa is finished he might make you one or two bespoke pieces.' She politely lets me know the idea of her husband doing any real renovating work is out of the question, and with two young children, I can't say I blame her.

Upstairs, the style continues, mixing traditional Greek and modern. Dark wooden units contrast with pale walls, and a huge bed is covered in a pale-pink duvet cover and colourful tapestry cushions. The bathroom is natural-looking too, using neutral shades of earth and grey. A glass sink against a stone background gives it a rustic, yet cosy feel.

'Thanks for showing me around, your villa looks wonderful. If I can get my place to look half as good as this, I will be a happy woman.'

The children are happily playing with some Duplo-style bricks and eating a biscuit as Ria pops the kettle on.

'You are welcome, and I am sure your place will be beautiful too. Just take your time with the interior design. The main thing is getting the building into shape.'

'Of course.' I smile brightly. 'Fingers crossed there will be no more problems.'

'I hope these are okay?' She pops a tea bag into water and I remind myself to bring some Yorkshire Tea over with me next time.

'Fine, thank you.'

Drinking tea from a stylish mug, Ria tells me she has lived in the street for three years.

'It was a challenge doing a house renovation and being pregnant, but it was the best move I ever made. It is so nice being close to the beach. And the neighbours are lovely. They think the world of the children, especially the older people.'

I suddenly think how the years are nudging by, and my next birthday I will be thirty-four. I have never really thought about being a mother, but then we always think we have more time I guess, and in the meantime I am enjoying being an aunt to George.

'It will be nice to have someone of a similar age around, even for a few months a year,' says Ria, kindly. 'Oh, and I am friends with Dimitri's aunt too. She and her husband are in their forties and really nice people. Dimitri is a great guy too, but I guess you already know that.'

She looks at me over the rim of her floral cup.

'I don't really know him on a personal level, although I know he is a hard worker. And, on that note, I should probably be off, work will be starting soon and I need to crack the whip before I catch the bus into Sidari,' I tell her and she laughs. 'Thank you so much for the tea, and showing me your home. It really is beautiful.'

'Thank you. And good luck with the renovation.'

She shows me out and I nip to the bakery, before arriving at the house at the same time as Dimitri and the young workers, and they wish me a good morning. The young men are yawning, and I wonder whether they were out again last night drinking.

'Ready for a hard day's work?' I ask breezily. 'I have bought you all some coffee and a Danish pastry. Keep the caffeine and sugar levels up.'

'Wonderful. Thank you. The coffee I will take, the pastry maybe when I have done some work, burn off a few calories first,' says Dimitri as the young men take the proffered breakfast gratefully.

While the men work hard and the cement mixer whirrs happily, I tell Dimitri that I am off to Sidari in search of some blue paint for the rear gate.

'There is no need. I actually have some,' he offers. 'Unless, of course, you want to go there.'

'I do actually. There's a shop I want to look at to get some ideas for the bathroom, it's on the bus route back.'

Ria's bathroom, a perfect mix of old and new, has inspired me so much that I want to pick up the first of the accessories. Even though the finished bathroom is a long way off, I can work them around the shades I choose.

Dimitri offers to drive me there, before thinking twice and saying there is maybe far too much work to do here at the house and I don't disagree with him, however much I would have liked that.

Descending from the bus half an hour later, I find Sidari is busy with shoppers, locals and tourists alike. The smell of garlic and BBQ meats drifts towards me as I walk past a café where a trio of old men are playing dominoes and drinking coffee at an outside table.

Setting the satnav on my phone, I make my way down a side street, passing graffiti-covered buildings away from the main drag. Passing a yellow-painted hotel with ivy-covered walls and metal balconies, I see the Venetian influence in the area. Looking up, I notice a couple sitting on the terrace of a tanger-ine-painted apartment drinking coffee and watching the world go by.

Walking past a leather shop, displaying heavy coats and

jackets in their window, reminds me that the winters can be a little cool here, but probably nothing compared to the winters we have back home. I pass a bakery, and the smell of something sweet and delicious drifts towards my nostrils as someone opens the door. Presently, I am standing in front of the metal sign of the hardware store.

The guy in the store is super friendly and a short while later, armed with the paint for the gate and some sample pots for the bathroom, I make my way towards the bus stop, stopping en route for an orange juice.

Seated at an outside table, I observe the steady trickle of holidaymakers, pale skinned and just arrived, browsing clothing stores and reminding me that the full-on season is just around the corner. A waiter is standing outside a restaurant, chatting to a trio of attractive young girls as he gestures to a menu board and they head inside as he scans the road for other potential diners. Already, it looks busier here than it was a few days ago and I have a sudden dread that the majority of the work being completed before I leave is nothing but a dream.

Finishing my drink, I catch the bus back to Roda, stopping at the large bathroom showroom, sandwiched between a bed warehouse and a tile merchants. I take photographs of the bathroom displays, before purchasing some new soap dishes and a hand wash dispenser. I hope I can achieve something as stylish as the bathroom in Ria's house.

I'm soon seated on the bus and passing the familiar sights whilst imagining what it must be like to live in Greece, spending days after work down at the beach, with a handsome husband, and two perfect children, before smiling to myself and realising that it is just a fantasy. I mean, does anyone live a life straight out of a romantic movie? Even beautiful people have to deal with laundry and all the boring bits. I remind myself how lucky I am to be the owner of a property here, and have been able to pay off a chunk of the mortgage on the apartment back home. I try not to think about the timescale of the finished refurb, however frustrating it might be, and focus on the positive. I am truly blessed and remind myself that there are people not so fortunate, as the bus trundles on.

Back at the apartment, I quickly drop off my purchases before taking the short walk to the house. I arrive just as Dimitri is changing his shirt and I have to avert my eyes from staring at his impressive six-pack. It's a hot day today and the men seem to be working at lightning speed, Dimitri barking orders at the young men; no wonder he is working up a sweat.

I'm thrilled to see the bedroom floor has been laid, and the remnants of the bathroom have been put into a new skip, the previous one having been removed.

'My goodness, you have been busy. Can I get you anything?' I offer, just as a beeping truck arrives, slowly making its way down the narrow street.

'Some cold drinks would be good,' he says, taking some money from his pocket. 'And it looks as though your kitchen has arrived.' He nods to the truck.

'Oh wow. Yes, of course, I'll grab some drinks. The kitchen is definitely something I can help with, especially the assembly of the kitchen units,' I tell him, thinking of all those self-assembly cupboards I have managed to put together.

'The units are fully assembled, they just need fixing to the floor and walls.'

'Really? Well, that is going to save a lot of time.'

I walk to the shop with a spring in my step, knowing the kitchen will be assembled much more quickly than I anticipated if the units are complete. If the bathroom can be finished too, then maybe the external rendering is not quite so important, as long as it is eventually completed. Along with my dream balcony.

Laden down with cold drinks, and some tubs of Pringles, as I approach the villa I hear the sound of Dimitri shouting. Surely something else can't have gone wrong? So much for the *gouri* hanging from the beams to bring good luck.

My heart sinks when I see Dimitri standing outside drenched in water, as the labourers frantically try and stem a fountain of water that is spurting from the ground.

'Oh no, goodness, what's happened?' I ask in shock.

The noise has brought Phoebe out of her house. 'They have hit a water pipe,' she explains.

I take in the sight of water cascading everywhere and resist the urge to scream loudly at the sky.

Dimitri dashes inside to switch off the water at the mains, and even the sight of his wet T-shirt sticking to his body can't quell my feeling of rising panic. The newly cemented front path has turned into a grey sludge as the men grapple with a cloth, trying to stem the flow of water, and shouting in Greek.

All the positivity I felt just a few minutes ago has drained away like the water that is running down the path, and I want to cry when suddenly the pipe stops spurting water.

'I can get the pipe replaced quickly.' Dimitri takes his phone from his pocket and makes a call.

I place the drinks and Pringles onto a wall with a heavy heart, as Dimitri directs the delivery guys through the sludgy path to deposit the units into the kitchen.

'Do not worry.' Phoebe looks completely unruffled. 'It is normal to have, what you might say, a few problems with a build. Some say it is good luck in a new house.'

'Good luck? You must be kidding.'

'You get the brush, I will bring the ouzo. This time it is for you.' She winks as she heads inside her house.

As I look around my drowned villa, I think she might be right. I do need a drink.

TWENTY-TWO

A short while later, having swept the water away and indulged in a shot of ouzo that I knocked back, I'm sitting with Phoebe feeling a little calmer. I don't know what I would do without Phoebe next door.

A plumber arrives in no time, and it's not too long before the punctured water pipe is replaced and there is a steady sound of hammering and drilling coming from the kitchen again. Dimitri assures me the kitchen, which is only a small space, will be completed by this evening.

'Did you ever think about opening the kitchen out?' asks Dimitri, glancing around the space. 'This is not a supporting wall.' He prods the space behind him.

'Now you tell me. Although actually, I quite like a separate kitchen. Maybe I could have one of those serving hatches. My gran had one in her house and she used to pass the plates of food through the hatch to the diners at a table on the opposite side.'

I have a picture of Dimitri wearing an apron cooking something up, and passing me a gin and tonic, and the faraway look in my eyes has Phoebe telling me to go off somewhere.

'Maybe you take a step back and go for a walk,' Phoebe advises. 'The more you see, the more you worry. You pay these people the money, remember.' She rubs her fingers together. 'If you do not see the problems, you cannot know they exist.'

'You know you are right, Phoebe. I am paying them, and a good price too. I just thought I could help things along by doing the garden and a bit of cleaning and tidying things away into the skip. But maybe I will leave them to get on with things now.'

Things haven't exactly gone to plan, but when a picture pops into my head of Yiannis falling through the ceiling and onto the mattress, I can't help but laugh. Especially as I know that he is now on the mend.

'Good, good.' We are standing outside at the front of the house and the lady across the road walks out of her front door. I lift my hand and wave, and she waves back as usual. Phoebe turns her head the other way.

'What's the story between you two then?' I ask, maybe feeling emboldened by the ouzo. I can't help feeling sad that two widows of a similar age are missing out on a friendship.

'She is no good.' Phoebe pulls a face, and dismisses my question with a flick of the hand but I press on.

'What do you mean no good?'

'Come inside,' she says and I follow her into her home.

Seated at her kitchen table, drinking a cup of lemon tea and resisting a slice of baklava, I listen as she begins her story.

'It was ten years ago at my sixtieth birthday party,' she tells me, her expression hardening. 'That was when I find out.' She sips her tea slowly.

'Find out?'

'Yes. That she was sleeping with my husband.'

My cup freezes halfway to my mouth. There was no way I was expecting Phoebe to say that.

'Oh my goodness,' is all I manage to say.

'It was a warm evening,' she says, recounting the event. 'The party was at the bar in the village. Many people were in and out, some sitting drinking and smoking at the outside tables. It was late and most people had left.' She stops and takes a sip of her tea. 'We were ready to leave, but I could not find my husband.' She takes a deep breath. 'And so I went outside and there they were.' She shakes her head.

'Go on,' I say gently.

'Wrapped in each other's arms.'

'Kissing?' I ask, knowing that a hug can often be misinterpreted for something very different.

'Yes, kissing.' She pours more tea from a jug. 'On my birthday too.'

'Oh, Phoebe, I am so sorry to hear that. Did they have too much to drink?'

She fixes me with her dark eyes then. 'Do you make the excuse for them?'

'No, no, of course not. So you say they were having an affair? Maybe I was wondering if it was just something they would later regret.'

'They have the affair, God forgive her.' She crosses herself.

It rankles me that she never asked for forgiveness for both her friend and her husband.

'Do you know long it had been going on?' I ask gently, taking a nibble of a delicious home-baked biscuit.

'No. My husband deny everything. But I know. The instinct of the woman.'

'Did you ever ask her about it?' I ask, wondering if they stopped speaking that very day.

'No. Never since the day of the party when I see them kissing,' she says, confirming my thoughts. 'She try to talk to me, but I say no. I told my husband to stay away from her, and I believe that he did.'

'So you stayed together?'

'Yes, for six more years before he died.'

'So you forgave him but not your friend?' I can't help asking.

'I took the vows, yes. I forgive him. Besides, he told me she was always interested in him, she started it.' She almost spits the words out.

'Well, he would say that, wouldn't he?' The words tumble from my mouth.

'What do you mean?' She places her cup down and frowns at me.

'I just wonder why the woman always gets the blame? They are usually the ones who are branded a homewrecker, even though the man is more than happy to go along with it. I mean, you can't force someone to have an affair, can you?'

The memory of my cheating ex rises to the surface, including the vile messages I received from his fiancée, yet she forgave him and even went on to marry him, instead of showing the cheating rat the door.

I'm expecting Phoebe to ask me to leave, especially when I think about it. She was Phoebe's friend after all, and she knew he was married. At least I had no idea about the bloke I met online who was supposedly single. Phoebe says nothing and it feels like an eternity before she finally speaks again.

'I did not want him to leave.' She sighs. 'I could never bear the thought of him living with my friend, just across the road, torturing me every time I see them together. I prayed every night for him to stay with me. To you, a young, modern woman, that probably sounds sad. But it is how I felt. The marriage vow I take, until death us do part.'

I'm sure there is also something in the holy book that says a marriage can be absolved on the grounds of adultery, but I don't say anything.

'Oh, Phoebe, it doesn't sound sad, and I didn't mean to be cruel,' I tell her gently. 'It just annoys me how women always get the blame when it takes two to tango, as they say.'

I wonder how much pressure Phoebe's husband felt in a

small village, to stay with his wife, but I know I could never be with a man whose heart wasn't truly in the relationship, always living with the fear that they may leave again in the future.

My whole sorry story comes pouring out of how I spent six months of my life with a man who was leading a double life. I met him online and he failed to mention his childhood sweetheart who was now his fiancée. I should have read the signs, but hindsight is a wonderful thing, isn't it? He would visit me at weekends, or occasionally during the week if he was working 'up my way'. I never went to his place, him explaining he was sharing a flat that was a bit of a dump, and that the landlord was in the middle of doing it up. It's amazing what you will believe when you are in love, or at least think you are. As my story unfolds, Phoebe's expression softens.

'Then I can understand your anger. And maybe I did not want to admit that I was not enough for my husband. Eliza was always prettier than me.' She sighs.

'I doubt that,' I say, looking at her pretty, hardly lined face. 'Who knows why some people behave the way they do? Ego maybe, flattered by the attention of another woman? But my boyfriend was in a relationship, and actively went looking for someone else. In my opinion, that is even more despicable than having your head turned. I'm not sure I will ever trust a man again.'

'You are young. Do not be soured by one bad experience,' she advises. 'Not all men are that way. As for my husband, I believe he stayed faithful until his death, but if I tell myself the truth, I know that things were never the same.' She sighs. 'I think the guilt would have been too much for him if he left,' she says, and I feel sad that her marriage ended up that way, after all those years together.

'Were you good friends with Eliza before that?' I ask and she nods.

'For over thirty years, when she first moved here with her

husband. They saved to come and live near the sea. Her husband, he had the bad chest.' She takes the cups across the kitchen and places them in the stone sink.

'And you don't think you could ever be friends again?'

'Too much time has passed. Ten years now.' She shakes her head. 'Some things are best left buried,' she says, but there is a sadness behind her eyes.

'How do you know, if you don't try? I have seen her glancing over at you. I get the feeling she might like to put the past behind you both. You are both widows now. You could be friends once more.'

'Pah. I do not think so.'

Her phone rings then, and her face lights up as she takes a call from her daughter. I gesture to the door to leave her to it and she waves me off.

All afternoon I think about how a friendship of over thirty years came to an end because of her husband's unfaithfulness. And yet her friend is the one she blames solely for the indiscretion and Phoebe still feels saddened and annoyed about it, but no one is unfaithful unless they really choose to be, surely? Maybe Phoebe's husband was weak, flattered by the attention of another woman, or maybe he had been unhappy in his marriage. I don't suppose Phoebe will ever know the answer to that now. I just think it a great shame that there can be no forgiveness on Phoebe's part and that two women have lost a friendship that they could probably do with in their older age.

Back at the house, Dimitri has already secured two of the kitchen units to the wall, and I offer to help with the base units, but he refuses.

'I am paid to do this job. I would not mind a coffee though.' He brushes his hair out of his eyes and smiles.

'Sure thing.'

'A double espresso. Maybe it will keep me going.' He smiles again.

Though the rest of the guys are working hard finishing things upstairs, his comment reminds me of how he promised to work until midnight if he had to in order to keep on schedule. I am beginning to learn that he is a man of his word.

Tomorrow the rendering on the outside of the villa will start, and I dare to imagine a smooth, white-walled building standing tall like the proudest house in the street. There will be pots of flowers either side of the front door, and at last I am able to envisage the long summer days I will soon be able to spend here in my dream holiday home.

Returning with the drinks, I watch Dimitri bending and stretching, his strong body hardly breaking a sweat, clearly very fit, his job no doubt keeping him in shape. His rippling arm muscles are flexing, and I struggle to keep my eyes on the little bit of work I am doing, screwing some hinges onto doors, despite his protestations. I haven't found a man so physically attractive in a long while, but that's all I am doing, admiring his physical appearance. Relationships are off the table for me, even if Dimitri had shown the slightest indication that he finds me attractive, which up to now, he hasn't.

'Is everything okay?' Dimitri asks me a while later.

'Yes, why do you ask?'

'You are very quiet,' he observes as he wipes his hands on some kitchen towel.

'I'm okay. I was just thinking about Phoebe and a conversation I had with her. She was telling me about her friendship with Eliza across the road before they fell out.'

'Hmm. I remember my aunt telling me a little about that. I was a teenager at the time, but I recall them having a huge row one evening in the street, when I was visiting my aunt with my parents. It seems Phoebe saw her husband coming out of Eliza's house, after she had returned home early.'

'Poor Phoebe.' I shake my head.

'The strange thing is, my aunt told me that Eliza always

swore it was innocent, he had been doing a job for her. He liked to help her out after her husband died. He was just being a good neighbour.'

'But Phoebe told me that they had an affair and he admitted it.'

'As far as I know, it was never his intention. Phoebe drove him crazy with her accusations. Some people say she drove the two of them together with her jealousy.'

'I don't believe that's possible if two people really love each other, surely.' I dismiss his idea.

'If you love someone, surely you trust them though?' He looks me in the eye. 'Why didn't Phoebe trust him? Without trust, there is nothing.' He picks up a hammer and returns to his work.

I find a crazy, jealous woman hard to reconcile with the kind woman I have come to know these past few weeks.

'Well, I can't argue with that,' I say. 'Human relationships can be so complicated, there is no doubt about that.'

'They don't have to be. If two people love each other, then that should be enough,' he states simply.

I'm about to reply, but the sound of his hammer blows tells me the conversation is over.

I think of Evie then, and how her marriage had slipped into the doldrums and wonder whether she may have acted on the attention from Kostas, if they had not decided to make more of an effort. Thank goodness they never threw everything away.

'You still have to work at it. Love isn't always enough,' I mutter to myself as I finish up with a base unit.

He glances over at me then. 'Did you say something?'

'Nothing important.'

Dimitri persuades the young men to stay until ten o'clock this evening, and it's just after eleven before he puts the finishing touches to the units himself, fastening the modern chrome handles onto the cream wooden doors.

'I really can't thank you enough for working so hard.' I glance around at the cream kitchen with the granite worktops, and glossy sage-green splashbacks. We are sitting on the floor eating the pizza we ordered from a box and sipping bottled beer.

'I told you I would. And before the midnight deadline. Maybe I will have a small lie-in tomorrow.'

'I think you deserve that. You can start at nine fifteen.'

'Slave-driver.'

I still have over a week of this visit left, and my spirits have been lifted by the installation of the kitchen. Knowing the roof is secured, as well as the ceiling in the lounge, is huge too. Exhaustion suddenly takes over, and I wish I could climb upstairs and crawl into bed in this very house.

Dimitri gets slowly to his feet.

'I am grateful to be staying so nearby,' he says. 'I will let Prudence out for the night and take a shower before bed. But first I will walk you home.'

'Really, there is no need.' One thing I can say is that it feels perfectly safe around here, and the apartment is literally a few minutes' walk away. 'It's been a long enough day for you already.'

'I would feel better if I did,' he insists.

'Okay. If you insist.'

We walk quietly and outside my apartment he doesn't linger, but says goodnight, and heads off.

It's been a good day today, and I hope tomorrow will bring more of the same.

TWENTY-THREE

As I go inside, I can't help wondering about Dimitri, and if he has a significant other. It's a nice place to live, but I wonder if there is much opportunity for romance in the village, with the people he grew up with. Perhaps most head off to bigger towns and cities, but surely some remain, favouring the beach location and marrying someone they have known all their life? He has never mentioned a girlfriend, but then, why would he?

As the questions go around in my head, I wonder why I even care. But there is just something about Dimitri that gets into my head and makes me think of him, long after he leaves.

Counting down the days until I return home, I have to be realistic about the time frame for the build, especially after discovering the builders will be heading off soon to their summer jobs. But I am grateful to Dimitri and the effort he has put in, and at least the roof is on to protect the house from the elements.

I do worry a little about it standing empty, but remind myself that I have Phoebe to watch over the villa until the next time I can return, and didn't Ria mention how the neighbours look out for each other? I have to put my trust in the people here and hope with all my heart that it won't be too long before I return to my favourite island.

Three days later, most of the rendering on the rear walls has been completed and I have even managed to paint the garden gate and bench the Greek shade of blue that can be seen everywhere. A new door has been installed at the front of the house, as it was quite rotten, and is now a welcoming door with a bunch of dried sage tied around the door knocker, said to ward away evil spirits. I'm sitting glancing up at the stone stairs to the balcony, daydreaming, when Dimitri seems to tap into my thoughts.

'Tomorrow, I will take you to see my friend. He can make your dream balcony rail. I will hopefully have it installed for the next time you come here.'

'Really? That would be wonderful.' I can already imagine myself standing there and just gazing out to the sea across the rooftops, or sitting reading a book in the sunshine.

'And I was wondering.' He looks uncertain for a moment. 'As it is on the way to Corfu Town, whether you would like to spend an afternoon there before you leave?'

'I would like nothing more,' I say, my heart beating just that bit faster at the thought of us spending the day together in one of my favourite places.

'Good. I would not suggest this if we were not so far on with the work, but I think we all need a little break.'

'I agree,' I tell him. I know they have worked above and beyond to get things to a certain place.

'We will soon finish rendering the outside walls, then there is only the bathroom. Unless, of course, you have come to terms with living with the blue bath. I could retrieve it from the skip,' he jokes.

'Absolutely not. I'm thinking clean lines, earth shades and

a nice white bath on legs. Maybe some exposed brickwork. I saw some lovely bathrooms at the showroom the other day. It would be good if I could order what I want before I head home.'

'I am beginning to realise you are someone who definitely knows what they want.'

'Oh, I do, although I'm aware that things don't always work out the way we expect them to.'

He studies me for a moment, and I feel heat rise in my cheeks under his gaze.

'Are we still talking about the house?'

'Maybe not. Life in general.' I shrug, not wanting to give too much away about my personal life and ruin the positive mood.

He finishes his drink then, and doesn't ask any more questions, before he resumes his work.

The next morning, we take a slight detour to the bathroom place near Sidari, and Dimitri quickly orders the bathroom suite I have chosen, along with some fixtures, to arrive on Thursday. I realise then how fortunate I am to have a Greek builder to help me with all of this.

The next stop is Dimitri's friend, who I am told has a workshop in the countryside at the edge of a village. We take a left turn, away from the highway and are soon surrounded by rolling countryside.

'Are you happy with how things have gone so far in the villa?' Dimitri asks as he drives.

'Yes, I am. I mean apart from a few hiccups, what with Yiannis and his back.'

'And the woodworm in the floorboards,' he says.

'Not to mention the water pipe in the garden,' I add.

'And the man-eating spider in the garden.' He turns to me with a smile on his face, and I can't help but burst out laughing.

We bounce along roads that are little more than dirt tracks and I ask Dimitri if he is sure his car will be alright.

'It's fine,' he reassures me as a chicken literally appears from nowhere, and crosses the road, and has him braking suddenly.

I glance along sweeping fields where men are bending and stretching, packing vegetables into plastic boxes ready to go to markets and shops. There are rows of red peppers and chillies, and fat red tomatoes growing on vines in the bright sunshine, alongside fields of courgettes and potatoes.

Eventually, we pull up outside a large house and are greeted warmly by Dimitri's friend, who leads us to his workshop at the back.

'Dimitri has told me about your project,' says Theo, a stocky man of around fifty years of age, with a balding head and a grey moustache. 'And your desire for a pretty balcony.'

'Yes, if it's possible, even though I am told it might not be very practical.' I cast a glance at Dimitri.

'Yes, but we must all have our dreams,' he tells me warmly as he leads the way to his workshop.

Inside, I glance around at some wonderful examples of his work. Fireplaces, lamp stands, and metal wall art jostle for space, along with some pretty wrought-iron gates.

'Your work is beautiful,' I tell him and he thanks me.

'I think, maybe, you like something like this?'

He shows me a wooden door with a metal insert at the top in a circular filigree pattern in black that seems to lift an ordinary-looking door to something truly extraordinary.

'That's it! That is exactly what I imagine.'

I can picture the white-painted stone stairs leading to the balcony with a beautiful rail. The French doors will be flung open in the early morning sun, the bedroom bathed in sunlight.

'No problem. I can make that for you,' he assures me, which is music to my ears.

'I'm not sure what I would do without you,' I tell Dimitri as we climb into the car. 'I would never have known about a place like this.'

'I am pleased to be of service.' He turns to me and smiles, and I feel a warm glow inside.

Driving through the bustle of traffic approaching Corfu Town once more, I can't resist glancing at Dimitri as we drive. He attracts an admiring glance from a woman in an adjacent car at some traffic lights, and it's not difficult to understand why. He's dressed smart casual today, his curling hair let loose, his sunglasses pushed to the top of his head.

We pass throngs of shops selling everything from tourist goods to stores displaying smart clothing in their windows, until soon enough we are pulling into a car park, close to a bridge that crosses over to the castle, giving a view of a river below.

The town is busy, and Dimitri tells me it is this way pretty much all year round, as we weave through the back alleys and tourist shops displaying their usual wares. Baskets of olive oil soaps with various scents sit alongside gift hampers of oils and herbs, neatly wrapped up in bows. Cats linger outside cafés hoping for a morsel of food; others laze beneath food tables, sated by diners' leftovers.

We pass a shop that has a stand outside displaying an impressive range of fridge magnets, next to a tall wooden stand displaying jars of honey and small bottles of the island's kumquat liqueur. The aroma of herbs from an open wood-fired pizza oven has my tummy rumbling.

Soon enough, we are in a park close to the Maitland Monument. It was built by the British, by Sir Thomas Maitland, the first lord high commissioner of the Ionian Islands, according to a plaque. We walk past what looks like an English village green then, where a cricket match is taking place.

'The whole of this park area is called the Spianada. Although I guess you already know that,' Dimitri tells me.

'Actually, no. I just think of it as a park.'

'Do you like to watch cricket?' he asks, as we stop and watch.

'No, cricket has definitely never been my thing. Or football. In fact, most sports, although I do enjoy watching ice skating and I do love walking, especially in the fine weather.'

My interest in ice skating puzzles me a little as I've only ever been on the ice once in my life, at a Christmas ice rink in Manchester, where I fell, skidded and crashed into a bloke around my age, taking him down too. He was literally frosty with me and I remember thinking that a bloke, no matter how good-looking he was, that could not laugh at himself – or even ask me if I was okay – would never make suitable boyfriend material.

'Have you ever played?' I ask Dimitri.

'Not really. What I mean is, I played with the boys in the village growing up, but I never took it seriously,'

An almighty cheer goes up then as someone has scored. Or made a wicket. Or whatever the terminology is.

'Not like this lot then,' I say, noting a batsman almost throw his cricket bat onto the grass in frustration.

'Not at all. It can be serious business here.'

Just off the green, we amble through the Liston, an elegant, arcaded promenade that houses bars and cafés close to the Spianada. Moving on, the Venetian influence is apparent once again as we pass tall, pillared colonnades and pastel-coloured buildings with iron balconies. One in particular catches my eye.

'That looks so beautiful.' I stare up at the impressive building. 'It's a bit like the one that is being made for me. It looks particularly good against the yellow walls.'

'So now you want us to paint it yellow?' He frowns.

'Absolutely not. White is fine, I wouldn't dream of changing the plans now, don't worry.'

We continue through a jumble of narrow streets with dark-green painted wooden shutters against pastel fronts, and I mention the Italian feel to Dimitri.

'It has that Venetian feel for sure, but many of the buildings were actually rebuilt by the British in a neo-classical style.'

'I'm impressed.'

'I have to confess, my father told me this when I was younger. As a builder he really loves the old buildings and their history.'

'And you, not so much?'

'In some ways, yes. I appreciate the craftmanship, but I prefer a more modern build, with clean lines.'

'Is your place like that?' I blurt out. 'I mean, assuming you have your own place. I know you are currently looking after your aunt's house.' Gosh why have I said that? He could still be living with his parents for all I know.

'Yes. I have recently refurbished the apartment I bought that was a little dated. It is very masculine, I suppose. Maybe I will show you sometime,' he says, fixing me with his deep-brown eyes as he steps a little closer.

'Right,' I mutter, before staring into a shop window at a tray of engagement rings.

'Are you thinking of buying some jewellery?'

'What? No, I was thinking of a gift for my mum.'

'She would like an engagement ring?' He raises an eyebrow.

'No, of course not, perhaps a bracelet or something.' I glance at the expensive jewellery as an immaculately made-up assistant strolls outside and asks if she can be of any help. I politely refuse and we walk on.

Half an hour later, having taken in the sights, including a very pretty church in an unusual shade of maroon and cream at the far end of the harbour, Dimitri suggests lunch.

'Lead the way, I'm famished,' I say, pleased to have diverted the conversation away from visiting Dimitri's apartment as I need to keep this professional. I know he had a drink with me at my place, but it felt less personal somehow, as it's a holiday apartment.

We head closer to the port and are soon shown to a table in a restaurant that overlooks the sparkling water.

'So, tell more about what you do at home?' asks Dimitri. 'I mean, your place of work and family.'

We are sipping cold beers as a waitress has disappeared to the kitchen with our food order.

'I process passports so that people can travel to wonderful places like Greece,' I say, pointing around the harbour.

'And do you enjoy it?'

'I do, actually. It can be frustrating at times though. Some people leave so little time to send in their application, then fly into a panic as their holiday approaches and there is no passport in sight.'

'I can imagine.' He laughs.

'But the wonderful thing is, as I have told you before, I can work from home some days, so I hope to do that from here eventually. Knowing I can stroll to a taverna in the sunshine after spending hours at my computer is far more appealing than walking through a park in the rain.'

'The flights can be expensive at certain times of the year,' he reminds me. 'But I guess you have considered all of that.' He takes a sip of his cold beer.

'Of course. And my job pays well.' There is no need to tell him about the amount of Uncle Jack's fortune and how my inheritance was very generous.

'Anyway, when I say tell me about your life back home, I suppose I mean all of it,' he says, his eyes on mine.

'What do you want to know?' I take a sip of beer, feeling slightly flustered. What can I tell him that doesn't sound totally boring? I live five minutes away from my parents, I'm single and don't really have any interests apart from watching films and walking through forests or along beaches. Oh, and cooking, I quite enjoy that, and can make a curry to rival any restaurant, according to my brother and he has visited a lot of curry houses. I did once join a group of dance majorettes as a teenager and can still twirl a baton rather impressively.

'Umm, I have a flat, old exterior, Victorian actually, but pretty modern inside, although very cosy,' I tell him, picturing the colourful rugs and plant pots, as well as a wall hanging brought back from Thailand on my travels. 'I like travelling, although more recently that has been mainly to Greece. I have a couple of friends and a best friend called Evie, who I have known since college. Is that enough for you?'

'No, do go on.'

'I drive a VW Golf and enjoy watching films, cooking, oh, and I like crafting, maybe a little knitting too. I also love walking through forests, but I'm not a great lover of hill walks.'

Dimitri puts his beer down. 'You are kidding me.'

'Why would I be kidding? I don't see what's so great about hill walking, getting aching calves and huffing and puffing, no thanks. Flat walks, yes, I've loved today for example, I—'

'No.' He shakes his head as he laughs. 'I mean you are kidding me because you like exactly the same things as I do. Watching movies, being in the countryside, cooking. But I also like making things to relax. My aunt Lena taught me how to sew.'

'Now it's my turn to say, you are kidding!'

'No, really. I mean, not all the time, but if I need to, I can sew. I can even crochet.' He grins.

'You can?'

'Yes. I once made a girlfriend a scarf,' he says proudly.

'Wow, you really are full of surprises.' I shake my head, thinking how wonderful it feels getting to know him a little more.

Just then our food arrives, mine a tasty-looking sea bass with oven-baked potatoes, with a delicious Greek salad. Dimitri has opted for a moussaka, the topping of which looks fluffy and delicious.

The sun is beating down on my bare arms and I feel a warmth washing over me as I sit here close to the water with my new friend, enjoying the delicious food. Does he really enjoy all the same things as I do? But then, why would he say it if he didn't? Maybe I just don't trust easily after my experience with my ex. As soon as we met he claimed to love everything I said I did, probably as a quick way to worm his way into my affections. I realised he hated walking on our third date when he began to complain two miles into a six-mile circular walk, asking how far away the pub was.

'Really? So do you have a favourite film?' I ask him. 'Although, I know it would be impossible to choose just one, at least it would for me.'

I take a bite of my delicious fish then, and a forkful of tasty crunchy Greek salad topped with a generous slab of feta.

'I agree, almost impossible to name one, but if I was pushed then I would say *The Bourne Ultimatum*. In fact, all of the Bourne films.'

'Good choice. So you like action movies, maybe thrillers?'

'In general, although I have been known to watch a romance in my time,' he confesses, and I can't help wondering who with. '*Marley and Me* gets me every time.' He thumps his heart with his hand. 'I love dogs.'

'Me too, although I don't have one because it wouldn't be practical in an upper-floor flat or fair on the dog when I am at the office.'

'Me neither. And for similar reasons. That is why I am happy to always look after my aunt's dog.'

'I'm not surprised. Prudence is adorable.'

'So you have told me a little about your life back home, but I notice you have not mentioned a boyfriend,' says Dimitri, before he dives into his moussaka and makes an appreciative noise. I eat more of my fragrant sea bass as I digest his words as well as the food, before I answer.

'Neither have you.'

'I don't have a boyfriend.' He frowns.

'You know what I mean,' I reply, with an eye roll.

'Now you are avoiding the question.'

'Why would I do that? No, I have no significant other as they say, and that's the way I like it.'

'When did you break up?'

'Almost a year now. I am happily single.'

'Yes, you mentioned that.'

'So how about you?' I ask, forking the last of the food into my mouth.

'The same.'

Sitting at this restaurant near the harbour we probably look like any other couple on a date, but the reality is I am sitting with my builder who has kindly offered to drive me into Corfu Town for a day out. But I really like him, and I can't believe we have so much in common. That is, if he is telling the truth. He could just simply have said all that stuff, agreeing with me and saying he liked the same things I do. I scold myself for thinking that way then, even though I kind of wish I had asked him about his interests first, just to be sure.

'I was engaged,' Dimitri tells me after a few moments. 'And my fiancée was someone who hated all of the things I just mentioned,' he reveals, before taking a swig of his beer. 'I thought she was the one, more fool me.'

'How long were you together?' I gently ask.

'Just over two years.'

'Then I'm sorry to hear that. Are you still friends? Sorry, if I sound like I'm prying.'

I have no idea why I am asking him this. Maybe I am just curious as to whether some relationships can end amicably, unlike my last one.

'In different circumstances, maybe we could have been. But even though she did not share an interest in my hobbies, she did like my friends. One in particular, it seems.' He pushes his empty plate away, and leans back in his chair.

'Oh no, I'm so sorry. That must have been difficult.'

'Yes, but it was almost ten months ago now. We have managed to remain civil despite everything, mainly just through social media, but I would not call us friends. Maybe I was kidding myself about it being forever as really we did not have much in common. Beauty alone is not enough.'

So she was beautiful?

I am wondering what happened to his friend but don't dare to ask, when he speaks again.

'As for my friend, he moved away so I don't see him these days,' he tells me, his jaw tightening slightly. 'And their relationship did not last either. Anyway, it is all history now.' He shrugs.

I quickly change the subject, getting back to movies as I don't want Dimitri delving into my last relationship too much, asking me if I am still friends with my ex. I mean, there was my six-year relationship, of course, but there is barely any interaction with him these days, even on Facebook. It makes me wonder how people feel when a partner remains friends with their ex. Would they always be wondering if there could be a chance of igniting a flame with them, especially if their current relationship hits a rough patch?

'As we both enjoy movies, we ought to go and see one,' says Dimitri, thankfully moving on from talk of exes. 'There is an open-air cinema not far from here. Maybe next time you come over, we could go and watch a film?' he offers. 'They have subtitles.'

It occurs to me then that my next visit will not be for another month, and then only for a long weekend, using Monday as a work from home day, working from the apartment.

'You might not be single next time I come over.'

'When will that be?'

'A month from now, just for a long weekend.'

'I definitely won't be.' He shakes his head.

'Oh.'

'I am joking.' He laughs. 'I will be working on your house, remember, then down at the harbour. I will have no time for anything but sleep.'

'You will definitely carry on with the build when the summer season begins?'

'But of course. Only for a few hours in the evening when the boat tours have finished. The labourers will probably be glad of the work too, they like the extra cash.'

The thought of things being actually finished, or close enough next time I visit, makes me almost burst with gratitude.

'You don't know how much that means to me. I thought things wouldn't be ready for months,' I tell him gratefully.

'Have faith.' He smiles. 'And Yiannis is feeling better every day. Things will speed up as soon as he is able to work again.'

We finish our delicious meal with coffees and a waiter brings some chunks of watermelon to round things off nicely and a tiny bottle of raki, which I sensibly refuse, remembering how strong it is. Walking back to the car I feel my spirits lifted by the wonderful day spent with Dimitri, along with the possibility of soon seeing my dream home become a reality.

The cricket matches are long over as we walk back through the park and couples are sitting having picnics and young families are playing football with children and I reflect on what a lovely day it has been.

'Thanks for bringing me here today, Dimitri, and for taking me to your friend. I can't wait to see the finished balcony.'

'You are welcome. It has been a lovely day for me also.'

'What would you normally do on a Sunday?' I ask, thinking of my own Sundays back home, usually a train trip into town with a friend, or Sunday lunch at my parents' house. Sometimes

Evie and her husband invite me to a pub to have Sunday lunch with them, which is always lovely, catching up with the latest things in the lives of sixteen-year-olds. It gives me kudos in the office when I can talk to some of the younger staff about current trends.

'Sunday is normally a day the family get-together, with my aunts, uncles and cousins. My mother is quite relaxed about that as long as we catch up at some point in the day. I will join them for a drink at the village pub later. You are welcome to join us.'

'Thanks, Dimitri, but I'm pretty tired. I am going to call my own parents, then I will probably have an early night. My father is always especially keen to know how work is progressing on the villa. Then I might browse some furniture online.'

'Of course. Well, if you change your mind, you know where I will be.'

Driving back to Roda, the traffic is busy once more, and Dimitri puts the radio on and his car is filled with Greek music. I close my eyes and picture us both sitting at the water's edge at the harbour, eating and chatting, the sound of the crashing sea in the background. The music takes me to another place, and as we sit at traffic lights I'm daydreaming about walking along a beach with a handsome man. I can't make out his face at first, but when we stop and he tilts my face towards his, moving in for a kiss, I can see that it's Dimitri.

'What are you smiling at?' he asks, bringing me back to the present.

'Oh, nothing really, just thinking of how much I enjoy being here in Greece. It always feels like I have come home.'

'You soon will be. At least, to your holiday home.' He smiles.

'I know. It still doesn't seem real, it feels like a dream.'

'Then you are very lucky. Not everyone has the chance for their dreams to come true.'

I think about his comment as we drive. He is right, of course, not many people are lucky enough to see their dreams come to fruition. And along with my home here, I think I may also have the beginning of a beautiful friendship, and feel truly thankful.

TWENTY-FOUR

'Thank you again, Dimitri, for a lovely day yesterday.'

It's late afternoon, and I stifle a yawn as I have been awake since very early this morning, just as the sun rose.

'It was my pleasure. Remember the bathroom arrives on Thursday, and we will start work right away.'

'Do you do the plumbing?'

'No, Yiannis is the plumber, unfortunately, but I can have everything ready.'

'Surely he isn't ready to return to work?'

I recall him doing a little work the other day, but plumbing requires a lot of bending and crouching sometimes in awkward places.

'He will do what he can, but do not worry, my father who has plumbing skills is going to help too. Yiannis knows he must take things easy.'

'If he's sure, that would be a great help.'

'He is. Even though my father is enjoying his retirement, I think maybe my mother wants to get him out of the house a little more, from under her feet. Although he does help his friend on his boat.'

'What does he do usually with his day?'

'He goes to the bar, plays dominoes with his friends, does a little walking in the hills. Sometimes a little fishing. In fact, he does what a lot of people do around here when the tourist season ends. Including myself when I am not working. Apart from playing dominoes, that is.' He pulls a face.

I must admit I have never really seen the appeal in that myself, but I guess it's a way of connecting the people to each other in the village, especially the older people.

'Well, I am grateful for the help. I hope he isn't letting his friend down on the boats.'

'It's fine, he will disappear when things get really busy though, like the rest of us.'

I notice him smiling as he takes a piece of kitchen roll and steps towards me.

'May I? You have a little something on your cheek.'

He stands so close, I feel lightheaded and I try to ignore the bolt of electricity that shoots through me as he gently wipes something from my cheek. He remains close, looking into my eyes, and I am sure he is going to kiss me, when I lose my nerve and break away.

'Gosh thanks, was it chalk? I don't want to be walking around with that on my face,' I manage to mutter.

'Yes, it was,' he says, which makes sense, as I had a piece of chalk behind my ear earlier, marking up some spaces on a wall.

I make my way to the garden, wondering what might have been had I not broken away, as Dimitri picks up some tools, and continues his work.

By Thursday every room in the house has been sanded and painted, brushed and cleaned, and now the new bathroom suite has arrived.

'Are you carrying on with the work?' I ask as Dimitri looks a little tired.

'Yes, my father will be here soon to help.'

Just ten minutes later his father arrives, and Dimitri introduces us.

'Claudia, this is my father, Eric.'

I'm shocked to be standing in front of the silver fox I met the other day in the bar.

'*Kalispera*, we meet again,' says Eric as he shakes my hand.

'You two have met?' asks Dimitri in surprise.

'Yes, at the bar last week.' He talks to Dimitri in Greek, and I can't help noticing that he looks a little embarrassed, as his father laughs.

'What did he say to you?' I ask him later.

'Just that I am lucky to be working alongside a beautiful woman, and have I asked you out yet,' he reveals.

'Well, we have already been out to Corfu together,' I remind him.

'True, although not really a date.' He touches me lightly on the arm, and annoyingly, there go those fireworks again. 'I told him, I don't mix business with pleasure,' he says, and I feel an irrational stab of disappointment. As well as confusion. I could have sworn he was going to kiss me the other day, when he removed the smudge of chalk from my cheek, but perhaps that is only in my imagination.

I busy myself with clearing up after the workers, and providing cold drinks and a healthy slab of orange cake I purchased from Thea's earlier, although this time it was on the house, and she sent her best wishes to Dimitri and his father.

'I did not realise it was your house my son is working on,' says Eric as he munches on a small slice of cake, saying his wife will kill him if he does not eat all of his evening meal. 'Although he did mention it was a house in the village. I thought you were here on holiday.'

'Well, I am staying in the holiday apartment. Sorry, maybe I am a bit cautious about telling people about my half-renovated villa.'

'I understand.' He smiles, and when he does I can see the resemblance to his son.

'I can't thank you enough for helping. I head home the day after tomorrow. I will feel so much better knowing all the major work is completed.'

A short while later, I head up to check on progress, when I hear raised voices. Upstairs, Yiannis is throwing his arms up and shaking his head at Eric, who retaliates in an even louder voice, both speaking quickly in Greek.

'What's going on? Is everything okay?' I ask, popping my head around the door.

'I am not sure this was such a good idea,' says Dimitri, clearly stuck in the middle. 'Yiannis thinks the next job is the wall boards, the bath later. My father wants to get all the plumbing done first.'

'Which makes perfect sense. It's a free-standing bath, the walls can wait, surely the plumbing must be a priority.'

'I agree. Maybe you will be happy to say that. It is your house after all.'

'Coward.' I laugh before telling the men my thoughts. Yiannis shrugs and I notice a smile curling around Eric's mouth.

Later that night, I have a bath and sink fitted, as both men remarkably seemed to work together well, after some initial differences of opinion. I had to stifle laughter when I spotted Eric pulling a face and shaking his head behind Yiannis' back several times, and vice versa.

The men disappeared just after nine o'clock, and I'm not too far behind them.

.   .   .

That evening, I'm sitting in my rental apartment, sipping a large glass of white wine on my balcony and I find myself wondering what Dimitri is up to this evening. He never mentioned anything earlier and behaved in a perfectly businesslike way, before wishing me goodnight and saying he would see me tomorrow morning. He seemed keen to let me know that he doesn't mix business with pleasure, despite sharing what I perceive to have been some intimate moments. But then, I am the one that seems to run away from them in an attempt to protect myself from being hurt.

I'm watching the sunset when I receive a text from Josh, asking if I am free to chat if he gives me a call. And I tell him yes, immediately.

'Hi, sis.' Josh sounds upbeat. 'So how's it all going with the house?'

'Much better now. Better than I could have hoped for, even.'

I fill him in on the little dramas, including the burst water pipe. I leave out the bit about me falling for the builder.

'But we seem to have a little more manpower now, courtesy of Dimitri's dad, who is a retired builder and has agreed to help out.'

'That's handy, him being in the trade.'

'I know. You sound happy, Josh, at least a lot happier than the last time we spoke.'

'I am. I've been painting a bit. Actually, I was wondering what you thought about this.'

He produces a striking watercolour in front of the screen, and I gasp at its beauty. It's a painting of a forest glade, the lighting so haunting it gives it an almost ethereal look.

'You really did that? It's gorgeous, Josh, really good.'

'Do you think so? Zoe said it was, and so did George.' He laughs. 'But I wanted to ask you. I'm right in thinking you will give me an honest opinion?'

'You know I would.'

'That's good, especially as I am going to pitch it to a local gallery. I've noticed some stuff in there selling for hundreds of pounds, and well, without sounding big-headed, I think some of my work is every bit as good.'

'Of course it is, it's fantastic! They would be mad not to want that. Oh, Josh, I'm thrilled for you, I really am.'

'Thanks, sis. Oh and me and Zoe have been having a bit of a chat, you know, about us. We went for a picnic last week in the Peak District, and stayed overnight. It's done us both the world of good, and got us thinking about something, but I'll tell you more about that when I see you.'

'Oh, please don't leave me in suspense,' I say.

'Okay. Well, it's nothing major, we're just thinking about a house move, somewhere closer to some forest or a beach, maybe something with a bigger garden for George.'

'That sounds like a great idea. I'm sure George would love that too.'

It makes me think of Phoebe's granddaughter who lives in a village and cannot really afford to move closer to the sea, but I have an idea about that.

I feel happy for Josh when we finish our chat, and really hope he and Zoe can work out any differences they have had. I think back to Zoe in the early days of her relationship with Josh, and she was like a different person then, so much more carefree, and she definitely laughed more. Perhaps they have just been sucked into a world that, deep down, they never truly desired. I hope they realise that before it's too late.

I'm just out of the shower and in my pjs around ten thirty, when I receive a text from Dimitri.

Still in the bar if you fancy a nightcap?

The temptation to get dressed and join him is almost too

hard to resist. But then, what would that look like at this hour. Would he be expecting an invite inside afterwards? I remind myself once more of his comment about not mixing business with pleasure.

Thanks so much but I'm in bed and almost nodding off. See you in the morning.

Of course. Kalinychta. X

I try not read too much into the kiss at the end of the text, even though it is the first time he has ended a message that way. Maybe he has just had one beer too many.

I toss and turn for hours then, wishing maybe I had gone to the bar, strictly for a nightcap that might have sent me off to sleep. I try my mind healthy app on my phone then, and eventually drift off listening to the sound of whales in the ocean.

TWENTY-FIVE

'Wow, everything is looking really good.'

Phoebe is inside, taking a tour of the villa, nodding in appreciation, especially at the free-standing bath with the clawed feet.

'Very nice. You are happy with all of the work?'

'That should be, "Are you happy with all of the work?"' I say.

'Yes. But what does it matter what I think?' she asks, and I laugh.

'No, I am sorry, Phoebe, I was correcting your grammar. You tend to say, "You would like" when actually it should be, "Would you like?" As it is a question and not a statement.'

'I see, I see. "Would you like?"' She repeats the phrase several times.

'Oh and I really am pleased with the house. Almost finished is good even for me, at least I literally have a roof over my head. And today I'm going shopping for a sofa, would you like to come with me?'

Phoebe agrees, and a couple of hours later, we have returned from a furniture shop, where I selected a stone-coloured sofa, and a gorgeous blue velvet chair that will look great in the corner. It will arrive at the end of June, during my next visit.

We are sitting on kitchen chairs, borrowed from Phoebe as she has several spare. Dimitri has promised to send me some photos of the newly installed bathroom when I return to the UK, and although there is still a little of the rendering to be completed at the back of the house, the major stuff is out of the way.

'And now, I have something for you. A housewarming gift.'

Phoebe appears with a bag and I open it to reveal a set of fluffy bathroom towels, two in a stone shade and one sea blue that will perfectly match the bathroom accessories.

'Thank you, Phoebe, that was thoughtful. They will go perfect with the décor.' I hug my friend.

'I cannot believe you leave again tomorrow,' she says.

'I will be back at the end of June for a few days.'

The time here has gone so quickly, yet I have become accustomed to the toing and froing, at least for now.

'I will miss you,' she tells me. 'And I know someone else who will miss you too.'

'Really. Who?'

'As if you do not know. I see the way Dimitri looks at you.'

'He has never told me directly that he likes me.' I shrug, although feeling secretly delighted by her remark. There is also the matter of him being five years younger than me, which I know isn't huge, but even so. He might not have any desire to start a family for years, whilst my own clock is ticking. Gosh, what on earth am I thinking? We haven't even kissed, and here I am thinking about babies. Time to literally give my head a wobble.

Dimitri and the team have worked hard today and Yiannis seems to be getting stronger every day. Today, he has been barking orders at everyone, and even Dimitri rolls his eyes once or twice and mutters something under his breath.

'My father was sorry he could not come today,' Dimitri tells me. 'He says he is a little sore in places he has not been sore in for a long time.' He smiles. 'He thinks maybe he has gone a little soft since his retirement, and maybe he ought to do a day's work here and there.'

'Maybe so. Use it or lose it, hey.'

'Also, I think having my father and Yiannis in the same room was perhaps not the best idea.'

'Perhaps not. Anyway, I am grateful for all his hard work yesterday. I hope you paid him,' I joke.

'I offered, but he would not take a penny.'

'In that case, what does he drink? I would like to buy him a bottle of something to show my gratitude.'

'Metaxa brandy. But I don't think it is necessary.'

'It would be my pleasure,' I insist.

I sweep up the last of the debris whilst the workers finish a little early to go and freshen up before they return for a bit of a party. The garden is neat and tidy, and I admire the brightly painted gate.

The front of the house looks like a picture too. I can't wait to bring some bits and pieces on my next visit, and to order some nice cushions to place on the sofa.

Yesterday, with the help of Phoebe, I wrote notes and pushed them through the doors of the neighbours to invite them for a drink and a little celebration, so I have been to Thea's for some treats and Phoebe has made a cheese pie, along with some Greek dips and flatbreads. We set it all up on a table in the garden, along with a platter of pineapple, grapes and watermelon.

Later, we are all gathered in the rear garden, and I raise a toast to my neighbours. Thinking about how far everything has come along since the sorry, grey building that first greeted me, I feel a little emotional as I address the assembled group.

'I would like to thank you all for being such understanding neighbours. Well, once you stopped waking to the sound of a drill so early in the morning,' I say, and they laugh. 'And I know the tourist season will be in full swing anytime soon, so I really appreciate the extra push from you guys.' I turn to Dimitri. '*Efcharisto* to you all, and please join me in a drink. *Yamas!*'

Everyone raises their shot of ouzo, before many of them step forward and present me with gifts. Ria hands me a stylish vase, and an elderly couple present me with a lavender bush in a pot.

'Place it on your windowsill, spiders, they do not like the smell,' says the smiling woman, glancing at Dimitri.

'So you have told the whole neighbourhood about my spider phobia?' I ask him.

'I think they may have heard the screams,' he says.

I laugh when I think of the evening I stood on the bench in the garden, and Dimitri rescued me. I receive a fruit cake from Eliza across the road and a bottle of Metaxa from a couple I have nodded to but never spoken to before. I am completely overwhelmed by their kindness, and have to hold back tears.

The neighbours eat some food and chat amongst themselves. Eliza talks to her immediate neighbours, but does not make eye contact with Phoebe.

Dimitri strolls over to me then, as I help myself to some of Phoebe's delicious cheese pie.

'It will seem strange you not being here,' he says, hands in his pockets, looking at the floor.

'Will it?' I dive into the pie.

'Yes. I've kind of got used to you being around.' He lifts his head and his eyes meet mine and the way he looks at me makes my stomach do a little flip.

'You have?' My heart is beating so loudly, I am sure he must be able to hear it.

'I really have.' He takes my hand in his. 'I will be counting down the days until you are back,' he whispers in my ear, and I almost drop my plate.

I steady my breathing and feel thankful that we are standing in a garden filled with people, or who knows what might have happened.

Just then, Phoebe appears.

'Would you like some cheese pie?' she offers Dimitri, and nods proudly at me as she gets the phrasing right. I give her a thumbs up.

'How can I resist?' He smiles, accepting a slice.

The rest of the builders head off, and I thank them once more, before I take a seat on the bench and Dimitri comes and sits beside me.

'Just think, next time you are here, you will be sitting here looking up at your balcony,' he reminds me.

'Oh, I can't wait.' I sigh.

'Can you imagine climbing out of bed in the morning, and gazing out at the sea view from up there?'

I have to check myself as I imagine him climbing out of my bed, and stretching, before drinking coffee.

'I can. I'm so lucky.'

The thought of it makes me sigh inwardly with pleasure.

'So, what do you have planned for your last evening here?' Dimitri asks.

'Not an awful lot. A little more work here, I guess, putting some finishing touches to the kitchen. Planting the lavender bush out here.'

Phoebe is tidying up, clearing away paper plates when people have finished eating.

'She will miss you, I think.' Dimitri nods in her direction.

'Do you think so? I know she has some friends here, and the people at church. It's a shame she doesn't have a best friend though,' I say, thinking of her estrangement with Eliza.

I think of her kind gift then, that will look nice in the bathroom. I've gone for exposed brick on one wall and blue wall panels dotted with silver flecks that remind me of sunshine glinting on the sea. I know it will look just perfect and will take far less time than tiling the walls.

'What time is your flight tomorrow?' asks Dimitri.

'Not until ten in the evening. I imagine I will leave around seven,' I tell him, dearly wishing I could be here for longer.

'Then I insist on taking you to the airport. I can take some time off tomorrow before you leave. Have you ever visited the Byzantine castle?' he asks.

'No, I haven't. Phoebe told me about that actually, she reminded me about the beauty of the mountains, away from the seaside.'

'She is right. There is so much more to discover than beaches and tavernas. There is a monastery not far from there too, with a café that looks down across the mountains. You did mention you like the forest surroundings.'

'I do, that sounds lovely.'

I've spotted a couple of planes flying overhead today, reminding me that the busy season is approaching, bringing hordes of holidaymakers here. The young labourers are needed in their parents' restaurant this evening, no doubt to host the arrival of some tourists.

When Dimitri leaves, I shower then take an evening walk along the beach in Roda, letting the wind sweep through my hair and allowing myself the last feeling of relaxation that being here always guarantees me.

I slip my shoes off and walk barefoot, thinking of Dimitri and his comments in the garden. He has got used to me being around, but maybe that is foolish to do so. He knows that it is a holiday home after all, so my visits here will always be intermittent. I'm almost at the end of the beach, about to turn back, when I notice Dimitri walking towards me from the opposite direction, with Prudence, and I catch my breath. It's quiet here, so he lets her off the lead and she comes dashing over to me.

'Hey there. How are you?' I stroke the top of her head, and she licks the back of my hand.

'*Kalispera*, this is an unexpected pleasure.'

'I thought you might be sick of the sight of me today.'

'I could never be sick of the sight of you,' he says sincerely.

We fall into step as he throws a ball towards the water for Prudence to chase after, and she leaps after it, as an incoming wave half engulfs her and she shakes herself briskly.

'When is your aunt back?' I ask, getting the subject away from me.

'The day after tomorrow. It is a shame you will not be here to meet her. I am sure you would like her and her husband. I am certain she would like you too.'

'Well, I look forward to meeting her next time I come over.'

We walk side by side and the chemistry between us almost has me reaching for his hand.

I try to distract myself by thinking about the neighbours a little, who seem interested in seeing the work on the house, and often come and watch the progress. There is always a cheery *kalimera* from everyone now, even those who complained about the noise originally. And, of course, I have already become good friends with Phoebe and Ria with the young children, who always stops and chats when she passes by, asking how things are going.

It's almost nine o' clock when Dimitri offers to buy us a drink.

'Sure, but maybe just a milkshake for me though, as we will be going out in the morning.'

'Good idea. They do the best ones there.' He nods to a small café with a terrace outside.

'What time shall I be ready tomorrow?' I ask.

'I thought we could leave around nine, maybe stop for some breakfast on the way somewhere.'

'That sounds good.'

Prudence lies at Dimitri's feet as we sip our delicious fresh fruit milkshakes, vanilla for Dimitri and strawberry for me. The waves are gently lapping at the beach as the sun begins its descent.

We chat about various things, and I can hardly wait to spend the day with him tomorrow. I think of our day in Corfu, and how we chatted about our shared interests.

Leaving me outside the apartment, he says goodnight, just as my bag slips from my shoulder. We both go to pick it up at the same time and our hands collide. He glances at me and moves in a little closer, before his lips gently brush mine. I whip the bag from him and turn towards the door.

'See you tomorrow then, nine o'clock sharp,' I mutter as I fumble with the key, my heart hammering in my chest.

Inside, I steady my breathing, as I wonder what on earth is going on here. Maybe I am going home at the right time tomorrow, because one thing is for sure, I think I need to put a little distance between us both. Even the slightest brushing of lips gave me a thousand jolts of electricity shooting through me. This cannot be happening. I think of Dimitri, his handsome looks, and hair blowing gently in the wind as we strolled along the beach, and find it almost unfathomable that he is single. But then, ten months is not a long time to be out of a two-year relationship I suppose. After all, I still feel bruised after being hurt by a cheat whose name I can barely bring myself to utter. Annoyingly, however much I am attracted to Dimitri, I just cannot see how it could work between us.

I'm in bed half watching a film, when I receive a text from Josh.

Safe journey home tomorrow. We will be at Mum's for a

few days, so catch up soon. Oh and I have a surprise for you. Xx

A surprise? I wonder what that's all about. Could Zoe be pregnant again? I certainly got the impression that things were a little better between them now, as he sounded much more upbeat the last time we spoke. I suppose it could be anything really, but coming up to Mum and Dad's implies something pretty significant. I'm super happy for them both, if they have worked things out, and there is no doubt a little brother or sister would be wonderful for George.

Whatever is in store, I guess I will find out soon enough.

TWENTY-SIX

Dimitri arrives at exactly nine o'clock the next morning, dressed in mustard shorts and a black T-shirt, his hair up in a man bun.

'Punctual. I like that,' I say, closing the door of the apartment behind me.

'I always try to be. Unless there is a good excuse, I find lateness a bit rude.'

'Me too.'

Thank goodness there is no awkwardness after the brief kiss last night. Maybe it meant nothing to him.

'Then I guess that is something else we have in common.' He smiles as we walk to his car, a silver saloon that is attractive, but not flashy, a bit like Dimitri himself. 'You look very nice,' he adds.

'Thank you.'

I feel nice today, and my white dress shows off my developing tan from my time here. I pop on my straw fedora and we head off.

'I feel a little guilty going off for the morning, but then the main building work is almost done.'

'You deserve a break,' I reassure him.

'You have worked hard too. I almost feel we should pay you a wage.' He turns and winks at me.

'I needed to keep an eye on you lot. Crack the whip.'

'Now there's an image,' he teases.

It occurs to me that maybe I have been around the villa a little more than I needed to be, once the work took hold, but maybe something – or should I say someone – has had me wanting to be in their presence. I hope Dimitri doesn't think that. He wouldn't, would he?

'Obviously, with it being my house I needed to oversee things,' I tell him, suddenly feeling a need to explain my constant presence. 'It has to be just right, especially any permanent fixtures.'

'Of course, I would be the same,' he agrees.

We turn off the coast road, and are soon climbing higher in the hills. Half an hour later, we pull into a village and park up. We are going to a restaurant Dimitri knows, which is good, because I wouldn't have spotted it almost obscured by trees.

There's an old water well in a tiny square in the centre of the village, flanked by a small church and a children's playground. As we walk, I notice a lot of the houses look to be in poor condition, with paint-peeling doors and rotten wood window frames; some of them are completely abandoned, and I comment on this.

'It happens a lot in the smaller villages. A lot of young people leave for the towns and cities,' explains Dimitri. 'There is nothing here for them, other than maybe farming or taking on cafés or restaurants handed down by their parents.'

As we enter the restaurant, we are welcomed warmly by the owner, and we are shown to a wooden table on a balcony outside with a spectacular view across the valley below.

'Wow, you were right about that view.' I glance at the lush, green plants, a common sight in Corfu due to its climate, alongside colourful shrubs with flashes of red and yellow in the verdant forest.

We dine on a delicious breakfast of eggs sprinkled with paprika and fried potatoes topped with feta and sprinkled with oregano, all served with slices of chunky bread. I enjoy a fresh orange juice whilst Dimitri sips his strong coffee.

'This food is seriously good, a lot nicer than some of the touristy places I have been to.'

'I have been here many times over the years. The owner knows my father. He takes a real pride in his food, whether it is breakfast or food for a large family gathering.'

Glancing around the sleepy village, and noting the number of abandoned houses, I ask Dimitri how the taverna has managed to survive.

'It's on a tour stop. Jeep safaris and coach trips stop here for lunch. It's how a lot of the traditional village tavernas survive,' he explains.

'That makes sense, I guess.'

'It does, the islands rely heavily on tourism. During the winter months the village restaurants make very little money, serving only the locals, although many families do come together and enjoy a Sunday lunch.'

We finish our delicious breakfast, and the owner offers us a raki, which is a little early in the day for me, but Dimitri accepts a small one to be sociable. They knock it back together with a *yamas*.

'I could get used to this,' I say with a sigh as we drive on, the window open and Greek music playing on the radio. 'I'm really not looking forward to the weather at home. My brother told me it's raining.'

'Are you close to your family?' he asks as we drive around a bend without any fencing along the road that looks down across the valley, which makes me feel a little nervous.

'I am. Especially my parents as I live so nearby, but I was

close to my brother growing up. I still am actually, even though he lives down south now.'

'My older sister moved away too. I stayed around here because I get regular building work, both renovating property and new builds in the surrounding area. She lives in Corfu Town now,' he tells me. 'But she visits fairly regularly, much to the delight of my mother. And me. They cook up a feast in the kitchen when they are together.'

I ask him whether things are still very traditional in the sense that women do a lot of the cooking.

'With the older generation, maybe yes, it is true. But many of my friends like to cook, as do I. Maybe next time you come over, I will cook for you.'

'Thank you, I would like that. Can you make those fried potatoes and eggs for breakfast then?'

'So you will be staying for breakfast?' He swings his head around and I want to die of embarrassment.

'Well, I mean, you know any time of day, that would be nice.'

I decide to be quiet for the rest of the journey, and just admire the scenery as we drive along the country roads. As we climb higher, a brown tourist sign soon points us in the direction of the ruins of the Byzantine castle called Angelo Castro. As we approach the castle, it looks as though it is perching on the clouds.

'Good job I didn't wear my high heels then.' I step outside the car and point down at my white trainers.

'It is not as daunting as it looks, the steps up are large and flat,' Dimitri tells me, before heading to a small kiosk to pay the entrance fee.

The old stone steps are flanked by ancient olive trees and the constant trill of cicadas as we make our way up the steps is soothing to the senses. As we climb higher, the ascent easy – Dimitri was right about the flat steps – the view becomes more and more stunning. When we arrive at the top, I turn and take in the panoramic view below that is simply breathtaking. A sea of blue, emerald and every shade in between, is lapping a small sandy beach and a valley beyond filled with trees has pops of colour from vivid red flowers on shrubs. A white boat glides along against the outline of distant hills, and the sight of it all almost takes my breath away.

'That's Paleokastritsa,' Dimitri informs me, following my gaze.

'Down there?'

'Just there.' He takes my arm and gently points it out. As he moves closer, I take in his scent, his closeness and feel my own heartbeat thump. If he tried to kiss me now, I'm not sure I would be able to resist.

For a few seconds, I just stand and gaze, then snap away with my camera phone, marvelling at the stunning vista below.

'Shall we have one together?' suggests Dimitri.

'Sure.'

He takes his phone from his pocket, and moves in closer to take the perfect selfie. When he shows it to me, we look like a happy couple relaxing in the sun and I have to admit I think we look pretty good together.

'That's lovely, will you send it to my phone?'

He fires the picture across immediately, and I can't resist sending it to Evie.

We take our time, exploring the castle ruins, climbing over rocks and reading the information boards. I can't help smiling at a teenage girl positioned on a wall, head thrown back and posing with the dramatic background as her friend takes a photo, no doubt for a social media account. I saw a café down below, just off the car park, and realise I am dying for a frappé. A text pops through from Evie in response to my photo, full of love hearts, and makes me smile.

'I think it's time for a drink soon, but first let me show you something.'

Dimitri leads me to a crumbling stairway, partly obscured by trees, and takes me by the hand, leading the way as we carefully descend the steps. A few seconds later, I am stunned to discover we are standing inside a tiny chapel cut into the rock. It has white walls and a small altar, even one or two religious artefacts on the wall.

'Oh my goodness.' I glance around taking it all in. It feels so cool down here, away from the burning heat. 'A church, it's beautiful. It's so tiny.' I touch its white, cool walls thinking of all the people who have been here over the centuries.

'Maybe it was larger at some point, but this is all that remains now, as a visitor centre. Much of the castle was destroyed in the Byzantine wars.'

As we descend the steps back towards the car park, I tell Dimitri how much I have enjoyed the castle visit.

We enjoy a drink at the café, overlooking the valley again, and I catch another glimpse of the sea stretching out into the distance. Glancing at my watch, I suggest we leave the visit to the monastery for another day.

'If you wouldn't mind. I don't want to be rushed getting ready this evening for my flight,' I explain.

Uttering the words, I wish I could stay here for a while longer, and discover all of the things the island has to offer. But I guess there is plenty of time for that in the future. Maybe I'm feeling it now because I am in such engaging company, something I have come to realise getting to know Dimitri, away from the villa build.

'Of course. We have all the time in the world.' He smiles.

Driving back to the village, I feel refreshed by the day out today, and still feel enchanted by the tiny chapel, with the almost hidden staircase. I admire the surroundings once more, still hardly able to take in that this could be something I do regularly, driving out to the hills.

'I can't tell you how much I have enjoyed today, thank you so much,' I tell Dimitri as he drops me off outside the holiday apartment.

'Believe me, the pleasure was mine.'

He moves in closer to kiss me, I am certain of it this time, and I feel my skin tingle in anticipation.

But I'm ready this time; to hell with the consequences, I think to myself. I'm about to close my eyes, when Dimitri is almost flattened by Prudence, who has jumped up at him.

'Prudence, here. Here.'

Dimitri follows the voice and his eyes widen in surprise.

'Auntie Lena, what are you doing home? I didn't think you would be back until tomorrow.'

I smile at the fact he still calls his aunt 'auntie', before remembering I used to call Jack 'uncle' too, which always amused him as I grew older.

'I was feeling homesick,' she jokes.

'Really?' He looks surprised.

'No.' She smiles. 'Although I was *actually* sick. Nothing more than a virus I think, or a cold,' she reassures him, noting his concerned look. 'But I wanted my own bed.'

Dimitri told me his aunt and her husband had been away on a month-long cruise and then stopped off in Thessaloniki for a friend's wedding.

'I was about to take Prudence out, although she has had an hour this morning on the beach,' he tells his aunt. 'And where are my manners. This is my friend Claudia.'

Friend, that is exactly what I am.

'Claudia! So pleased to meet you. Phoebe has been telling me all about the work on the house. It is looking good.'

'Thank you so much, it's good to meet you too. Your nephew and his team have been working very hard.'

We chat for another minute or two, before Dimitri strolls off, the intimate moment between us vanished. He tells me he will collect me later to take me to the airport.

Inside the apartment, I close my eyes and try to imagine Dimitri's lips on mine, holding me in his strong arms.

Maybe it was a good thing Prudence appeared when she did. Because I can't imagine how I would feel to be leaving this evening, knowing we had shared a thrilling kiss.

TWENTY-SEVEN

As I watch the sky grow darker from my window seat on the plane, I can feel my eyes grow heavy. I'm sitting next to an older gentleman, who after a pleasant hello has plugged his headphones in and is watching a movie on his tablet.

An hour into the flight, after thinking about his goodbye hug at the airport, I dream vividly of Dimitri. We're in the holiday apartment and he's smiling at me as he brings me coffee in bed. I stretch my arms out above my head, his side of the bed still warm, the white cotton sheets wrapped around me.

'Mmm, thanks, coffee, just what I need.'

'Milk and sugar with that?'

'What?' I'm pulled out of my delicious dream by a smiling cabin crew member brandishing a coffee pot.

'You did say you wanted coffee.' The blonde lady in the navy uniform smiles.

'Yes, yes, thanks.' I sit up and rub my eyes. 'Although on second thoughts, maybe a hot chocolate. It's probably a little late for coffee.'

I take my drink and avoid eye contact with the bloke next to me, who thankfully seems engrossed in his film. I hope I wasn't talking in my sleep, or even snoring.

I stay awake for the next couple of hours, thinking about my house in the village, and how much I enjoy being there, and how much it has been enhanced by getting to know Dimitri. But even if he wasn't there, I love the place, and after an initial blip with the complaints about the noise, I have come to know some very lovely people in the street.

Besides, apart from some jokey flirtation, there hasn't really been a hint of anything romantic between us until just recently. I definitely think things have shifted between us now though, as there have been a few moments when I felt something pass between us.

I am certain we would have kissed again today, had Prudence not interrupted us, and what then? Would we have gone inside, and spent the last evening in my bed together? Is that what he would have liked, some conquest to brag about to his mates at the bar, not long after I boarded a flight? I push those silly thoughts from my mind, telling myself that Dimitri is not that sort of man. Or is he? How could I possibly know, having only recently got to know him?

I feel a little relieved that things didn't go any further between us, despite what I now know to be a definite mutual attraction. All the determination I have felt about not letting another man into my life is just so difficult as I feel such a strong pull towards him. Why could Yiannis not have been the only builder on the job, I ask myself, before silently laughing.

I concentrate on thinking about the soft furnishings for my home then, excited to show my parents when they come out for a visit, Oh and little George. How he will love to splash about in the sea and take the little train into Sidari and through the villages that I always enjoyed doing as a child when we holi-dayed there. Josh and I would enjoy stopping for ice cream at cafés in mountain villages and listening out for the tinkling of the bells that would signal the sight of the mountain goats.

The flight passes uneventfully, with me treating my mum to some heavily discounted perfume. I've already bought Dad some packets of Greek tomato and herb seeds for his green-house, which I think he will be thrilled with. I also treat little George to a toy aeroplane that makes a taking-off sound when it's pushed along.

'Did you have a nice holiday?' asks the bloke next to me, who has finished watching his movie.

'I did thanks, did you?'

'Oh lovely, although it was more of a viewing trip. My wife and I have been looking for a holiday home, but haven't managed to find the dream place in our price range. Anyway, it seems one has been reduced greatly after a year on the market, so I've been to check it was still in good condition which it was, so it looks like we will make an offer.'

'That is wonderful, I'm so happy for you.'

We chat about our respective holiday homes; his is a little further north near Kassiopi.

'I would have liked to have done some work on a house, but I'm a bit older now, and don't have the energy to renovate,' he tells me, and I think of my dad saying the same thing. 'That's the thing about life. You don't always have the money when you're younger, but all the energy in the world,' he reflects. 'I have a decent pension now but it's the other way round.' He smiles. 'Seize the day whilst you're young, if you can. And try and save for a decent pension,' he sensibly advises.

I think about his comments as I walk through the airport to find a taxi. Seize the day while you're young. Maybe instead of worrying about relationships and cheating boyfriends, I ought to start doing exactly that. Life is for living, and tomorrow is guar-anteed to no one.

.   .   .

'You shouldn't have done that, but thanks, love.'

Mum takes the gift gratefully, spraying a little perfume onto her wrist and admiring the scent. Dad as I predicted is delighted with his seeds and looking forward to growing some huge Greek tomatoes.

'So where's Josh?' I ask.

'He'll be here shortly, they were up early to take George to the park.'

'I bet it's been lovely having them here.'

'Oh, it really has. Right, tea or coffee?' asks Mum, before heading into the kitchen.

'Coffee, please. I'm still tired after the flight, I think I need the caffeine.' I stifle a yawn.

It's Sunday, so at least I didn't have to log in for work.

'I take it I've missed breakfast?' I make a sad face as I take in the faint smell of bacon after one of Dad's Sunday breakfasts.

''Fraid so. The kitchen closes at ten.' Dad glances at his watch. 'Although I suppose I could make you a bacon sandwich.'

'I was only joking, but if you insist. Who can refuse a bacon sandwich?'

I show my parents pictures of the house, even though I've sent them updates, and Mum claps her hands together. 'It's looking wonderful, isn't it. I can hardly wait to come for a visit.'

'It looks good, the builders have done a decent job,' agrees Dad. 'If I was a few years younger, I would have definitely given you a hand, but I'm not great with heavy lifting.'

'I wouldn't expect you to, Dad, and it's money well spent. A holiday home in Roda, for all of us,' I say and Mum can't keep the smile from her face.

I'm enjoying my bacon sandwich when the front door opens, and the whirlwind that is George comes charging into the room.

I give him his little plane, and he immediately runs off to

play with it in the long hallway with the wooden floor. Mum bustles about in the kitchen and we are all sitting around drinking tea, me devouring my bacon sandwich, to the sound of the aeroplane noises and George mimicking the sound.

'So,' I say to Josh, dunking a biscuit into my tea as Mum throws me a look that tells me it's not a very polite thing to do. 'What's your news then?'

Josh and Zoe exchange a look as I await the announcement of what I am sure will be their pregnancy news.

'We're moving house.'

'Yes, you mentioned that when I spoke.'

I'm wondering how that is big news, although I am a little surprised given the financial situation my brother told me they were in.

'The good news is we've found a place that could be perfect. It's around a forty-minute drive from here.'

'You're really coming back up north?' I ask him excitedly.

'We are.' He looks at Zoe and she curls her hand around his. 'We've found a gorgeous Victorian semi on the outskirts of Manchester. In fact' – he pauses for a moment – 'we've put an offer in.'

'That's fantastic! And are you both happy about that?'

I glance at Zoe, who is grinning from ear to ear.

'I'm more than happy.' She says and I throw my arms around them both.

'What's brought this on?' I ask, when we come out of our group hug.

'Where to start?' says Josh.

'Let's just say, we are both burnt out,' Zoe answers honestly. 'The cost of living down south, not to mention the mortgage, is just astronomical. It makes financial sense to move up north. We can both find similar jobs in Manchester, but we will have money in the bank after our house sale.'

'And you never know, the painting might take off. I sold my

painting for three hundred pounds at that gallery I told you about,' Josh tells me proudly.

'You did! Well done, Josh, that's fantastic.'

I feel so proud of my brother, who looks a lot less stressed since the last time we met up.

'And I can see how it makes financial sense moving up north. Wow, I can't believe it. It will be so good having you closer, and I will get to see George a bit more too. I'll babysit any time you want, and George can have sleepovers.'

'You'll have to fight me first,' Mum says with a big smile. 'I'm already thinking about colours for decorating the guest room. It's wonderful news, isn't it?' she says, looking absolutely thrilled.

'The best news ever,' I agree.

We head out that evening to a pub for dinner, and as I eye the rather limp-looking salad that accompanies my lasagne, I long for a Greek salad.

Back home, Dimitri sends me a picture of my finished balcony in his friend's workshop, with his friend standing proudly beside it and I almost squeal with excitement. He tells me it will be installed before my next return.

I can hardly believe that my holiday home is a whisker away from being completely ready, to head over and spend time there whenever I like, as can my family. It's been such a good day. Soon enough my dream home will be finished and my brother will be living less than an hour's drive away from here. It's been a day of such wonderful surprises!

TWENTY-EIGHT

The following weeks seem to drag, as I literally cross the days off on a desk calendar I have at work. Some of my colleagues teased me when I bought it, asking who on earth still has that kind of thing, but I like to cross the days off as it makes it feel more tangible and satisfying somehow, seeing all the crossed-out dates.

My office friends are more than impressed by the villa renovation so far and tell me how envious they are.

'I've never been to Greece, it looks dreamy,' says our office apprentice, flicking through my phone pictures. 'And so does he,' she says, her eyes falling on the photo of me and Dimitri on the steps of the Byzantine castle.

'That's Dimitri,' I tell her.

'The builder?' Her mouth falls open.

'The very same.'

'Oh, he's fit,' she says, her eyes lingering on the photo. 'Is he single?'

'He is, as it happens. But I don't think he is the type to get involved with someone he's working with.'

'Shame, hey,' she teases. 'Although you have been out

together?' she says as she hands me back my phone after viewing the pictures.

'It was just a trip to a castle, he was showing me around the area a little. We're just friends,' I tell myself.

'In that case, maybe I'll come and pay you a visit soon, so you can introduce us,' she says with the cheeky confidence of an eighteen-year-old before adding, 'I'm joking, he's too old for me.' Which I was thinking myself.

Even if I wanted to, I can't see how we could possibly have a future together. I'm not sure he could deal with the wind from the Mersey for one thing, and I certainly can't up sticks and move to Greece so easily, especially following Brexit.

I'm here in England, he's there in Corfu, and I don't care what people say about long-distance relationships; they rarely work. I selfishly kind of wish he would disappear after the build, never to be seen again, but his aunt lives nearby and as they are pretty close, I'm sure I will run into him from time to time. We could be friends though, I guess. I gaze out of the window and wonder exactly what it is I want. And every time I do that, annoyingly a picture of Dimitri flashes into my mind.

'So how's everyone in Corfu?'

A few days later, I'm out for dinner with Evie at a new Italian place in the city centre.

'You wouldn't happen to mean Kostas, would you?'

'Not at all, I meant your new neighbours.' She flicks me on the arm with a napkin.

'Sorry.'

'You should be. I've told you, me and Nick couldn't be happier,' she tells me, and I believe her.

'They're fine, really lovely, actually.'

I tell her about the little party and the gifts they gave me.

'Ah, how sweet.'

'It really was. The people there have good hearts and Phoebe tells me they are happy to see the house looking good once more.'

'And how are things going with Dimitri?' She takes a forkful of lasagne as she awaits my reply.

'Dimitri and I are friends, nothing more.'

'Is that why you sent me a photo of the two of you together at the castle?' she asks knowingly.

'I just thought it was a nice photo, with a stunning vista.' I shrug.

'Yeah, right. Oh, and the two of you look really good together.'

'Oh, Evie, it's all so complicated.' I sigh. 'I can't deny a physical attraction between us, and actually we have almost kissed, but somehow something has always stopped us. Which got me thinking, maybe it isn't meant to be.'

'That's your trouble.' She takes a sip of mineral water. 'You think too much. Sometimes you ought to just go with your heart, and enjoy the ride. And don't talk about what happened in your last relationship,' she continues as I am about to speak. 'Anyone can fool you over the internet. You have got to know Dimitri these past weeks, you even know some of his family.'

'I know, and you're right, of course. I suppose it's just the physical distance between us. It stops me from getting too involved. I don't think I could deal with having my heart broken again.'

'I get that, but don't be miserable out of fear of getting hurt. Have some fun, you would be mad not to.' She grins. 'Just have faith that things will work out just the way they are meant to.'

'When did you become so wise?'

'Maybe it's being friends with you for so long. Anyway, this time, I think you should take my advice. What will be will be,' she says firmly. 'It doesn't mean you should stop living because you fear being hurt again, that would be leading a very small life.'

'That's me told.'

Over dessert, a creamy panna cotta, I bring the subject round to Josh and how I am looking forward to him moving closer.

'That's so great, isn't it? If George has a sleepover at yours, maybe we could take him out somewhere?' she suggests. 'I really miss visiting farms and funfairs since the girls have grown up. These days it's just lifts to horse riding, or collecting them from friends' houses late at night.'

'George would love that, although it still isn't too late for you to have another little one you know.'

Evie looks horrified. 'Absolutely not.'

I mull over our conversation later, and realise Evie is right in so many ways. I can't stay in a cocoon avoiding romance, even though I am perfectly happy on my own. At least I was.

But that was before Dimitri came along, and turned things upside down. And I don't just mean my villa.

TWENTY-NINE

I've had photo updates from Dimitri over the weeks and I'm thrilled to see the rendering on the rear walls has been completed, and the bathroom finished. There's a chrome heated rail on the walls, and the towels are neatly stacked on a corner shelf. I can hardly wait to get back there and see it in real life.

The front garden looks inviting too and all of the interior painting has now been finished. I gave a key to Phoebe, who has agreed to take delivery of a huge bed and bedding next week, so at least I will be able to stay there on my next visit.

It's nice to receive updates from Dimitri, yet I kind of wish he would call me for an actual chat, but maybe he is trying to keep things professional. He also lets me know that the balcony is almost in place and will send me a photo when it is.

After dutifully crossing off the days on my desk calendar every morning, it's finally time to head over to Corfu for another long weekend, and before I know it, I am hailing a taxi at the airport to take me to Roda. The plane was full of holidaymakers, and I wonder how the builders are getting on in their summer jobs down at the harbour. I'm looking forward to the holiday vibe of the summer season, as I did when I was growing up. It excites me to think that next time I come out, it will be with Mum and Dad to reveal the holiday home to them, so that they can make use of it later in the year too.

Climbing out of the taxi, I pay the driver and realise this will be the first time I will be spending the evening in my house rather than at the holiday apartment.

I text Dimitri and inform him of my arrival, although I expect he will out on the boat with the tourists. En route to the villa, I call in at Thea's bakery, and grab myself a slice of feta and spinach pie and she greets me with a hug and a wide smile.

'I am so excited the house is finished. Are you looking forward to spending your first night there?' she asks, sliding my lunch into a paper bag.

'I really am. I can hardly believe it.'

'Oh, and I have a housewarming present for you. I hope you like it.'

She reaches beneath the counter, before presenting me with something wrapped in lilac tissue paper. It's a black-and-white framed photograph of the village harbour in days gone by.

'It is a copy of a photo my grandfather took when Roda was a small fishing village. I hope you like it.'

'Thea, it's perfect! Thank you. I can already see it on the white walls of my house, it really is so thoughtful.'

Passing the village green near the church, I notice Dimitri getting out of his car, parked just off the main street. He opens the passenger door with a smile, and a young woman with tumbling dark curls steps out. It definitely can't be his older sister, as even from here I can see that she is the wrong age.

My appetite suddenly deserts me, as I head towards my house.

'Claudia, you are here.'

Phoebe appears as soon as I walk up the path, interrupting my disappointed thoughts.

'You are okay? Sorry, are you okay?' She smiles.

'What, yes, I'm fine.' I plaster a smile on my face. 'How are you?'

'Good, fine. Yesterday, I stayed with my granddaughter overnight. I have just come home.'

'Oh lovely, are they well?'

'*Nai*, very good. Jason, he grows up so fast.' She smiles again as she mentions his name. 'I am sure he grows every few weeks in between my visits.'

As I search for my keys and invite my first visitor inside, I think of how I am a short walk away from my own parents, yet Phoebe's granddaughter has almost an hour's drive from her village, as she is unable to purchase a house in the area she grew up in.

Even in the space of a few short weeks since I last visited, the temperature has soared, and now, at the end of June, it's a warm and balmy evening.

I glance up at the steps leading to the bedroom, noticing the balcony is covered in blue plastic sheeting. I'm about to head up and take a look, when my phone rings. It's Dimitri.

'Claudia, are you at the villa yet?'

'I've literally just arrived. I'm about to remove the blue plastic from the balcony.'

'Wait there, I will be over in two minutes. I want to see your face as you see it.'

'Right, okay sure. I'll head inside and make a brew,' I say, gesturing for Phoebe to follow me.

It feels so good now that the gas and electricity are connected. It feels almost like a home; it's just awaiting some furniture and finishing touches and it really will feel like a second home.

'Come.' Phoebe guides me upstairs, and flinging the bedroom door open there is my bed, assembled and waiting, complete with crisp white bedding.

'You've assembled the bed! I was kind of expecting to sleep

on a mattress this evening, and then spend the day putting it together tomorrow.'

'You think I did that?' She laughs. 'No, it was Dimitri, he has the muscles.' She lifts her arm and touches her biceps. 'But I help with the bedding.'

A few minutes later, Dimitri arrives. Alone.

'Claudia, hi, how are you?' He squeezes me in a hug, and despite trying to deny having any attraction towards him, I feel my pulse quicken.

'I'm fine, thank you, thanks for coming over, and for putting the bed together. I really did not expect you to do that, you have gone above and beyond.'

'It did not take long.' He shrugs.

'Are you not busy at the harbour?' I ask.

'I have taken a few tourists out today, but the last trip has finished. I have just returned from taking a friend somewhere.'

So the striking brunette was a friend?

'It's good to see you,' I tell him.

'You too. And before we reveal your balcony rail, take a look at the garden,' he says, heading downstairs and out towards the rear of the house.

Phoebe tells me she will finish making the tea, and Dimitri leads me to the back garden. The rendered walls of the house are gleaming as bright as snow in the sunshine. I notice two new pots against the wall. To my surprise, the white wall has a centrepiece of a blue shuttered door at the centre, which, when opened, reveals a mirror.

'Oh my goodness, who did that? It's beautiful.'

'I found it in a reclamation yard, and thought it would look good, so I bought it for you. I think it looks like a real Greek garden now.'

My eyes fall on two pots sitting on the floor against the wall, one a terracotta pot filled with a thriving rosemary plant, the other a coloured heather in shades of mauve and yellow in an amber-coloured glazed pot.

'And the plants?'

'A gift from me also. I think the garden looks perfect.'

I can imagine sitting on the bench in the morning sipping coffee and listening to the sound of birdsong.

'I couldn't agree more, it looks wonderful! Thank you so much, Dimitri.'

I want to kiss him on the cheek, but something stops me.

The grey concrete stairs leading to the bedroom have been whitewashed, and I follow Dimitri as he leads the way to the top of them. The original rusty handrail has also been spruced up and painted black, much to my delight.

'Are you ready?' He can't seem to keep the smile from his face as he places his hand on the blue tarpaulin sheet.

'Ready. Although I feel as though we ought to have a bottle of champagne or something.'

'To smash against your beautiful new balcony?' He frowns.

He removes the sheet with a flourish, and I stare at the intricate, black metalwork of the balcony. It looks even more beautiful than I could have ever imagined, even though I had been shown a photograph. In between the curls and patterns are one or two tiny birds.

'It's wonderful,' I say, almost holding back a tear as I slide my hand along the metalwork, and gazing out at that distant sea view. It's everything I have ever dreamed of.

Downstairs, Phoebe has made tea and set out fruit loaf, which she spreads with butter, and it's so delicious I ask her for the recipe. I think about the old recipe book in the drawer then.

'So, it would seem that my work is here is done,' says Dimitri later as I walk him outside.

'It is, and I can't thank you and the team enough for your hard work.'

'You have paid us well,' he reminds me. 'And the Metaxa went down really well with my father.'

'It was nothing, I'm glad he enjoyed it.'

We hesitate for a moment, neither of us seeming to want to leave, unless it's just me who feels that way.

I want him to say something, as I can't believe that's the end of our time working together, but the fact is he was hired to do a job. After hesitating, I decide to bite the bullet and ask him over for dinner.

But as I am about to do so, his phone rings.

He covers his phone with his hand for a second, before wishing me all the best for the future.

'No doubt I will see you around,' he says, before quickly shaking me by the hand, and then he's gone.

THIRTY

I unpack a few bits and piece and place them in my new home. A few books on the bookshelf, purchased at Manchester Airport, a silver frame containing a family photo, and a paperweight that Evie bought me. I fling the French doors open upstairs and stand on my balcony, closing my eyes and breathing deeply. Not to mention trying hard to shake Dimitri from my mind.

I place some toiletries in the bathroom, before flopping down on the bed and trying it for size. It's perfectly comfortable.

An hour later, Thea from the bakery taps on my front door, and asks me if I fancy going for a drink at the village bar.

'Gosh, I'd like nothing more, thanks, Thea.'

'Although, you know, I do not have late nights. I open the bakery very early in the morning, and stay open later than usual in the summer, with the resort being busy,' she explains.

'Of course. Please come in,' I offer.

I show her around the villa, and she confesses her nephew has shown her some of the progress since my last visit.

'He talked about you a lot,' she reveals as I grab my handbag from newly erected black metal coat hooks in the hall – something I managed to put up myself.

'He did?'

'Yes. It was Claudia this, Claudia that.' She looks at me knowingly.

'I've probably talked a lot about him too, back home, but usually about the work he has been doing.' Which is true, of course. There is no need to tell her that I was keen to drop his name into the conversation at any opportunity.

'Look. This will match perfectly.' I pick up the photo she gifted me from the hall table and place it against the white wall. Some bright flowers in a vase on the hall table will set it all off nicely, I think.

'I see what you mean. Maybe some flowers on the table,' she says, reading my mind, and I laugh and tell her I had just had the exact same thoughts.

We walk to the bar, order our drinks and take a seat outside in the early evening sunshine. It's pretty quiet at this hour, some people still down at the beach now that the summer is here, the bars becoming livelier as the sun goes down. Maybe tomorrow evening, I will take a stroll down to the beach myself, maybe even persuade Phoebe to take a walk with me.

'I met Dimitri's aunt when I was here last, who I have only just remembered is your sister.'

'Yes. It is nice having family nearby. I guess we are all pretty close. You are bound to see Dimitri around.' She smiles.

'Does he live nearby too?'

It occurs to me then that I have never seen Dimitri's apartment. In fact, I'm not sure exactly where it is.

'Only a ten-minute walk away, at the far end of the beach. I can't see him ever leaving Roda, he loves it here.'

'I can understand why.'

'Have you seen my nephew today?' she asks.

'Yes, I saw him on the main street when I first arrived. He was getting out of his car with a woman.'

I don't know why I tell her this. I could have just mentioned him being at the house earlier and the unveiling of the balcony. Yet I do.

She frowns a little, before twirling the stem of her wine glass in her hand.

'That was probably Athena.'

Athena?

'He used to date her,' she tells me. 'But he tells me he feels nothing for her now. She has been back here to visit her grand-mother who is ill, I believe. Perhaps they were just having a catch-up.'

I recall Dimitri saying he had just been out dropping a friend off somewhere. Even so, the wine seems to lose its taste as I take a large gulp.

To break the slightly awkward silence growing between us, I ask Thea about her business, which she tells me is doing well. 'Especially during summer season when the apartments are all rented out. Many people call in for their bread in the morning. I have to work half the night baking, but of course I am grateful to save some money for the winter months. The locals keep the shop ticking over, especially when the planes stop coming in October.'

I recall Dimitri telling me this.

'Do people still fly over from Athens?'

'Yes, thankfully, for people like yourself who have holiday homes.' She smiles. 'But, of course, it does get cooler here in the winter, with some rain even, but maybe not as cold as in the UK.'

'Definitely not as cold as there,' I confirm.

After another drink and a long chat, it's almost nine and Thea tells me she ought to get off and have an early night, before a very early morning.

'Of course. And it's been really lovely chatting to you. It feels so good to have friends here in the village.'

'I'm happy to have you as a friend too. See you soon, enjoy the first evening in your new house.'

'Thank you, and thanks once more for your thoughtful gift. Goodnight, Thea.'

Back at the house, I take a glass of water out onto the balcony, and watch the sunset. There's the distant strains of a song playing at some bar on the main street, drowning out the faint sound of the crashing sea I can normally hear, but I don't mind. It makes me feel connected to the people here when I hear noise and activity all around.

I also can't help wondering how Dimitri is spending his evening. I recall him shaking my hand in a very businesslike manner, and wishing me well before he departed. I'm not sure exactly what I was expecting, but I do know one thing.

I can hardly wait until our paths cross again.

I stretch out the next morning, having had the best sleep ever. The sun is rising, and I fling open the French doors and make a coffee to take outside. I breathe in deeply, still hardly able to believe this place is actually mine. It's Saturday today too, so I don't have any work to do.

After some breakfast and a video call to my parents, showing them the finished villa, I head to a car hire place next door to rent one for the weekend.

Back home, I study the map and decide to take a drive to Paleokastritsa Beach, the place we viewed from the summit of the Byzantine castle. I'll have some lunch there, and spend a couple of hours on the small beach nearby, enjoying the sunshine.

I nip next door and ask Phoebe if she would like to join me, but she tells me she is seeing a friend from church in a few hours' time, but thanks me anyway. She agrees to a walk on Roda Beach in the evening. 'And maybe a small ouzo,' she says with a wink.

'I look forward to it.'

I pack a beach bag, then set the satnav in the car before driving off. It's such a glorious sunny day, I open the car window and enjoy the feeling of the wind in my long hair, rather than switching on the air con.

It's a lovely drive, passing tourist spots and residential areas in turn, as the landscape changes from villas with lush plants in the gardens to mountain villages with tiny churches and olive groves. I spot chickens on land adjoining houses, surrounded by mesh fences.

I pull up at a roadside truck stop in the middle of nowhere and buy some fresh peaches and a slice of watermelon, along with a bottle of the island's kumquat liqueur. I can't say I have ever really tried it, so will sample some later poured over ice.

The owner of the wooden stall thanks me, and drops a small bunch of grapes into a brown paper bag, free of charge. I take a photo of the scenery below from this viewing point and a photo of the old Greek man, standing proudly beside his stall.

As I continue driving, my mind keeps flicking back to the sight of Dimitri with his beautiful ex. Thea told me they were no more than friends. Dimitri told me they could hardly even be called that, but had manged to remain civil to each other. Even so, they looked close when I saw them.

As I approach the beach at Paleo, as it's known by, I can see that it's very busy. Large tourist coaches inch their way down a tiny road lined with tourist shops and ice-cream kiosks as they make their way to a car park. If anything is going to distract me from thinking of Dimitri, it's the sight of the blue water. I give up hope of ever finding a place to park when, miraculously, someone pulls out of a space in a parking area near the beach. I deftly park, and cross the road to a restaurant that overlooks the water.

It's bustling with diners, and I consider grabbing a takeaway gyros from a kiosk and taking it to the beach, when a waiter appears and guides me to a table where a young couple are settling their bill. It seems the Greek gods are smiling on me today as I'm so lucky to have this table, that is directly overlooking the small, crowded beach.

Beyond the sand, people are floating in the blue-green water on pedaloes, or swimming. I glance up at a paraglider in the sky as a boat guides them safely into the shore. In the distance, at the top of some mountains, I can make out the outline of the castle, and can almost hear the crickets as I recall climbing the steps to the summit.

Sitting here, dining on the most delicious sea bass and a Greek salad, just watching the world go by, I can't help but feel blessed. I hope that next time I come over, I will be accompanied by my parents and enjoying a meal together at a seafront taverna.

Settling down onto a sunbed, which thankfully there are still a few left of as most people seem to be in the restaurants, I pay the sunbed guy and stretch myself out, slipping my sundress over my head. If anything is going to clear my mind, it's lying here in this glorious sunshine listening to the gentle sound of the waves caressing the golden sand. I'm almost dozing off, when I hear my phone ringing in my bag.

'Hello?' The signal isn't too great here, but I can just about make out Dimitri's voice.

'Hi, did enjoy your first fright in the mouse?' Crackle, crackle goes the phone line.

'What?'

'The house. How was your first night?'

'Oh, the house!' I'm laughing now. I'm still missing words, but we should just about manage to have a conversation.

'I had the best sleep.'

'The vest what?'

'The best sleep.'

'Oh good. Where are you now?'

'I'm on a beach, watching some boats.'

'You are watching some goats,' he says and I roar with laughter.

'This is useless. I will text you.'

'Test me?'

'Hang up, Dimitri. The signal is awful.' I realise I am almost shouting as a man on an adjacent bed gives me a funny look.

I tap out a text telling him where I am, and then inviting him for dinner tomorrow evening at the house. I will make him the casserole from the old cookery book I found in the drawer.

There's no immediate reply, and I wonder whether or not I have done the right thing.

Fifteen minutes later, having glanced at my phone at least half a dozen times to see that he still hasn't replied, I feel so stupid. Although I wonder why he was calling me in the first place. Especially now that his work at the villa is finished.

An hour later, I gather up my things and decide to head back to Roda. I am a little preoccupied as I make the journey back to the village, but when I pass the wooden stall on the roadside, the owner lifts his hand and waves.

Driving on, I giggle to myself when I think of Dimitri asking if I was watching goats. Where on earth did he think I was? Sitting in the hills somewhere?

I'm looking forward to changing and going for an evening walk with Phoebe later, stopping for a little drink and watching the sunset on the beach. I'm sure Dimitri never received my text with such a poor signal, so decide to put it out of my mind.

I'm thinking about all of these things as I pull into my road, and the first thing I can see is an ambulance. Oh no, is that why

Dimitri was calling? And here was I inviting him over for dinner!

I hold my breath as I park up behind the ambulance and head over to where a small crowd have gathered. I see Phoebe near the ground and I catch my breath, but as I draw closer I can see she is crouching down next to someone. Eliza is spread out on the floor, being assisted by a paramedic, who is placing an oxygen mask over her face.

'Oh my goodness, what's happened?' I ask Thea.

'Eliza collapsed in the middle of the road. It is her heart I think, they had to resuscitate her.' She clutches her chest.

The sight of Phoebe clutching her old friend's hand and repeating her name almost brings a lump to my throat.

The ambulance people address the small crowd in Greek, asking if anyone would like to go with her to the hospital. Phoebe stands and enters the ambulance with her then, still holding on to her hand.

THIRTY-ONE

I tell Phoebe I will follow her to the hospital, before going inside and doing a quick change, as well as grabbing a phone charger to charge the phone in the car. The hospital in Corfu is around forty minutes' drive away so I will need it.

'Would you like me to come with you?' offers Thea. 'Or maybe I will call at the hospital later when the shop has closed?'

'No really, I will drive. I have no phone battery right now, but I will call you later when my phone has charged and let you know how things are.'

'Okay.' She nods. 'And let me know if there is anything I can do.'

I'm soon driving to the hospital, recalling the stricken look on Phoebe's face as she held on to her friend's hand.

Turning onto the highway, I think about all the people who hold grudges, even if deep down, they want to forgive. Maybe it's because we always believe there is more time. But the future is promised to no one, as all too often, unforeseen circumstances can deny a person the chance to reconcile.

The traffic is quite busy being summer season, but just less than an hour later, I am pulling into the car park of the hospital.

Grabbing my bag and phone that has charged enough to send messages, I enter the cool reception area of the hospital, where I find Phoebe sitting fidgeting with worry.

'Claudia.' She stands when she sees me. 'I am so happy you are here. I never gave a thought to how I would get home. I was going to call my granddaughter.'

'Don't worry, I wasn't far behind the ambulance. My phone had died,' I explain. 'How is Eliza doing?'

'She is having the operation.' She blesses herself. 'The passing by of the artery.'

'She is having a bypass? Gosh, she is lucky they caught her in time.'

I sit with Phoebe for a while before seeking out a doctor for an update, as it is getting late.

'You might like to go home and get some sleep,' he suggests. 'Eliza will be heavily sedated after the operation. Phone the hospital later, and see how the operation went and maybe return tomorrow,' he advises.

I grab us some coffee for the journey home and Phoebe sips it in silence beside me.

'Such a waste of years,' she says eventually as we drive. 'A long time.'

'I can understand why you fell out in the first place,' I say gently. 'Don't be too hard on yourself.'

'But I remembered your words.' She turns to look at me. 'My husband was not blameless, he was weak. And we have both been lonely women. I just could not forgive her, even though I missed her,' she admits.

'Well you are here now, when it matters. And you will be here again tomorrow when she wakes up,' I try to reassure her, knowing how much courage it must have taken for Phoebe to be here. I take hold of her hand and she squeezes it tightly.

We sit in almost silence, when my phone rings. Phoebe answers for me and puts it on loudspeaker. It's Thea and

Phoebe fills her in on the situation. 'Sorry, I meant to call you but the reception in the hospital was so bad,' I explain.

'Don't worry. I will phone the hospital tomorrow, and maybe take her a treat if she is up for a visitor later in the day.'

'I'm sure she would love that.'

We arrive back home, and after Phoebe heads into her house, I lie on my bed, scrolling through my phone.

To my dismay there is still no reply from Dimitri and I feel like a fool asking him for dinner. What was I even thinking? When he had finished the work on the house he simply said he would see me around, hardly an expression of any desire to spend time with me.

A wave of exhaustion takes over then, and I'm just dozing, when I hear the sound of hammering on my front door. To my surprise it's Dimitri.

'Dimitri. What are you doing here?' I'm thrilled to see him standing in front of me.

'I came to see how Eliza is. And to see you.'

'At this hour?'

'It's only eight o'clock.' He raises an eyebrow.

'You could have phoned,' I suggest.

'That's true, but I misplaced my phone. Turns out I left it on the boat, I have just been to retrieve it,' he explains. 'As I was passing, I thought I would call in.'

I tell him all about Eliza and how Phoebe is willing to put the past behind them.

'Then something good has come out of it.' He smiles. 'I am pleased to hear it.'

We stand in the hallway for a moment, my senses stirred by his closeness and I pull my short cotton robe around me tightly.

'I sent you a message earlier, but maybe you didn't see it as you didn't have your phone,' I tell him.

He takes a second to reply, and I bite my lip anxiously, wondering if dinner at my place really was a bad idea.

'I didn't see the message, I am so sorry,' he says, scrolling through his phone, frowning slightly. 'I would love to have dinner with you,' he says, and I am surprised at how relieved I feel.

'Great.' I feel excited by the thought of him spending the evening here.

'And please, let me know if there is anything I can do,' he says.

'I will do.'

'Right, well I am off to meet my father at the bar. I will call you tomorrow. Goodnight.'

'Goodnight, Dimitri.' There is no kiss, even on the cheek.

It's now almost one in the morning, me having tossed and turned for hours, when I decide to call the hospital. It appears Eliza is just out of surgery, and her operation has gone well. I call Phoebe, because I can still see her lights are on, and give her the news.

'Thank you, Claudia. Now I will sleep.'

'Me too. Goodnight.'

The next morning I retrieve the recipe book from the drawer and head off to the supermarket to buy the ingredients for the evening meal. It's a lamb casserole, flavoured with star anise, and I also have a recipe for flatbread using only flour and Greek yoghurt.

As I load my shopping basket, I feel a thrill at the thought of Dimitri dining in my house this evening. Maybe we can really talk, aside from building talk, that is. I choose a bottle each of a red and white wine. At least I can have a lie-in tomorrow, before my flight the day after.

I manage to gather all of the ingredients, and also pop in a couple of magazines for Eliza that Phoebe can take with her when she visits with Thea later today.

Back home, I arrange the ingredients in a pot, and set it on the stove to simmer, before giving everywhere a tidy. Once my house preparations are done, I spend the afternoon in the sunshine, tidying up the garden.

I head up for a leisurely bath, and light a candle in the lounge to ready myself. By the time Dimitri arrives just after seven, the room is filled with the welcoming scent of vanilla from the melting wax, and the delicious casserole.

'Something smells good,' he says as I welcome him inside. He's dressed in long dark shorts and an apricot-coloured polo shirt. His hair is loose and he smells wonderful, as always.

'Do you mean the cooking or the candle?'

I feel inexplicably nervous welcoming him into my home as it feels so intimate somehow.

'The cooking, I think. Is there a hint of cinnamon? Oh, but wait, I am getting vanilla now,' he says as we make our way to the lounge. He hands me a bottle of ouzo and I thank him, but tell him I will probably stick with wine.

'Maybe a good idea to have just one shot. People have been known to do foolish things after a few of those.' His eyes meet mine, and I rush off to the kitchen to check on the food and do a little taste. It needs more herbs, so I throw in a load of cinnamon and replace the lid.

'So how is Eliza doing?' asks Dimitri as I pour him a glass of red wine.

'The operation was a success apparently. She will be there for several days. It was nice watching Phoebe reconnect with her old friend. Your aunt went with her to visit earlier.'

'That is good to hear. All those wasted years.'

'That's what Phoebe said. I think it brought it home to her.' We spend a moment in silence, in our own thoughts. 'So how was your day at the harbour? I'm keen to know.'

'Busy, thankfully. And I have also taken on a job to refurbish an old restaurant that someone has bought in the countryside. I'm looking forward to doing that, although it will be after the summer season has finished.'

'Sounds good. Gosh you will hardly have a minute to yourself.'

'It's okay, the restaurant owner knows it will not be ready until next autumn, he is in no rush. It will be a slow project as it is little more than a ruin.'

He tells me the village in question hasn't had a restaurant for many years, and the word is the locals will welcome it very much. He also tells me that two overseas buyers have bought two of the village houses that have fallen into disrepair.

'There is hope that the small villages can be brought alive again, and I am grateful because it is a steady income for me.'

'That sounds wonderful. I am really pleased you have the work, Dimitri. I can definitely vouch for your hard work.'

I glance around my cosy home.

'This was quite easy. And a pleasure for me, as the home-owner is rather attractive.'

I always knew the attraction was mutual, but even so his comment has me feeling a little flustered.

I'm about to stand, when Dimitri pulls me gently by the wrist down next to him.

'Why do you always run away from me?' he asks. He is so close, I am sure he must be able to hear the sound of my heart beating like a drum.

'Do I?' I stutter.

'You do.' He leans back then, lacing his hands behind his head, and studying me. 'I wonder what you are afraid of?'

'Afraid? Who said I am afraid of anything?' I smile nervously, before grabbing my wine and taking a glug.

'I'm not sure, I was hoping you might tell me. I know

nothing about your personal life really, only your job,' he says, holding my gaze.

I think of how Dimitri told me everything about his ex, and I divulged nothing about my ex, but I find it just too humiliating to discuss. Then I remember that Dimitri's ex is, in fact, back in town.

'And what will happen if I don't run away and stay right here?'

Dimitri moves closer then, and this time I lean into him. Just as the shrill of the smoke alarm in the kitchen makes me jump to my feet.

I am greeted by the sight of smoke spiralling from the pot, and when I lift the lid, I smell the unmistakeable aroma of burnt meat.

'Oh no, how has this happened? I only checked it ten minutes ago,' I say, cursing the timing of the smoke alarm.

I realise then that I had turned the heat up earlier and forgot to return it to a simmer.

'Maybe I have had a narrow escape, if you have added this.' He raises an eyebrow, pointing to the jar of mixed spice.

'Oh no. I tasted it earlier, then added more of what I thought was cinnamon. That is a mixed spice that I use for baking fruit cakes.'

'May I?'

Dimitri grabs a spoon and dips it into the casserole.

'Actually, not as bad as I thought.' He laughs. 'It is like a lamb-flavoured Christmas cake,' he says and I can't help laughing.

'Oh dear. Shall we order a pizza then?' I say, not wanting the evening to end.

'Or we could go out?' suggests Dimitri. 'Unless you would prefer to stay at home?'

'Let's go out. I'll open the window a little to give the smoke a chance to clear,' I say, before grabbing my bag.

'Sure. There's a nice place near the beach,' says Dimitri as he finishes his glass of wine.

We chat as we walk, but I can't help feeling the mood has shifted, although when we are seated at a waterfront table, the stars reflecting on the water, I feel myself relax. We both order lamb kleftiko, having both missed out on my lamb casserole.

'Do you remember me telling you about my life here, and I mean all of it,' Dimitri asks as we wait for our food to arrive.

'Yes, of course.'

'It occurred to me then that I know nothing about you. You say you have no boyfriend at home, but how can I be sure?'

'What do you mean?' I ask, aghast.

'I mean, people come on holiday, they think the Greek men look for a holiday romance. But maybe the women who come here do the same,' he suggests as he picks an olive from a bowl.

'And yet it was you who kissed me the other day.' I'm silently fuming. 'Unless a peck on the lips has replaced a kiss on the cheek? And you really think I have a boyfriend back home?'

'I am so sorry.' He holds his hands up. 'But honestly? I'm not sure what to think. I thought we were growing closer, then you run away. Maybe foolishly I hoped you thought of me as more than just your builder.'

A waiter arrives then and places a basket of bread down on the table.

'It's a bit complicated.' I sigh. 'I really don't have someone at home, I wouldn't do that. But I guess I am just trying to protect my feelings.'

'You think I would hurt you?'

'Not exactly, but I find it hard to trust. My ex wasn't exactly all he seemed.'

Even now, thinking about how he cheated on both myself and his now wife makes my blood boil, but I am prepared to tell Dimitri everything. Especially as he thinks I may have someone back home.

As our meals arrive, I'm about to tell him my story, when I see the expression on Dimitri's face change. I follow his gaze to the woman with the tumbling hair who he gave a lift to. His ex, Athena, who is sitting with a group of girls. She blows him a kiss and waves, before striding towards us. She's stunning, dressed in a short silver dress, with legs that seem to go on forever.

'*Kalispera*. Are you having a nice evening?' she asks Dimitri.

'Yes, fine. Athena, this is Claudia,' he says, introducing me.

'Oh hi, good to meet you. I have heard all about your villa.' She smiles. 'Right, I will leave you to enjoy your food.' She places a perfectly manicured hand on Dimitri's shoulder. 'Are we still okay for tomorrow?' she asks, before she departs.

'I have already told you, yes,' he replies, his jaw tightening as she heads back to her table.

'And you wonder why I have trust issues?' I say, trying to keep my voice even. 'Here you are, dining with me and making plans with your ex for tomorrow?'

He sits quietly for what feels like an age and I sigh in frustration, my appetite having completely deserted me.

THIRTY-TWO

'It's not what you think.' Dimitri breaks the silence that's fallen between us.

'Oh, really?'

'Please, I am so sorry. I have no idea why she came over. Maybe I have been foolish in driving her to see her grandmother. Please let me explain.'

A part of me wants to scrape back my chair and head off, but I am not going to be accused of running away again.

'Go on.' I take a glug of my white wine.

'Her grandmother is very ill, and she lives in a remote village. Athena no longer has her driving licence, so she asked if I could drive her there, once or twice. This will be the last time.'

'And she has no friends who could take her?'

'I have thought about that.' He sighs. 'Although she tells me the friend she is staying with does not have a car, I hope I have not encouraged her.'

'Why would you say that?'

'Because I get the feeling she is interested in me, now that her most recent relationship has ended.'

I feel the warmth of the evening turn cold.

'So maybe I have been giving her the wrong impression.' He sighs.

'Are you sure it's the wrong impression?'

'I have no interest in her, romantically,' he says, looking into my eyes. 'You have to believe me. We are history. Do you think I could ever trust someone like her again? I regret agreeing to her requests.' He shakes his head.

'Yet you are taking her tomorrow?'

'I have already arranged to do so, so I will honour that. But I will make it clear it will be the last time,' he says, sounding genuine.

'If you say so.' I am trying to remain calm, but what am I to think? His beautiful ex is back in town, and I will soon be thousands of miles away.

'Please, Claudia, you must believe me.' He reaches across the table and takes my hands in his, and a mixture of desire and confusion races through me.

I can hear Athena's voice behind us and the sound of her shrill laughter. I paint on a smile and try to enjoy the rest of the evening, but even the beautiful location can't lift the heaviness I feel in my heart. When Dimitri escorts me home, I leave him at the door.

'Can I see you tomorrow?' He looks at me pleadingly. 'I will take Athena in the morning, then I will be working until five o'clock on the boat. Maybe tomorrow evening, I can cook for you at my place?'

So, Dimitri is inviting me to his flat, a day before I leave?

'Maybe. I have to log in tomorrow as I will be working from home.'

'I will call you tomorrow.' He gives me a peck on the cheek, before walking off.

It takes me a long time to get to sleep, going over the events of the evening. I can't shake the picture of Athena from my mind, and how she placed her hand on his shoulder, but eventually I drift off and wake bright and early to the sun streaming through the windows once more.

I invite Phoebe in for coffee. She sniffs as she enters the kitchen.

'You burn the dinner?'

'I did, but I think even the stray cats in the street would turn their nose up at it, I'm sure.'

I tell her what happened with the spice mix and she roars with laughter.

'A lamb-flavoured Christmas cake, I like it. Dimitri has humour. So you see him again?'

'He has invited me to dinner this evening, at his place.'

'Don't be too hard on him,' she tells me, when I tell her my concerns about his ex. 'He is a kind man, who likes to help people. But remember, it is you he talks of all the time.' She taps her nose and smiles. 'Now, I know that you have work to do,' she acknowledges as she stands to leave and I give her the magazines to take to Eliza. 'You have been very kind.'

'Nonsense, you have done so much for me too. We're friends, right? It's what friends do.'

After a breakfast of fruit, Greek yoghurt and honey, I spend the morning working, occasionally wondering how the conversation is going in the car between Dimitri and his ex. Is he really so certain that they will not rekindle their romance? After all, I will soon be back in England. But perhaps the time has come for me to let my guard down as Evie suggested, and have a little fun and expect nothing more, although I have never really been someone who is into casual encounters.

Later that afternoon, I log off and nip outside to stretch my legs and go for a walk along the beach. Dimitri's aunt is there with Prudence, who jumps up at me in greeting.

'*Kalispera*,' she says.

'*Kalispera*.'

She asks about Eliza and I inform her Phoebe will be visiting her later.

'I have no doubt she will be inundated with moussaka from the neighbours when she returns.' She grins. 'Although I get the impression Phoebe will be happy to look after her.'

'It's funny how things have worked out between them, isn't it?' I say, having heard the story of their estrangement from Phoebe.

'It really is,' agrees Lena. 'I think they have both been very lonely. Phoebe is a stubborn woman, although don't get me wrong, I can see why. It just seems so sad, that with both of their husbands gone they could have been company for each other.'

'Well, maybe this last chapter in their lives will bring them both some happiness,' I suggest.

'I hope so,' Lena agrees with a smile.

The beach is quite crowded today, so Lena has Prudence on a lead, especially as there are a lot of children playing with a ball.

'She will go crazy after that ball,' Lena says as Prudence strains at the lead. 'I am just heading to a quiet stretch of beach, if you care to join me,' she offers.

'I would love to. I have been at my laptop all day and I need a good walk.'

Presently, we arrive at an almost deserted stretch of beach, and Prudence races off as soon as she is released from the lead.

'You know, I really admire you,' Lena tells me as we walk. 'Buying a house that needed some work doing. It must have taken some courage.'

'A little, but it was easy for me to choose Roda. I spent a lot of my childhood holidays here, in the hotel near the sea.'

'Yes, Dimitri told me about that.'

We stop at the water's edge, and she tosses a pebble into the water. Prudence races after it, before abandoning the search and racing back on the sand, shaking herself.

'He likes you, you know.' She casts me a glance, to see my reaction.

'I like him too. He's a lovely guy.'

'Well, I would obviously agree with that.' She smiles. 'But what do you really feel about him?'

I can't think of how to reply for a moment and she apologises.

'Forgive me. I have no right to ask you, it's just that I know he has grown very fond of you.'

At the end of the beach is a tiny café, and Lena offers to buy me a coffee, so we take a seat at an outdoor table beneath a parasol and continue our conversation.

'It's so difficult. I think I have feelings for him too,' I admit. 'I have grown to know him quite well doing the refurbishment, and there is no denying I find him attractive.'

'But?' She stirs her cappuccino.

'I can't see a future,' I tell her honestly. 'I have no plans to emigrate, which since Brexit I would need to do, and I can't see Dimitri in the North of England.'

'I can understand that. But you never know what could happen if you open yourself up to the possibility, surely?'

'Maybe you are right. But then, there is the small problem of his ex being back in the village.'

'Do not worry about her,' she says, with a dismissive wave of the hand. 'She is back to see her dying grandmother.'

'Yes, he told me that.'

'My nephew has a soft heart, he can never say no to helping anyone. But he has no interest in her. She, stupid girl, lost her driving licence because she was caught drink driving,' she says, shaking her head. 'They were never a good match. She is imma-ture, whereas Dimitri has always had an older head.'

I take in Lena's words as I sip my delicious frappé. She thinks her nephew has an older head, so maybe the five-year difference between us might not be so significant. For the umpteenth time, I wish I hadn't allowed myself to develop feelings for him; everything would be so much simpler then, but I guess nothing in life ever is.

I walk back with Lena, who tells me it is time for her to get back to work also. She is a sewing machinist and has a room in the rear of her house where she makes children's clothes, supplying them to markets and a clothes shop in Corfu Town that she visits once a week.

'Enjoy dinner with my nephew this evening.' She smiles. 'Believe me, it isn't every day he invites someone to his place.'

'Thank you. And thanks for the coffee.'

Inside, I shower and change into a lime-green shorts suit, with a black vest underneath. The colour suits my hair colour I think as I give a little twirl in front of the mirror.

I'm trying to stop the butterflies in my stomach as I glance at my watch. Dimitri will be here to collect me in twenty minutes. I debate pouring myself a drink, when the phone rings. It's Josh.

'Hey, sis, put the phone onto video, George wants to say hi.'

I switch to camera, and Josh lets out a little wolf whistle when he sees me.

'Going somewhere special?'

'No, I usually hang around like this, it's just something I threw on,' I joke.

George appears then dressed as a pirate, and brandishes a sword in front of the camera.

'He wanted to show you his outfit. I've just collected him from a pirate-themed party at one of his friends' houses after nursery.'

'Did you have fun, George? You look amazing.'

'Yes, thank you. And I won a prize in musical statues,' he tells me proudly, lifting up a small gold whistle that he proceeds to blow loudly.

'Lucky you. I'm glad you had a good time. I hope you will come and see us again soon when I'm back in England.'

'We will, won't we, Daddy?' he says, turning to Josh.

'We certainly will.'

George waves, then dashes off, swishing his sword.

'Good luck with getting him to bed, after all that sugar.'

'Oh, I know.' He laughs. 'He's got a couple of hours to work it off though, I'll let him run around the garden.'

'Of course, I keep forgetting we are two hours ahead.'

I tell him all about my impending date with Dimitri.

'Brilliant, I think you should go for it.'

'You do? I texted Evie earlier and she told me the same thing.'

'Why not? You're always there for everyone else. It's about time you had a little fun. I know you helped Evie get through her marriage slump, and you have always given me nothing but good advice. Maybe it's time to concentrate on your own happiness.'

'Thanks, Josh, and I know you're right, but a long-distance relationship is hardly ideal is it? It's the last thing I was expecting to happen.'

'Just go with the flow. I know it wasn't exactly Greece, but I moved hundreds of miles away to be with Zoe. Love can conquer anything, if it's meant to be.'

'Do you really believe that?' I ask doubtfully.

'I do as it happens, yes.'

Zoe pops into the room then, and says hi and chats for a second, before dropping a kiss onto Josh's head, and saying she will go and prepare dinner. I don't think I have seen them look as happy as they are in a long time.

Five minutes after finishing the call, Dimitri is tapping at the front door. I open it and his eyes widen.

'Wow. You look beautiful. But then, you always do.'

'Thanks. Although you wouldn't say that if you had seen me earlier dressed in old joggers and a T-shirt, which I dripped honey on from eating some baklava,' I tell him and he laughs.

Outside, there is no sign of his car.

'We are walking?'

'Yes. No more than ten minutes, if that is okay?'

'Gosh, sorry yes, your aunt mentioned your place wasn't far away.'

'You have been discussing me?' He grins.

'What? No, I bumped into her earlier at the beach when I was taking a break. She mentioned it when we were talking about living here. Do you think you will stay around here?' I ask as we walk.

'I imagine so. I could never be too far away from the village. My friends and family are here.'

We stroll side by side in the early evening sunshine, Dimitri casting the occasional glance at me and smiling. I'm surprised when we take a walk down a side street not far from the beach, to what appears at first glance to be a block of holiday apartments.

'They once were,' Dimitri tells me when I remark on this. 'They were sold off several years ago. I was lucky to be able to secure a large one-bedroomed place.'

He lets us into a public area with a cool, marble floor and potted plants dotted about in the entrance.

Dimitri's apartment is on the first floor, and he leads me inside to a cool, stylish interior. The main lounge is white walled with a huge black-leather sofa and some striking art on the walls. The large window at the end of the room gives a side view of the sea. At the far end of the long lounge leading from the kitchen, a table has been set, with a candle at its centre.

'Would you like a glass of champagne?'

'Champagne? What's the occasion?' I ask as I follow him into the kitchen, which is just as stylish as the lounge with navy units and pale-grey marble work surfaces, although maybe I should expect nothing less from a builder. It does have a masculine, yet welcoming, feel. Dimitri most definitely has a good eye for design.

'Do we need an occasion? Although maybe it could be a late toast to your new home.'

He pops the cork on the champagne, and pours us each a glass.

'So what are we eating?' I glance around but there's only a single pot on the top of the stove.

'A meze. Most of it is in the fridge, the rest on a low heat in the oven. Please, sit down.'

He guides me back to the lounge, where there is a bowl of olives on a maple-coloured coffee table. I glance around at the room, which could be in any modern European city; the only clue to it being in Greece is the sight of a Greek flag out of the window, fluttering in the breeze near the sea.

A short while later, I am seated at the dining table as Dimitri brings out dish after dish of delicious-looking food. There are stuffed vine leaves, meatballs, dips, bread and olives, as well as some deep-fried whitebait. He retrieves a small moussaka from the oven, and some tasty-looking roasted potatoes dusted with oregano and lemon.

'You made all this?' I stare in amazement at the crowded table. 'Wait, you did make it, didn't you, or is this courtesy of a local restaurant?'

'You insult me.' He looks at me in mock horror. 'I told you I like to cook, although a lot of the meze is shop bought,' he admits. 'But I made the moussaka and the potatoes.'

'Well, it looks wonderful, thank you so much. I've been saving myself for this all afternoon. Well, apart from the tiny piece of baklava,' I tell him, remembering I had mentioned that.

'So how was your day?' I ask him.

'Busy. We had some really fun guests on a boat trip earlier, with a man who liked to sing, and the children laughed a lot. It is so nice to see people enjoying themselves on holiday.'

'How is Athena's grandmother?' I can't stop myself from asking.

'Do we have to ruin the mood?' He edges his chair closer to mine and tops my glass up with champagne.

'That's not what I am trying to do. Why would I?'

'Then forget about her. I dropped her off for a visit, went and had a coffee, then brought her back. I told you it was the last time. Besides, her grandmother is very unwell now and will be going into a hospice in the near future.'

'I'm sorry to hear that, I really am. And I'm sorry for ruining the mood, as you say.'

The champagne has gone to my head a little, and I feel myself begin to relax more. The food was delicious, the company engaging, and I really don't want the night to end.

'Shall we take these outside?' asks Dimitri and I nod.

We finish up with a Metaxa that we enjoy outside on his balcony. The sea has blackened, distant lights coming from the bars at just before midnight.

'I've had a lovely evening.'

'So have I. You mean a lot to me, Claudia. I haven't felt this way about someone in a long time.'

I let his words sink in, realising I feel the same way about him.

'It's a pity I live so far away, isn't it?'

'But you have your second home here now. Tell me all about the city you live in back home.'

I tell him about Merseyside and the surrounding areas and how sometimes we travel into Chester by train.

'I think you would like it there. It's a pretty city, with some Roman ruins and great restaurants. Oh, and it has a racecourse.'

'Horse racing?'

'Yes, it makes for a great day out.'

'Then we must do that sometime.' He smiles. 'I would also quite like to watch Liverpool play football. In fact.' He swirls his brandy around in his glass. 'How would you feel about me visiting you over the winter?'

'You would come to England?' I ask in surprise.

'Why not? I don't have as much work over the winter, and I can take a flight from Athens.'

'And you would do that?'

'Would you like me to do that?' he asks searchingly.

'I would love that. I'm not sure how you would cope with a winter in the North of England though.'

I have a vision of us snuggled up on the couch then, beneath a cosy blanket, watching a Christmas movie and sipping mulled wine.

'I am sure I would not even notice the weather, if I was with you.'

'Oh, believe me you would.' I laugh at his cheesy line.

We go inside and sink back into the sofa, and Dimitri plays some music from a sound system. It's slow mood music perfect for the evening.

I'm aware of his closeness, every nerve in my body tingling. He has just told me he hasn't felt this way about someone in a long time, and however much I try to deny it, I know I feel the same.

I take a final sip of brandy, and he takes the glass from my hand, and edges closer.

And when he finally takes me in his arms and kisses me, there are no interruptions, and I don't run away.

It's just perfect.

THIRTY-THREE

I almost don't want Dimitri to take me to the airport as I hate goodbyes and it is especially hard this time.

I'm packing the last things into my case, when Phoebe calls in to tell me that Eliza will be allowed home in a couple of days, on the premise that she will be looked after.

'I have a key. I have been to tidy her home, and I will make casserole for her return. And then I buy her a pet camel.'

'What? Oh yes, that sounds nice.'

'You do not hear a word I say. What would she do with a camel?'

'I'm sorry, Phoebe.' I flop down onto the couch and sigh. 'It's just for the first time, I am really not looking forward to going home today.'

'You have been hit by the Cupid's arrow,' she says, sitting down beside me.

'I'm afraid I have.' I relive the passionate evening we shared together that was everything I imagined it would be.

'Why are you afraid?'

'Oh, I don't know. I have tried to just relax and see what

happens in the future, but I really have fallen for Dimitri. I never expected any of this to happen.'

'We find love in unexpected places. It is destiny.'

'Do you believe that?'

'I do. Love will find a way if it is meant to be,' she says firmly.

'Maybe you're right. And he did say he would come and visit me over the winter months.'

'He did? Then he must be a man in love.'

When Phoebe leaves, I sit with my own thoughts while I wait. I'm expecting Dimitri in a few hours; I have a night flight and he is working on the boat. But I almost cancel my flight and stay here. I have enough money to live on, and it is a much simpler life over here. I pull myself together then, as in reality my inheritance would soon run out and there is barely enough work here for the locals, so finding a job would probably be difficult. And as much as I can work from home sometimes with my current job, I still need to be in the office sometimes.

I also think of my family. My parents are not getting any younger, and there is also the fact that my brother and little George will soon be moving closer to us. Could I really turn my back on everything for a life here? Maybe I ought to count my blessings, as at least I can travel here as often as is possible and see what happens in the future. I think of Josh's words and how he said I ought to seek my own happiness, and not just be concerned with helping others find theirs.

He's right, of course. But sometimes it's easier to see what your loved ones need. Figuring out your own happiness is a whole different thing.

A few hours later, Dimitri walks through the door and takes me in his arms and kisses me.

'You do know you are making it so difficult for me to leave,' I tell him, when I finally come up for air.

'Then stay for the summer. Come and work on the boats with me.' He snuggles my neck.

Maybe if I was ten years younger I would, and enjoy one long, heady summer without a care in the world, spending evenings on the beach drinking beer and making new friends. But I have job and a flat back home.

'It's a nice idea but it's not that easy,' I say reluctantly.

Why do we always meet the right person at the wrong time in our life? But then again, love will always find a way, if it is meant to be.

'Then I will count down the days until I see you again. When exactly will that be?' he says, circling his arms around my waist.

'Hopefully next month. I can maybe fly over some weekends, and work from here on Mondays.'

'Will that not be very costly for you?' He frowns.

'I can afford it,' I reassure him. 'I am paid well, and I also have some money left in the bank from my inheritance.'

'I feel bad that I cannot come to England during the summer, but I am far too busy here,' Dimitri explains.

'Please, don't worry. I look forward to welcoming you when the season finishes, if you really mean you will come to England.'

'Try stopping me.'

He pulls me closer then, and kisses me, leaving me breathless once more.

'When do we need to leave for the airport?' he whispers in my ear.

'In around an hour.'

'Perfect,' he says, before taking me by the hand and leading me upstairs.

And I can only pray that I am doing the right thing, and not opening myself up to the possibility of having my heart shattered into a thousand tiny pieces.

THIRTY-FOUR

'Safe journey to you. I will look after your house,' Phoebe reassures me as Dimitri and I step outside to his car for the journey to the airport.

Phoebe mentioned her granddaughter coming over next weekend, as her husband is working a night shift. She says Sofia is taking her out for a meal, in between Phoebe looking after her old friend.

'She can stay at my house overnight if she likes,' I offer.

'Your house?' Phoebe looks completely surprised.

'Just until you sort your guest room out, of course. It is quite a drive home for her after a long day.'

Phoebe's second bedroom is tiny, and overflowing with furniture, and boxes of old books and personal items that belonged to her husband, that somehow she hasn't got around to disposing of.

'You are right. I have been selfish holding on to my husband's things. I need a guest room for my family.'

'You do,' I say gently.

'But are you sure she can stay?' she asks again, uncertainly.

'Honestly, it's fine. I would rather the villa is not standing empty.'

Phoebe kisses me on the cheeks. 'When they leave, I will clean the house until it shines. Thank you.'

'I know you will.' I smile.

This time, I am going home happy in the knowledge that Phoebe's friendship with Eliza will soon be back on track. I get the feeling the two women still have a few more adventures in them yet and look forward to hearing all about them in the future.

We drive in silence, Dimitri taking my hand in his when we stop at traffic lights, and I allow myself to feel happy and content. In fact, I could burst with happiness and wish I could stay here for just a short while longer, although I know I will be back soon. The last thing I expected when I embarked on the villa purchase was to fall in love with my builder, but I guess fate had other ideas. It seems you can never deny something that is written in the stars.

At the airport, I am reluctant to be free of his embrace, but eventually it's time to go through security.

'Call me when you are home.' Dimitri kisses me one last time, and even though I am not one for public displays of affection, I don't care who is watching.

I hear them announce my gate so make my way through the airport, away from Dimitri, fighting back tears as I walk.

I sleep during the flight, and arrive at Manchester Airport feeling miserable for the first time, although I am sure the feeling will pass.

It's a little cool in contrast to the warm evening in Greece and I pull my jacket tightly around me as I make my way to the car park to retrieve my car. Back home, I realise it's almost three in the morning in Corfu, so I flop down onto my bed and send

Dimitri a message to tell him I have arrived home safely and will call him tomorrow. My phone rings within seconds.

'Dimitri, hi, I thought you would have been asleep.' It feels so good to hear his voice.

'I was sleeping lightly, maybe half-listening for your message. I wanted to hear your voice,' he says sleepily, and I imagine him in his huge bed, wishing I was there beside him.

It seems unbelievable that just hours earlier I was in Corfu saying goodbye to the most wonderful man. I am certain of that now. I accept that maybe this could lead to something more lasting, maybe not. But I think I owe it to myself to at least give things a try.

'I have a calendar on my wall. I will cross the days off until you return,' he says and I laugh.

'No way, I thought I was the only one who still does that.' I tell him about my desk calendar at work.

'That is it. We are kindred spirits.'

'Maybe we are.'

I hear him yawn a minute later, so wish him goodnight, even though I hate putting the phone down.

THIRTY-FIVE

I keep looking at flights and am almost tempted to return to Greece the following weekend. But I am sustained by video calls from Dimitri, and manage somehow to not allow my heart to rule my head.

'Absence makes the heart grow fonder,' my mum reminds me as I have Sunday lunch with my parents. 'Don't go running over there every five minutes, you don't want to appear too keen,' she continues as she thinks men ought to do all the running. 'Faint heart never won fair lady, and all that. Besides, you need to have a chance to miss each other,' is another piece of her advice.

'Do you think so? Isn't there also a saying, "Out of sight out of mind"?'

'Oh, don't be silly.' She laughs. 'You have only been apart for five minutes. Your grandfather went to war you know, and all my mother had for years was letters. True love can survive anything.'

'Maybe you're right, but I suppose only time will tell.'

Is it true love? I wonder. If it is, then maybe it really can survive the distance.

I'm halfway through Mum's delicious apple crumble and custard for dessert, when Mum takes a call from Josh.

'Oh, that's marvellous! Your sister is here, do you want to tell her too?'

I take the phone from Mum, who is smiling from ear to ear and Josh tells me that they have had an offer accepted for the house near Manchester.

'And we've had a lot of interest in our place here, so fingers crossed we should be in before the end of the year.'

I daydream of us all sitting around the table at Christmas, little George playing with his toys.

The following week in work passes in a blur, as it is the height of the holiday season and more passports than ever are being processed, along with the usual last-minute applications from people who make daily calls for updates.

It's a Friday work from home day, and at lunchtime I'm sitting in my tracksuit eating some lunch and thinking about messaging Dimitri. I imagine him out in the sunshine, chatting to tourists on the boats, and have a yearning to be there too. But maybe Mum is right, about appreciating time together even more if you spend time apart.

I'm thinking about this, when I receive a message from Dimitri, telling me an Amazon driver is trying to deliver a gift to me, but cannot find the apartment.

'A gift?'

'Yes. He has called my number, saying he cannot find the apartment. Maybe you could go outside and look for the van.'

'Sure, it's perfect timing, as I am just taking a break. I'll call you back shortly.'

I walk downstairs, excitedly wondering what gift Dimitri might have sent me. Maybe it's something Greek to remind me

of Corfu. Or perhaps it is something more personal, like a piece
of jewellery.

I take a glance outside, then walk to the end of the path, in
search of the delivery driver. Whatever I was expecting, it
certainly wasn't what I find, strolling towards me in the street.

'Dimitri!' My hand flies to my mouth as I am almost rooted
to the spot. 'It's you, it's really you!'

I practically run to him, before sinking into his soft embrace,
wondering whether I am actually dreaming.

'So, are you going to invite me in?' he asks, after kissing me
right there on the doorstep. 'It's freezing out here.'

'I can't believe you are here.'

I can't stop looking at him, wondering if I close my eyes, he
might just disappear.

We are sitting on the sofa, him clutching a coffee.

'Oh, and if you think it's cold now, just wait until
December.'

'I had to come. I heard Liverpool are playing an important
match tomorrow.' He grins.

'Ah so you really are crazy about them?'

'I am crazy about you,' he says, placing his coffee cup down
and kissing me. 'I could not stop thinking about you, so I
thought I would surprise you.'

'You have certainly done that.' We're sitting snuggled
together. 'I think this might be the most romantic thing anyone
has ever done. Aren't you meant to be working on the boat
though?'

'As it is only for the weekend, it was easy to arrange cover.
There are plenty of people willing to take over for a few days,'
he explains. 'I had to see you, I could not wait for another few
weeks. I hope I haven't ruined your weekend plans.'

He clearly doesn't share my mum's philosophy of thinking
absence makes the heart grow fonder, I'm delighted to say.

'Well, I was thinking of doing a little shopping, maybe

eating out, followed by a relaxing day on Sunday, starting with a long lie-in.'

'That sounds perfect. But maybe first, we need to go to a supermarket.'

'What for?'

'The ingredients for that Greek breakfast I promised you.'

Strolling hand in hand through town heading to a large store, I feel like the luckiest girl in the world.

'Tomorrow, we could go on a city sightseeing bus if you like,' I tell him, as we walk. 'It takes in all the main tourist attractions, as well as some of the places the Beatles sang about in their songs. Penny Lane, Strawberry Fields and so on.'

'Perhaps I need to go shopping for a warmer coat first.' He pulls his jacket tightly around him, and I tell him he can borrow one of my dark woollen scarves if he likes.

'And I hate to tell you, but Liverpool are playing an away match at Chelsea, I think.'

'So I came all this way for nothing?' He shakes his head, and I push him playfully on the arm.

'Then we could finish off with a meal at the Greek taverna on Bold Street, if you like. Gosh, I still can't believe that you are actually here.'

'Maybe I was hoping to try the local delicacies of England. You do not eat English food in Greece, do you?'

'Of course, what am I thinking? You will be spoilt for choice here, there are restaurants with every international cuisine you can think of. Probably more than English restaurants actually, but there is always fish and chips.'

'You're going to take me to the chippy?' he asks in the worst Liverpool accent ever, that has me roaring with laughter.

As we head home with our shopping, I feel pure joy in my heart. I have no doubts now.

Dimitri couldn't bear to wait any longer to see me, so whatever the future holds I know I will face it with a certainty that we will do our best to make things work. It wasn't so long ago that I was unprepared to take a risk on a new relationship, happy on my own, too frightened to let anyone into my heart again.

But that's the thing with love: it can creep up on you when you least expect it.

And once that happens, as a line in a certain song says, *Love changes everything.*

EPILOGUE

'So how is it working out for you, having two homes?' asks Thea.

We are standing in the bakery, me sampling a new cake creation of hers.

'Wonderful. And so is this, by the way.' I wipe crumbs from my mouth having devoured the cherry and almond cake. 'You definitely need to make a load of these to sell.'

'I will. You know, in a few weeks I will be overrun with customers before the season ends. August and September can be very busy. I could barely cope last summer, so if you fancy a part-time job...?' she asks as she places some bread rolls into baskets.

'Are you serious?'

'Why not? You could give me some recipes for the UK holi-daymakers.' She smiles.

'That's true, although I'm sure they would rather eat your delicious Greek cakes, especially the baklava. Anyway, that's me leaving,' I say, glancing at my watch. 'I told Dimitri I will join him on the two o'clock sail round the island.'

Bookings are picking up and the boats take tourists out every two hours on trips.

'Have a great time. See you tonight for dinner at mine,' she reminds me.

'I'm looking forward to it.'

Sitting at the front of the boat, watching the glistening water, and listening to Dimitri as he gives little commentaries as we sail past places of interest, I feel once again like the luckiest girl in the world.

Around thirty passengers, mainly English, are enjoying a drink from the bar, turning their faces towards the sky and feeling the first warmth of the summer sun with smiles on their faces.

Sailing past tiny islands, and white churches, watching the sea changing from dark blue to shades of turquoise, I suddenly realise I could get used to living here. Mum and Dad have already been over for a visit, and are planning another trip in September. It isn't too far from the UK, and hasn't Thea just offered me a job at least in the summer months? Besides, I still have quite a lot of savings left from my inheritance.

I snuggle into Dimitri as he takes the wheel of the boat.

'Are you okay?' he asks.

'Wonderful. I'm just dreading leaving again in a few days, that's all.' I sigh.

'You do know, you don't have to?' He kisses the top of my head.

'I've been thinking about that. A lot. Of course, I would have to go home and sort a few things out, but maybe I could live here.'

'You could?' Dimitri lets go of the wheel, for a second, before taking my face in his hands and kissing me. 'You really could see that?'

'I could. It's getting more and more difficult for me to leave, and with Josh moving closer to my parents, I feel a little less guilty about settling somewhere else.'

As I say the words, I realise it had been a little bit of a stumbling block to my relocating, but my parents becoming more involved in George's life lately has given them a new lease of life. I stare out across the sea with a feeling of contentment I haven't felt in a long time. I belong here.

'Any chance of another beer?' An English guy's voice brings me back to the present, and Dimitri calls to a young worker to fetch some. I'm so lucky to have two homes, both in places I love, but I guess home is where the heart is. And right now, it's here in Greece, with a guy called Dimitri.

A LETTER FROM SUE

Dear reader,

I want to say a huge thank you for choosing to read *The Greek Villa*. If you did enjoy it, and want to keep up to date with all my latest releases, just sign up at the following link. Your email address will never be shared and you can unsubscribe at any time.

www.bookouture.com/sue-roberts

I hope you loved *The Greek Villa*; I certainly enjoyed returning to Greece once more, this time to Corfu, a place I have visited many times over the years.

I found this book such a joy to write, and particularly enjoyed writing about the small, pretty resort of Roda, that has easy access to Sidari. I hope it gave you all of the holiday feels!

I am so thankful that many of my readers love the Greek islands too, and continue to buy my books. I also appreciate some of the wonderful messages I have received on social media. It means so much.

If you did enjoy the story, I would be very grateful if you could write a review. I'd love to hear what you think, and it makes such a difference helping new readers to discover one of my books for the first time.

I love hearing from my readers – you can get in touch on my Facebook page or through X.

Thanks,

Sue Roberts

 facebook.com/Suerobertsauthor
x.com/SueRobertsautho

ACKNOWLEDGMENTS

Once more, I would like to thank my wonderful editor, Natalie Edwards, and the team at Bookouture for their involvement in getting this book out in the world to all you lovely readers! There is so much work that goes on behind the scenes to produce a novel, and I thank everyone in the team.

I do hope you enjoyed taking the journey to Corfu. It was one of the first Greek islands I visited many years ago, and when I returned recently, it was every bit as charming as I remember! The Venetian influence is evident in the buildings, as well as French and British touches. (Cricket on the green!)

I was inspired to write about a house renovation, after watching a TV programme about a couple who did just that, as well as opening a restaurant.

I would like to thank my family and friends, for their holiday stories, and details of the things they get up to, which often inspires my writing. Also, the café owners and workers in the Sidari restaurants, always greeting us with a smile and recommending local dishes. (I can highly recommend Greek taverna Konaki.)

A huge thanks as always, to all of you bloggers and readers, who share and introduce new readers to my books. Your support is invaluable.

Thank you for some of the lovely messages I have received from you dear readers, telling me how much you love my books. It is always such a joy to receive such messages, especially being told that the escapist nature of my novels, take people away to a better place when they are feeling a bit down. It is a privilege to bring a little sunshine into someone's life!

Finally, thanks to my husband Derek, who keeps me topped up with coffee and good humour when I'm flagging a bit. And my wonderful daughters Rachel and Vicki who proudly display all of my books on their bookcase. I can't imagine life without any of you.

PUBLISHING TEAM

Turning a manuscript into a book requires the efforts of many people. The publishing team at Bookouture would like to acknowledge everyone who contributed to this publication.

Commercial
Lauren Morrissette
Hannah Richmond
Imogen Allport

Cover design
Debbie Clement

Data and analysis
Mark Alder
Mohamed Bussuri

Editorial
Natalie Edwards
Sinead O'Connor

Copyeditor
Jane Eastgate

Proofreader
Becca Allen

Marketing
Alex Crow
Melanie Price
Occy Carr
Cíara Rosney
Martyna Młynarska

Operations and distribution
Marina Valles
Stephanie Straub

Production
Hannah Snetsinger
Mandy Kullar

Publicity
Kim Nash
Noelle Holten
Jess Readett
Sarah Hardy

Rights and contracts
Peta Nightingale
Richard King
Saidah Graham

Made in the USA
Las Vegas, NV
07 August 2024

93476805R00152

**Is this villa in Greece a disastrous fixer-upper…
or a dream come true for Claudia?**

After receiving a life-changing inheritance from a beloved, quirk
older relative, thirty-two-year-old **Claudia** has done something wi
they would approve of – she's bought a run-down villa in Greece
Though she's never seen it in person, she's sure that with a lick of
paint, it will be everything she's ever dreamed of…

But, arriving at her new home on the gorgeous Greek island of
Corfu, Claudia is met with a shock. The cracks look more like
chasms, plants are growing through the tiled floor, and the view
of the sparkling blue sea would be perfect – if there was a
window instead of a hole in the wall.

With the local villagers thinking she's mad to take on the villa,
Claudia panics she's made the biggest mistake of her life. **Until
local builder Dimitri comes to her rescue…** Between his caring
nature, his rippling muscles and deep brown eyes, Claudia can't
believe she's found her knight in shining armour. And they grow
close over glasses of Greek wine beneath the stars, after long,
hot days working on the villa.

But just when Claudia begins to see a future with Dimitri, his
ex-girlfriend throws a spanner in the works. Though he reassure
her that it's over between them, Claudia starts to feel like he's
keeping secrets. Then a pipe bursts, flooding the villa, and all
Claudia's hopes are dashed at once…

**Should Claudia call it quits and head back to her old life?
Or is Dimitri hiding the perfect surprise, one that could help
Claudia finally build her dream life in Greece?**

ⓑ www.bookouture.com

ISBN 978-1-83525-354-0

90000

9 781835 253540

Cover images © Shutterstock. Designed by Debbie Clement